# The *Fine Art* of *Kindness*

By
Robert Philip Bolton

Also by Robert Philip Bolton
*The Artist as an Old Man (Self Portrait)*
*It's What Eddie Did*
*The Fable of Flitcroft Point*
*Jacko. One Bloke. One Year.*
*The Boys and Men of Auckland's Mickey Rooney Gang*
*The Fine Art of Kindness*
*Six Murders*
*Underneath The Arclight*
*To The White Gate*
*My Marian Year*
*The Boltons of The Little Boltons*
*The Tapu Garden of Eden*
*For Viktor. The story of Mussorgsky's 'Pictures at an Exhibition'*
*The Collected Short Stories* (in which is combined *Nana's Special Day and other stories, The Dolphin and other stories,* and *Quickies.*)

Robert Philip Bolton was born in New Zealand in 1945. He has been writing most of his adult life. Most of his work is about New Zealand and New Zealanders. He lives in Auckland.

*The Fine Art of Kindness*

By
Robert Philip Bolton
Cover design and production by Stephen Bolton
Copyright © Robert Philip Bolton
ISBN: 978-0-473-42584-5 (v3a 11/25)

*For Billy*

# FROM THE AUTHOR

*The Fine Art of Kindness* is a work of fiction. Apart from references to real places and people which are obviously in the public domain the characters, places and events it depicts are entirely the products of my imagination. However, I did receive help and advice for which I was grateful.

Thanks especially to Lindy Lely, the Starship Volunteer Coordinator at Auckland City Hospital, and Andrea Newland of the Starship Foundation, for their patience and kindness, their time, information and advice.

But while their help was invaluable in the preparation of this small book of fiction, the value of their *real* work, day after day, and the work of all the Starship grandmothers, grandfathers and many other volunteers and donors, working quietly behind the scenes in support of Starship's objectives, as well as the hospital's medical professionals, is impossible to measure.

Similarly, the Women's Refuge movement in New Zealand works constantly and quietly in the interests of women and children and I am indebted to Wendy Valler for her information and advice, helping me understand the movement's work.

Thanks also to my wife, Kath, for her advice and encouragement, to Gail Batten and Max Ross for their help, and to my son Stephen for his cover design.

# PROLOGUE

'ZELNICK,' ANNOUNCED THE voice on the phone.

'Mort. How are you?' answered old Jack Landseer cheerfully. 'Long time no hear.'

Landseer liked Zelnick. He always had. Despite his flashy suits, heeled boots, gaudy ties, huge gold watch on one wrist, heavy gold bracelet on the other, and heavily-bejewelled fingers – he even suspected Zelnick sometimes wore lipstick – he had always, since he bought the Steele twenty-five years ago, found the strange little man, now in his sixties, to be easy to deal with and utterly honest. And that, to a plain and practical country man with an open mind, was more important than appearances.

'Well, my friend,' said Zelnick, 'I am afraid this is the last time you will hear from Zelnick. At least about this thing of us. Perhaps other things, perhaps not so, I do not know. But about this thing there is no more. It is over you see. Finished. The end. The last. The very final last.'

'I see,' said Jack Landseer quietly. Wondering.

'I keep the very best for last you understand,' said Zelnick.

'I see,' said Jack again. 'But it's not really *you* is it, Mort. Deciding I mean.'

He enjoyed teasing the wily old dealer.

'You insult Zelnick, my friend. It is I who give advices. Good advices. From here, the heart, and here, the brain. Both are important you must understand. And now this.'

'So, the very best and the very last. What is it this time?'

'Before I say, my friend, before I tell, I must ask of you.'

'Ask away,' said Jack. He knew basically what was coming; he just didn't know, couldn't even guess, the number.

'My vendor – so secret and private as usual – is wanting one hundred and eighty thousand dollars,' said Zelnick.

Jack pursed his lips and then smiled; almost laughed aloud. He had just finished his breakfast when the phone rang. He was now standing in the kitchen, dressed, ready for the day. And now this.

'That's a lot of money, Mort,' he said.

'A lot of money he says. I know already, my friend. But what can I say? A lot of money of course.'

Jack could almost hear the dealer shrugging apologetically over the phone. 'But the seller won't get it all,' he said teasingly. 'There's your commission, Mort.'

'But of course, my friend,' said Zelnick. 'Vendor understands. For many years we have done business. As you of course know. And business is business, no?'

'Tell me about it. But you're rather early for this, Mort. It's not even eight o'clock on a Friday morning.'

'I want to get it out of my brains now, off my desk, gone, vamoose, before I open, before the masses of people come and it gets busy. So busy. You've got no idea how very very busy is Zelnick. This business. My God.'

Jack smiled; again he almost laughed aloud. He knew business would be slow in Parnell on a hot Friday morning in early January; most people would be on holiday.

'That's alright, Mort,' he said soothingly. 'So, what are we talking about? A hundred and eighty thousand. What is it? Do you think it's worth it? What's your advice?'

'Is Lindauer, my friend Jack,' said Zelnick. 'Gottfried Lindauer. You know? The little Austrian. Or Czech I think. Who cares? Bloody foreigner. Worth it? Are you a crazyman?'

'And?'

'Mere Rangipaeroa. Handsome old famous lady with a feather and a cloak and a moko and a tiki and a pipe and every damn Maori thing. So beautiful. Exquisite. She's not been seen by nobodies for seventy-three years. Imagine it. Except two owners. Just two. Can you believe this what I tell you?'

Jack pursed his lips again, frowned, in surprise, in silent admiration for the collector who had kept something so special so secret for so long.

'Authentic?'

'I am a liar now? I am a fraud already? My friend, Jack. Authentic? I am Zelnick. My reputation.'

'Then it's probably worth a lot more than that,' said Jack cautiously.

'Between you and me and the post gate probably is true,' said Zelnick. 'But our vendor friend is not greedy. Not a tiny little bit of it even. As usual just wants a quick sale. No auction. No publicity. No newspapers. No pictures. No interviews. Nothing complicated. We together trust you, my friend Jack. Only you. Always we have trusted. Agree? Quick and easy. No publicity. Just so.'

Jack Landseer thought for a moment but for no more. He didn't have to. Not for a forgotten Lindauer.

'Then a quick and easy sale you have, Mort,' he said. 'If it's everything you say.'

'Everything, my friend. But our secret, eh?'

'Our secret.'

'Is alright? A hundred and eighty thousand?'

'It's fine. Well, if you say so it's fine,' said Jack although he could imagine what his son Alan would say. But in return he would say to Alan that it was worth a lot more. Indeed, a bargain. A real bargain.

'I will come down tomorrow, my friend Jack,' said Zelnick. 'About eleven o'clock. For the cheque, no?'

'Saturday?'

'But of course,' said Zelnick. 'Is good for me. Closed Saturday.'

'Bring the painting too,' said Jack. 'I want to hang it here. To see it.'

'Of course, my friend, I will bring her. Not so big but so valuable. You must add to your insurance. With all the others. So valuable.'

'I'll take care of it today,' said Jack. 'Now. But they might ring you to confirm.'

'Is good. They ring me. They know me well. No worries,' said Zelnick. 'So, tomorrow I will come, in my own car, not the van, with the security men. Two men. They will cost.'

'That's your problem,' said Jack with a laugh.

'You are a hard man, Jack,' said Mordacai Zelnick. 'This I know. A very very hard man.'

# 1

OLD BETTY KRILICH could have cried. But she didn't. Instead, she sat in the gutter in her long and somewhat shabby camelhair coat, her faded-denim clad legs apart, her knees high, her little tartan shopping trundler lying broken on the footpath behind her, and wondered what she should do next.

'Bloody hell.'

Thus was her wondering expressed aloud.

Her arms were resting between her raised and spread knees and she had a large egg in each hand, the only two which had survived; the others — a dozen or so — lay broken on the footpath, their golden yolks and gelatinous albumen soaking through the flimsy brown paper bag in which they had been held and so mixing with the fine gravel and pebbles and filth and grime of the pavement. Beside them lay two large cauliflowers — their virginal lumpy whiteness now irreversibly corrupted by the dirty footpath upon which they had landed, bounced and rolled — two tightly wrapped dark green cabbages, each as large or larger than a basketball, which had also bounced and rolled on the pavement and were therefore somewhat darkened and bruised, and an iron-bark pumpkin with specks of black gravel embedded in its hard but not invulnerable silvery-grey skin. The rest of the produce, fresh from her garden – a large bunch of silverbeet, a plastic bag bulging with heads of broccoli, and long stems of streaky wine-coloured rhubarb tied together with string – had remained contained in the little lidless trundler.

The red and rubber-tyred wheel which had come off the shopping trundler had rolled away and lay on its side a few metres distant. Sitting there on the kerb, her feet in the gutter, her legs apart for comfort and her knees up around her ears, her elbows between her legs, her arms held out in front, a precious egg cradled in each hand, old Betty Krilich was only a hundred metres or so from home; but it might as well have been a hundred kilometres.

'So what the hell am I going to do now?' she said. To herself.

'Betty,' said a voice from behind. It was, she could tell from experience, the voice of an old man. She turned around and looked up at the speaker, an old fellow for sure, but still reasonably handsome, and well-groomed, she could tell, despite being dressed for gardening. He was wearing a working man's leather boots, leather gloves on his hands in the right one of which he gripped a pair of soft-handled secateurs. His white hair and rimless spectacles made him look professorial.

'Who are you?' she asked.

'This is a fine kettle of fish, isn't it.'

'Who are you?' she asked again.

'Jack Landseer, Betty,' said the old man. 'Remember? I live there.' He was pointing his closed secateurs over his shoulder to the brick-and-tile house behind him which was set far back from the street at the end of a long front garden which was so perfectly planned and maintained it had the appearance of a public park.

'Jack Landseer?' There was a question in Betty's tone but she quickly decided that the name meant nothing to her.

She stood up, somewhat awkwardly, shuffling, and leaning far forward, her bottom out to maintain her balance given that she was carefully cradling an egg in each closed hand. Once standing she turned around to face the man. She stood, looking at him curiously – she was about his height – now holding her egg-holding hands to the warmth of her belly.

'How do you know my name?' she asked. 'Betty.'

'That's your name. I know that. Everybody calls you that,' said the old man.

'They call me Old Betty, don't they,' she said. 'It's derogatory. They think I'm a bit nutty.'

'No they don't,' said Jack.

Betty looked at him curiously, her head to one side, thinking.

'Yes they do,' she said at last. 'But I'm not.'

'Not what?'

'Nutty.'

'I know *that*. Anyway, your wheel's come off,' he said. 'Needs a split pin. No problem.'

'It's a problem to me,' she said.

'I can fix it, love,' he said. 'Piece of cake. I'll take it home – right here – and fix it.'

'Don't call me love.'

'But first we'll get you home.'

'You don't know where I live,' she said indignantly.

'Yes I do. Of course I do. One hundred and seventy-two. Down there.' The old man pointed with his secateurs down Northumberland Road, the main road from the Karapuke shops south to the State Highway, in the direction of Betty Krilich's house. 'Everybody knows that.'

'Do they?'

'Of course they do,' said the old man. 'You're famous.'

'Am I?' Betty was surprised.

'Tell me about it,' said the old man. 'Now where were you going?'

'You know the women's refuge? The safe house?'

'No,' said the old man.

'Good,' said Betty. 'Best you don't.'

'Is that where you were going?'

'Never mind that now. I just need to get home,' said Betty. 'Get this mess sorted out.'

'No sooner said than done,' said the old man. 'Just wait here. I'll get my barrow.'

And so Betty waited, her egg-holding hands held close to her body, and watched curiously as the unfamiliar old man, Jack something, who seemed to know her, strode back to his garden, slipping the secateurs into his back pocket as he went, and pulling off his gardening gloves and stuffing them into a side pocket. She saw him walk to a big professional-looking steel wheelbarrow which stood where he had left it at the head of a long row of roses adjacent to the long drive which ran down the length of the garden to a double-garage attached to the side of the house. She continued to watch, puzzled, as he tipped the few rose prunings from the barrow onto the lawn; evidently he hadn't progressed past the first few plants before he had noticed her sitting in the gutter beside her broken shopping trundler. And she watched as he returned pushing the empty barrow. He stopped when he reached the broken trundler where he set down the wheelbarrow.

'What are you doing?' she asked.

The old man didn't reply; rather he bent, easily, and effortlessly lifted the broken and half-full shopping trundler and gently placed it in the wheelbarrow in such a position and at such an angle that its remaining contents of freshly-harvested produce – those which had not spilled onto the pavement – were safely contained.

Betty was surprised. She looked surprised.

The old man then bent to retrieve the spilled goods lying on the dirty pavement: the pumpkin, the caulis and cabbages; and then, with a booted foot, he nudged the broken eggs and their wet, transparent and shredded paper bag into the gutter. Betty watched; she could see he was untroubled by stiff joints or any other such condition common in men and women his age. Evidently – like her – he was healthy, fit, strong and capable.

Having made the observation she collected herself and her thoughts and stepped forward somewhat annoyed.

'I can do that,' she said abruptly, sounding rude and ungrateful when in fact she was neither. 'Hold these.'

She handed the two warm eggs to the old man and then quickly gathered up the goods in question and placed them carefully in the open top of the trundler.

'I'll take them now,' she said, her hands held forward to accept the eggs.

'Right-oh,' said the old man who handed back the two eggs and then picked up the red wheel which had come off the shopping trundler and wedged it between its broken parent and the side of the wheelbarrow's steel tray.

'Now,' he said as he took the loaded wheelbarrow in hand and turned it down Northumberland Road. 'Let's get you home safe and sound.'

He looked at her again to make sure she was recovered and ready to walk home with him and his wheelbarrow.

✪

Jack Landseer was used to Betty's odd appearance; she always wore clothes that were once exceedingly fashionable (and expensive) but were now dated, shabby, and utterly inappropriate. Indeed, some of her clothes would have once looked elegant and refined at a ball, a cocktail party, a symphony concert, the ballet, a gallery opening or the theatre, while others clearly belonged at an old-fashioned rock festival. But now, in the small rural service town of Karapuke, whatever she wore made her look both strangely eccentric and oddly distinguished. Whether she knew what others thought of her wardrobe was not known but if she did she certainly didn't care. She couldn't afford to: it was the only wardrobe she possessed.

Betty Krilich was tall – taller than most women of her or any age – and slim and upright and eminently dignified despite her late years and evident borderline penury. To the old man she was like a human version of her own house: an elegant old mansion whose fading paintwork, dirty windows, sagging verandas, rotten steps, loose roof shingles, broken chimney pots, overgrown front yard and broken concrete drive, couldn't diminish its fine underlying architecture nor the quality of the materials with which it was built.

On this chilly Monday morning in July she was dressed in her camelhair overcoat – which was limp and tired-looking now but was expensively fashionable once – over a pair of widely-flared faded blue jeans; around her neck was a red mohair scarf. She'd always had masses of thick and wavy hair, now perfectly white, which she wore up in a casual fashion held roughly in place by coarse tortoiseshell combs which weren't taming enough to stop a few long and curly strands of whiteness to fall, loose and unruly, to the sides of her thin and remarkably unlined face. She never wore a hat. Her spectacles had radiant-blue frames, dotted with diamantes, which swept up to a point above and beyond her eyebrows; like almost everything she wore they were designed and made at a distant time to follow the dictates of a now-scorned fashion. The only modern item of dress – perhaps her only wardrobe extravagance – were the expensive white sneakers, of a recognizably famous brand, with neon-green laces, which she chose and wore for comfort.

'I walk everywhere, you know,' she used to say by way of an unnecessary explanation. 'I need good and comfortable shoes like this.'

Bright, modern and incongruous, her expensive and comfortable trainers were the only exception to her overall but unconscious projection of an old woman accustomed to quality, with an innate sense of good taste, but compelled by her limited budget to wear clothes from another era.

And so, as Jack Landseer – tall, upright, himself smartly dressed (even for working in the garden) – strode purposefully down Northumberland Road, pushing his wheelbarrow and looking directly ahead, Betty Krilich, comfortable in her expensive walking sneakers, easily kept pace with him while holding a precious egg securely in each hand.

She wanted to talk, to ask him something, but at the same time she didn't. She didn't especially want to engage with this man whom she didn't know – he said his name was what? Jack something – and yet she was curious about him. He seemed to know her. He definitely knew at least her first name. Should she know him somehow? She looked across at him as they moved together down the long flat road but he didn't return her look. She looked, trying to remember, but she couldn't. She wanted to ask him to stop and look at her, so she could stare at his face, but she didn't. He just marched on with his wheelbarrow, looking straight ahead as if she were not there.

Jack Landseer knew Betty's house well; in fact he'd known it almost all his life although he'd been inside it only once and that was many years earlier. And anyway he had to drive past it often enough, down Northumberland Road, to get to the State Highway which led to the motorway.

'Here we are, Betty,' he said as he reached the top of the drive of one-seven-two. 'Home again, safe and sound, good as gold.'

'Thank you,' said a grateful Betty although she couldn't help wondering how she was going to transfer everything in his wheelbarrow to her kitchen at the back of the house. 'Thank you very much.'

'Call me Jack,' said Jack. 'Now we'll get your stuff inside and I'll take the trundler home and mend the wheel.'

Betty was on the broken concrete drive by then but she stopped, paused, and looked around at the old man with an expression of doubt – apprehension, almost fear – on her face.

Her hesitation didn't go unnoticed by Jack; and so, when he added: 'Well at least I'll get the wheelbarrow to your door,' he saw at once the relief on her face.

She smiled weakly. 'That'd be good,' she said. 'On the front porch. I can manage after that.'

And so she led Jack as he pushed the wheelbarrow down the drive of broken concrete, across myriad cracks filled with rank weeds, and then at an angle along a narrow and equally-derelict path across the unmown lawn to the front porch. She went ahead of him and up the three shallow wooden steps to the porch where she carefully laid her two eggs on a coir mat and then turned to help Jack lift her produce from the open top of the broken shopping trundler and set them carefully on the floor of the wooden and somewhat rickety porch.

'Job done,' said Jack. 'Right as rain.'

There was an awkward moment of silence then as if neither of the old pair knew what to do next. Betty wanted to ask him in. No she didn't: she felt *obliged* to ask him in but she didn't *want* to and so was torn between her innate courtesy (against which she was always struggling) and her privacy (which unfortunately but not accurately manifested itself as a dislike of strangers) of which she was inordinately jealous. It was the sort of internal conflict of conscience she didn't enjoy and did everything she could to avoid. Indeed, she even resented any person, situation or event she considered the cause of any discomfiture of conscience. But sometimes – and this was such a time – resentment was unreasonable and avoidance was impossible; the conflict had to be faced. And so she determined to thank her Samaritan as graciously as she could sufficient to make the offer of further hospitality unnecessary.

Although Jack Landseer was a plain and practical working man, rarely if ever subject to the internal emotional conflicts now at work in the emotionally complicated mind of Betty Krilich, he wasn't insensitive to them in others. Thus was Betty enormously but silently grateful when, as if reading her thoughts, the old man went to the back of the wheelbarrow and, after dropping the red wheel into the empty shopping trundler, and ensuring that the trundler itself was secure in the wheelbarrow's belly, he lifted the barrow by the handles and simply said: 'Right-oh, like Gough I'm off.'

'Thank you, Mr–'

'Call me Jack,' said Jack again. 'Jack Landseer. Remember? I'll bring your trundler back in a couple of days. Tomorrow probably.'

'Yes, that'll be fine. Thanks–' said Betty, adding, after a pause: '–Jack.'

Jack merely smiled at that – at Betty calling him Jack – and gave a little farewell salute by flicking his forefinger away from his forehead.

## 2

TO KEEP BUSY, not without purpose but to be always useful and productive, was Betty Krilich's philosophy; especially to help vulnerable children and their loving mothers. Being always useful, productive and helpful helped her remember what was important in life, now and in the future. And it helped her forget the unimportant past; the regrets; the awful regrets; the wasted years.

Gus knew. Dear Gus she called him. He tried to tell her then but she wouldn't listen. She was enjoying herself too much. It won't last, darling, he used to say. You can't go on like this. I don't mind for myself but I mind for you. And he was right. All those wasted years. Wasted money. So selfish. And self-centred. And self-indulgent. It was shameful and she hated – not too strong a word – hated to think of it.

But those days are gone, she thought. That was a different me. A long-ago me. Not the now me. The real me. Now I keep busy. Busy being productive and useful and helpful. Helping others. Especially children. Mothers and children. That's it. That's what's important. No time to waste. Must never waste a minute. Never again. Never a minute.

So now she was annoyed to be wasting *more* than a minute. She had wasted time and effort in setting off for the refuge with a full trundler only to return, her bounty undelivered, burdened with an obligation to that man Jack. Now she was wasting time, waiting fruitlessly, unproductively, on the front porch, waiting for him, that Jack, to be out of sight so he couldn't see what she was about to do. She watched him impatiently, unreasonably annoyed, as he wheeled his barrow – within the deep steel tray of which lay her little disabled tartan trundler and its red rubber-tyred wheel – across the lawn path, down the short drive of cracked and broken concrete and out to the public footpath. She watched and waited, frustrated, as he, with a cool and thoroughly methodical deliberateness – as if he were purposely trying to annoy her – strode away to the right along Northumberland Road back to his own house. And she watched, relieved at last, as he looked back at her, just before he passed out of sight behind the tall and unruly *pittosporum* hedge which marked the boundary on that side of her property, and nodded what was meant – she assumed – to be a final goodbye.

Despite her impatience, and unable to overcome her innate courtesy, she – reluctantly – gave a little wiggly-finger wave of acknowledgement although she quickly realized that it was probably too little a wave given too late; he probably didn't see it.

'Too bad,' she said. To herself. 'Too bloody bad.'

She was on the front porch, with her produce at her feet, her two eggs safely cushioned on the coir mat at the front door. But the front door was permanently locked and bolted; she never used it, never used the haunted hall which led to it, nor any of many large, dusty, empty and unfurnished rooms which were off the hall, all of which were decorated with– (she shuddered at the arrival of the thought and quickly blocked its progress).

So she had to make three trips from the front porch, down the steps, around the side of the house, down the long, unused and cracked, broken and dangerously uneven drive which led to the unused garage and the back yard, through the flimsy wire-netting barrier she called a gate but which wasn't a real gate, up the few unnaturally steep wooden steps to the back door, through the warm glassed-in sun-porch she used as her bed sitting room, and into the kitchen. There she laid the two eggs on a damp dish-cloth, on the bench, and the produce – the soiled cauliflowers, the huge bruised cabbages, the pumpkin, the splaying bunch of shiny and crinkly silverbeet leaves, the broccoli, and the bunch of stout, pink, fibrous and juicy rhubarb stems – on the table. She removed her old camelhair coat in the sun-porch and replaced it with an all-purpose plain cotton wraparound housecoat. Then she sat at the table on an old wooden chair, one of only two in the little kitchen.

'What a bugger,' she said. To herself. She rested her elbows on the table. 'A proper bugger.'

She sensed – no, she felt – soft pressure on her left leg.

'Hello, Norman,' she said brightly.

And as she leaned back in her chair Norman, a middle-aged spayed male she rescued from the RSPCA, more black than tabby, and somewhat overweight, sprang lightly onto her lap – judging the distance perfectly as cats do – and purringly began nuzzling up to her chin; she could feel his wet nose.

'You don't love me,' she said as she knuckled his bony cheek. 'I know you, you rascal. You just want something to eat.'

Norman was one of Betty's three cats; he was the oldest, biggest, strongest and bossiest while black-and-white Duchess was small and delicate and especially affectionate, and long-haired Mittens, the youngest, was grey and limp and soft and shy. They didn't get on well, the three cats, but managed to tolerate each other as cats do when thrown together by chance. But at night they overcame their antipathy and slept together on Betty's cot: Duchess near her head, Mittens at her waist and big Norman at her feet; he liked to have immediate access to the cat door.

'Well, come on, young man,' said Betty as she gently tipped Norman back to the floor. He looked up and meowed in mild protest. 'Too early for your dinner. But no time to waste for me. I've got to do something to save these caulis. Cut off the dirty bits and make a nice creamy cauliflower soup I think. The kiddies will like that. They will. I know. And nourishing too.'

She stood up and moved to the bench taking the two cauliflowers with her. Norman moved too, pressing against her leg around which he curled his tail sinuously. She laid the cauliflowers on the bench and bent to fetch a wooden cutting board; and as she bent she massaged the top of Norman's head with her fingertips.

'He'll bring the trundler back tomorrow I hope,' she said to Norman but really to herself. 'I'll have the soup ready. And I think I'll pull some carrots. And, of course, I'll need more eggie-weggies thanks to you-know-who.'

Norman looked up, opened his mouth to show its pinkness, and display his rough tongue and his little white teeth as sharp as needles, and gave a silent meow in reply.

☼

Old Betty Krilich had lived in Northumberland Road for more than thirty years. She moved there from Wellington after her mother died and left her the Karapuke house. She had already lived alone in Wellington for seven years after her husband had died so suddenly, so unexpectedly. Well, it was sudden to her, unexpected, although evidently, according to the coroner, based on the post-mortem and the evidence of Gus's doctor, and of course on his will, he, Gus, would not have been surprised at his own sudden death. Indeed, thinking about it later, remembering many of the things he had said and done, Betty realized he may even have expected it.

'He more or less told me,' she said to Margaret, Gus's old and faithful spinsterish secretary. It was at the funeral. Margaret was weeping and it dawned on Betty then – for the first time, (God, I'm stupid, she thought) – that Margaret, who was more Gus's age than Betty was, had probably been secretly in love with Gus for years. She felt sorry for Margaret then. 'More or less told me but I wasn't listening,' she said to Margaret. 'Too absorbed in myself,' she added sadly.

The weeping Margaret had agreed: 'Yes, I know,' she had said.

But what did she know? thought Betty. Which? That Gus knew he was ill? Knew he was going to die? Or that she, Betty, was too absorbed in herself to realize what Gus (and probably Margaret too) knew? Betty had wondered about that then. But now she knew the answer. What a shit I was, she thought. All those wasted years. Such a shit. And how kind, devoted and loyal was poor lonely Margaret.

'I was a shit, wasn't I,' she said to Norman. It wasn't a question.

Norman followed Betty into the sun-porch, looking up at her eagerly – still hoping for food – but chose to jump onto the end of the cot, which was covered in a rug of multi-coloured knitted peggy squares, when she opened the back door and went out into the chilly yard. Resigned to hunger for a few more hours he curled himself into a furry ball, covered his nose with his right front paw, and was instantly in a state of feline nap.

The hens ran clucking to the door of their long and narrow coop, with stretched necks and long strides, when they heard and then saw the back door being opened. Betty carefully stepped down the steep staircase – there was no handrail – and laughed.

'You biddies all got fed this morning,' she called jovially to the noisy hens – brown shavers and white leghorns – numbering a score or more. 'It's carrots I'm after now. Carrots for my soup.'

Betty's house was set well to the front of what was a large section – a genuine old-fashioned New Zealand quarter-acre section – which meant that the front yard was especially small and devoid of trees or shrubs or garden or anything ornamental, living or not. And the grass and weeds grew rank together as though in the unfavoured field of a lazy farmer.

But while the front yard was small, unkempt and uncared for the long back yard was neatly planned and laid out, intensely planted and highly productive. The hen house was in the north-east corner together with a row of compost heaps, at various stages of decomposition, set against the boundary hedge of mixed *pittosporums*. The drive from the street — of badly-fractured concrete — ended at a dilapidated and unused garage set near the house against the southern boundary behind which was Betty's little glasshouse within which she raised all her vegetables from seed. Behind the glasshouse, running parallel to a tall wooden fence, stood a double row of fruit trees including winter-bearing lemon, orange and grapefruit, feijoa and tamarillos as well as summer apples, pears, plums, peaches and apricots. Meanwhile the old fence supported the rambling dun-coloured hairy and smelly vines of kiwifruit while half-a-dozen bright and shiny passion fruit plants sent their curling tendrils up and across the walls and roof of the derelict garage.

And down and across the rest of the entire spread — a rectangle defined by the back of the house, two boundary hedges and the tall wooden fence — was laid out a vegetable garden divided into regularly-sized manageable plots by neatly-trimmed grassed paths.

It was down one of these paths that Betty now went to pull a handful of long *Egmont Golds* which she had sown directly in the past summer in accordance with her garden calendar. While she was there, on her knees, she pulled a couple of radishes — long magenta-and-white French breakfast, her favourite — which she rubbed clean on her housecoat as she walked across to the current compost where she laid the already limp green-tops of the carrots and radishes before walking back to the house.

It was a large and sprawling bungalow of the nineteen-hundreds, her house, painted a now-powdery cream. Within its sturdy kauri walls, and below its aged shingled roof, was a wide passage leading to the unused and permanently-locked and bolted front door and providing side access to four spacious bedrooms, a large lounge, an equally large dining room as well as a big bathroom, a small one for the bedrooms, two toilets and a study. It was, indeed, the largest house in the neighbourhood; it was also the shabbiest.

Despite its generous proportions, and the large number of its commodious but unfurnished rooms, Betty chose to live only at the back of the house in only four of its rooms: the east-facing sun-porch (glassed in, years ago, by her father) which served as both her bedroom and living room and was only a doorway away from the adjacent kitchen – which also served as her laundry and which also looked east and out to the long back yard – and the cold-water bathroom and separate toilet, two small and gloomy rooms across the hall from the kitchen. As she never used any of the other empty rooms of the house her privacy was as complete in the house as it was in the back yard. Indeed, she was rarely – never – disturbed by her neighbours who considered her a harmless hermit-like recluse; and although they surreptitiously looked out for her – an old and eccentric lady living alone – they had no idea of the layout of her back yard nor how she occupied herself there or within the few back rooms of her always darkened house.

Now, in the utter and treasured privacy of her back yard, she laid the bunch of hard carrots on the steep back steps and sat beside them for the few minutes it took to enjoy the fresh, cool, crisp and peppery white flesh of her two long radishes. And while she was there the usually affectionate Duchess emerged slinkily from the house and leaped directly down to the path where she began chasing a brown and curled leaf which had attracted her attention and was now being patted about by her right front paw curled into a quartet of vicious hooks.

'Sorry, darling,' she said to busy Duchess. 'I'm going to use your lovely gravy beef to help make my soup. You'll all have to have tins today. Or Whiskas.'

But the little black-and-white Duchess – preoccupied with slaughtering her leaf – took no notice and so Betty laughed, stood up and returned to the kitchen and the cauliflowers which were waiting there to be transformed, with the fresh carrots, and a stock of more than a kilo of gravy beef, into a hot and nourishing soup made with love to be enjoyed by the mothers and children now residing in the safe house of the Karapuke women's refuge in Church Street.

3

'DAD?'

'Alan.'

'Where the hell were you?'

'I was in the workshop.'

'I had to ring three times. I was a getting a bit worried.'

'I was in the workshop,' said Jack again. 'I can hardly hear the phone from there.'

'That's why I got you the cell phone. You can use it anywhere. Take it anywhere. In your pocket.'

'I hate that thing,' said Jack. 'I told you. Everything's too bloody small. My fingers.'

'So what have you done with it?'

'In the kitchen drawer I think.'

'What were you doing in the workshop anyway?'

'Just fixing something. Nothing really.'

'Nothing heavy,' said Alan. 'You know what the doctor–'

'He said I'm fine.'

'But the angina.'

'I'm fine,' insisted Jack. 'The angina's nothing so stop worrying. A wheel came off a shopping trundler. It needs a split pin that's all.'

'What the hell are you doing with a shopping trundler?'

'It's not *my* shopping trundler. Anyway, what do you want?'

'I just wanted to make sure you're okay. All the trucks are out, everyone's at morning tea, Miriam's doing the accounts, the branches are all busy, customers happy, the phones are quiet, the whole place is peaceful and quiet for a change. Like a morgue. Nothing till the bank manager at eleven. Coming down from Auckland for a meeting. So I took the chance. Whose shopping trundler is it anyway?'

'Just a friend's,' said Jack. 'I better get back to it.'

'A lady friend?'

'Yes,' said Jack, somewhat annoyed by the persistent questioning. 'Men don't have shopping trundlers do they.'

'Is she a new friend?'

'What's this all about? She's not really a friend at all. Just a neighbour. Someone I know. I've known her for years.'

'Does she know about the Braithwaites and that? The Steele and the McCahon? And the Lindauer? Christ, dad–'

'She knows *nothing* about me or anything,' said Jack curtly. 'We're just neighbours. I'm doing her a favour and that's it. Okay?'

'Okay, dad,' said Alan. 'I'm sorry, okay. But I can't help worrying about all that stuff in the house and no security and strangers–'

'She's a poor old lady of eighty-eight so she's hardly going to be–'

'Forget it, dad,' said Alan, somewhat embarrassed. 'Forget I mentioned it.'

'Alright then,' said Jack resentfully. He didn't like being bullied by his own son.

'So, are you alright out in the workshop?'

'I told you, I'm putting a split pin in the axle of an old shopping trundler. And that's it.'

'Nothing heavy. Not too strenuous.'

'Nothing like that.'

'Are you warm enough out there? It's quite cold today.'

'Look, I'm fine. But I've got to go now. How's Miriam?'

'She's fine.'

'And what about Michael? Any change?'

'Not really,' said Alan. 'He just lies on his side staring at the wall all bloody day. Day after day. Says nothing. Does nothing. If it wasn't for Miriam.'

'Poor bugger,' said Jack.

'All the drugs don't help,' said Alan.

'They knock him out I suppose.'

'That's about it.'

'What can you do?'

'Miriam gives him something to eat sometimes. Soup or something like that,' said Alan. 'Has to feed him like a baby.'

'Poor Miriam.'

'She doesn't mind,' said Alan.

'Tell me about it,' said Jack. 'She's a bloody saint.'

'Now, are you sure you're okay?'

'I'm fine,' said Jack. 'Can't help thinking about Michael though. On my mind. It's horrible.'

'I know.'

'Anyway, I better go. I'll see you later. Love to Miriam, eh.'

'Will do, dad.'

'And Michael too if he wakes up.'

'Will do. See you Sunday.'

'Tell him I'll see him then,' said Jack. 'Sunday.'

Jack stood by the phone in the kitchen for a minute or two trying to calm down. For some reason Alan's phone call annoyed him. And he was worried – and felt so helpless – about Michael, his younger son.

'Bloody kids,' he said. To himself. 'Sixty years old and he's still a worry.'

He shook his head sharply in an attempt to shake out the thoughts about sick Michael.

When he felt better he made his way from the kitchen to the attached double garage, past his two cars – standing side-by-side like big brother and little brother: first, his beloved nineteen fifty-five blue Zephyr Six and, against the far wall, a nineteen seventy Rolls-Royce Silver Shadow which was about due for its monthly outing to Landseer Farm on Sunday – and into the workshop which was in fact an extension of the garage. It, the workshop, was built and equipped to his own specifications when he bought the house. That was when he retired, just after Catherine died, twenty-five years ago.

'You go ahead and retire,' Alan had said. 'Everything'll be fine. Business is booming. You know that. Buy yourself a nice place in town. You're still young enough to enjoy life. Even on your own.'

'Sixty's young to retire,' said many of his sixty-year-old Combined Club friends who couldn't afford to retire.

'Alan's running the business now,' he said. 'And he's good. He doesn't need me hanging around the place.'

'But you're on your own now,' they said. 'Why did you buy a big family-sized house when you're on your own?'

'Why on earth did you buy that place?' asked Alan. 'In Northumberland Road of all places?'

'What's wrong with Northumberland Road?'

'It's so busy. All the traffic to and from town and the highway.'

'It's not that bad,' said Jack defensively; indignantly. Alan didn't know it but he had always planned to live on Northumberland Road. One day.

Annoyed that he had to explain himself – to his son as well as to his friends – and knowing there was at least a little envy behind the questioning of his friends, he nevertheless tried to furnish credible-sounding explanations.

'I've bought that old Zephyr and I'm going to restore it,' he said. 'I need a big garage for the cars. And I need my own workshop and tools.'

'But you never drive the Rolls,' they said.

'Yes I do,' he replied. 'I maintain her very carefully and drive her regularly. She's an investment.'

'But all those rooms,' they said. 'Such a big house for one old bloke.'

'I need wall space,' he said. 'I'm investing in art.'

'Why? You never cared about art before.'

'Well I do now,' he replied somewhat resentfully. 'And I like the garden. I'm going to grow roses. I love roses. And, anyway, I've always wanted to live in town; close to the doctor and the Combined and the showgrounds for rugby and that.'

'But Northumberland Road? It's so busy.'

'I really like Northumberland Road. I really do,' he said.

'But that old painting?' said Alan. 'You never liked art before. Who was Steele anyway?'

'He was pretty bloody famous actually,' said Jack.

'Pretty bloody expensive if you ask me,' said Alan. 'Twenty-four grand. That worries the hell out of me, dad.'

'Alan. Why don't you leave your father alone?' asked Miriam. Rhetorically. Frequently.

'I don't know what's got into him,' said Alan later. 'He's never been arty-farty. He's always been so bloody down-to-earth. So practical.'

Indeed, Jack had always been a practical man, always enjoyed working with his hands. In the early days of the business – when he left school at fifteen to work for his father – he did most of the mechanical maintenance and repairs on the company's trucks and vans. Now, seventy years later, despite being a ball of muscle (as he said), fit as a fiddler, (as he said), a box of budgies (as he said), generally healthy, fit and strong, his doctor had mentioned his heart: a bit of angina there, Jack, he had said, almost in passing. Not bad. But best to take it a bit easy at your age. It's only your age. And keep the pills on you.

It was advice which he heeded with sensible moderation – walking, working in the garden – but which Alan had interpreted as a direct instruction to do nothing.

'I can't do *nothing*,' he had insisted. 'I'd rather die being busy. Doing something.'

But Alan – conservative and cautious in all things – didn't have to worry. A man of eighty-five is naturally less able than a man of sixty; it's a self-regulating process.

Before he re-entered his workshop Jack stopped briefly at the door. He wanted to admire it. He liked its orderly tidiness; the way the woodworking bench ran the length of the wall to the right, with fixed vices and all his woodworking tools mounted on the wall above. He liked the way he had organized the engineering bench which ran the length of the other side, the side to the left, together with all the tools for engineering and metalwork mounted on the wall above. Each bench was lighted from above, along its entire length, by its own strip of fluorescent tubes and a wide window set into each wall to let in natural light. Meanwhile the few heavy power machines – for woodworking and engineering, necessarily bolted to the concrete floor – were fixed in a line down the middle of the workshop's length, each with its own source of power and its own lighting for close-up work.

Most of the tools, equipment and machinery were now rarely used but he liked to remember that he was once active in the workshop almost every day and that it and its machinery were always there if he needed them. Even now he was sometimes called upon to make or repair something which, according to Alan, couldn't easily or quickly enough be made or repaired by the men in the firm's own now-extensive workshops. Jack didn't quite believe Alan about that but he accepted the patronage graciously and enjoyed the work.

After no more than a few moments of such melancholy contemplation he moved to Betty's little tartan trundler which was lying on its side on the engineering bench. He used a pair of pliers to finish the job which Alan's phone call had interrupted: to divide the tines of a shiny new split pin and turn them back around the axle. Then, unable to stop there, as a matter of course, a matter of pride, he turned over the trundler and replaced the other old split pin with another new one drawn from his plentiful stock of such miscellany stored in a plastic tray of labelled compartments which he kept under the bench. If one's gone the other's bound to go soon, he thought. A few drops of oil to each end of the axle, to each wheel, and a trial spin of them both, confirmed – he was sure – that Betty's little tartan shopping trundler was good for many more of her walking kilometres.

'Just like a bought one,' he said as he lowered the flimsy and light-weight little vehicle to the floor.

After lunch he set off for Betty's house. He started by pulling the repaired shopping trundler behind him although only a few steps into the short journey he decided it was easier to pick it up and carry it. Once there he again made his way up the broken concrete drive and diagonally across the lawn path to the front porch where the day before he had sensed Betty's discomfort at his presence and then her relief when he said goodbye and left her and her vegetables and eggs together on the porch.

4

'I'LL BRING BACK your trundler in a couple of days,' he had said. 'Tomorrow probably.'

And that was today.

He stepped up and across the narrow porch to the front door which comprised eight panes of dimpled glass held in place by old putty, brittle and crumbling and losing its hold; there was a Yale lock, a tarnished door handle – no more than a grip – and a matching doorbell twist. Swinging the shopping trundler in his left hand he used his other hand to twist the doorbell but it turned freely, without resistance, without ringing, evidently disabled, and so he knocked loudly with his knuckles on one of the loose panes of glass.

He saw, through the dimpled glass, the approach of a vague, indistinct, distorted shape. It stopped, and he heard Betty say, a little nervously he thought: 'Who is it?'

'It's Jack,' he said loudly. 'Jack Landseer.'

'Who?'

'Jack Landseer.' He shouted it this time. 'I've brought back your trundler. All tickety-boo and right as ninepence.'

'Oh dear. I see,' he heard her say. 'Take it around the back will you. To the back door. But mind you shut the gate.'

'Good-oh,' he said cheerfully. 'Round the back it is then.'

And so he went down the long side of the big house, along the uneven concrete drive which led to the ramshackle garage. He could see the garage was not used — at least not for housing a car as he knew from experience that it once had — as its wooden doors, rotten at the bottom, hung crookedly on rusty hinges and were fastened by an old and corroded padlock; and anyway the whole double-door opening was draped in a green tangle of jasmine which would, in the summer, he knew, be covered in small, bright and highly-scented flowers. The side of the building, the side facing into the back garden, was covered in a green tangle of something shiny but dormant; he guessed correctly that it was passion fruit.

A fence of lightweight chicken wire was stretched at an angle from the corner of the garage to the adjacent corner of the house to which it was attached by a batten and three large dull brass cup- hooks. Jack assumed that the wire netting was a fence and the batten-and-hooks arrangement constituted the gate which Betty had enjoined him to shut. And as he lifted and lowered the shopping trundler over the fence and unhooked the batten from the house he could see the probable reason for the enclosing fence and why its flimsiness was sufficient for its purpose: a flock of large and healthy-looking hens — variously brown and white — enclosed in a long and narrow run with a hen-house attached, set in the far corner of the section. They clucked alarmingly and flapped their wings uselessly at his appearance. Jack assumed they were protesting his presence in their domain but in fact they associated any human shape with the potential delivery of food. When none was forthcoming they reduced their excited clucking to a soft and sociable croaking and resumed their heads-down bobbing and browsing.

As Jack rehooked the flimsy gate Betty appeared at the top of the steps which led up to the closed door of the glassed-in porch. He was surprised to see that that she was wearing a sturdy all-purpose wraparound house coat in plain cotton. He'd never seen her in such an ordinary workaday outfit.

'Your trundler, Betty,' he called as he approached the steps. 'All ship-shape and Bristol fashion again.'

'Thanks,' said Betty. She smiled weakly. 'I do appreciate it you know.'

'My pleasure,' said Jack cheerfully. He lifted the trundler by the handle and proffered it up to her standing at the top of the steps with the porch door half-closed behind her. 'Where do you want it?'

'Just leave it there,' said Betty. 'It'll be fine.'

She turned back to the door.

'But I could—'

'I'll get it later,' said Betty quickly, over her shoulder. She pushed open the door and was gone leaving Jack standing at the bottom of the steps, holding the shopping trolley at his side, looking up dumbly at the closed door.

'Bugger me,' he said as he lowered the trundler and checked that it would stand upright on the crooked and broken concrete apron at the foot of the steps.

He turned then and looked properly down the back yard. The hens had settled and were now scratching in the dry bare dirt of their run, scratching and bobbing and pecking away at whatever things edible they found there, although a few looked up the yard at him from curiosity.

'Bloody chooks,' he said quietly, to himself, as he surveyed the scene, duly impressed – as any gardener would have been – by the planned orderliness of the back yard.

There were twelve rectangles of cultivated garden, four rows of three, all the same size, separated by grass paths, carefully mown and with neatly-trimmed edges. All but one were dedicated to seasonal vegetables, some low-growing, some tall, some staked and some only recently planted. He recognized the patches of silverbeet, cauliflower and cabbage as the sources of those vegetables which had spilled from Betty's trundler, as well as rows of lush-green spinach, unready broccoli of a medium height, thriving broad beans and Brussels sprouts, a corner dedicated to a few large-leafed rhubarbs, and a few other plants that were too young and too small to be quickly or easily identified. Over the only fallow plot stood a mobile but vacant chicken coop, with rubber wheels at one end, the exact width and length of the garden rectangle.

To the right, behind the end of garage, he could see a small glasshouse, its panes glowing with internal condensation and greened with moss at their edges. And beyond the glasshouse, two rows of fruit trees – one row without leaves – running parallel to the boundary fence all the way to the section's end which was roughly defined by a ragged tecoma hedge.

'Bugger me,' said Jack again. To himself. As a gardener of sorts he couldn't help admiring the garden while nevertheless being perplexed by the personal nature of its architect and only operative.

He was about to leave at last when he heard the back door open; he turned to see Betty standing again at the open door.

'Excuse me,' she called tentatively and Jack wondered why she didn't – couldn't bring herself to – use his name.

He waited. Looking up at her looking down at him.

'I made some soup,' said Betty. 'For the refuge.'

'I see,' said Jack who didn't see at all.

'The women's refuge. In Church Street.'

'I see,' said Jack again.

'It's in a sealed pressure cooker.'

'Oh,' said Jack.

'The soup, I mean,' said Betty. 'You see, the thing is–'

'Jack,' said Jack by way of a prompt.

'–Jack,' said Betty somewhat awkwardly. 'The thing is, it's big and heavy and I can't get it there. To the refuge. I could put it in the bottom of the trundler but it's too big see.'

'Oh,' said Jack again.

'So, the thing is, I hate to ask but could you give me a lift in your motor car?'

'I see,' said Jack.

'You have got a car haven't you?'

'Tell me about it,' said Jack.

'Eh?'

'Yes, of course I've got a car.'

'Yes, I thought you would have.'

'When?' asked Jack.

'When what?'

'When do you need a lift? In my car?'

'Oh, the sooner the better,' said Betty.

And so Jack held up the forefinger of his right hand, to signal a decision, and said: 'Right-oh. I'll go and get the car now and be right back. Would that be okay?'

'Oh, that'd be splendid,' said a genuinely pleased Betty with a genuine smile. 'I'll be waiting at the gate.'

'Okey-dokey,' said Jack. 'Back soon.'

✿

'This is a really nice car,' said Betty as she settled herself on the bench seat of Jack's Zephyr, her catering-size sealed pressure cooker of soup at her feet. 'How old is it?'

'It's a nineteen fifty-five,' said Jack.

'My goodness,' said Betty. 'Such nice condition.'

'Built in Lower Hutt and fully restored by yours truly.'

'It's lovely,' said Betty. 'It really is.'

'Tell me about it,' said Jack. 'I don't use it much though. Vintage. It's like a hobby.'

'It's nice,' said Betty approvingly. 'A nice English car. A *proper* car. Now, do you know where the refuge is?'

'No,' said Jack, as he turned the car around and headed back up Northumberland Road in the direction of town.

'It's at the very far end of Church Street,' said Betty.

'Okey-dokey,' said Jack.

'But the thing is, you're not supposed to know.'

'Eh?'

'It's not a secret exactly, the safe house, but we don't advertise it,' said Betty.

'No, I suppose not,' said Jack but he didn't know what he was talking about. The subject was a mystery to him.

'For obvious reasons.'

'Yes. I see.'

'We know some people – undesirables shall we say – they probably know the address,' said Betty.

'Do they?'

'Probably,' said Betty. 'But, you know, we've never had any trouble.'

'That's good,' said Jack. He didn't know what else to say.

'Anyway, the thing is, don't tell anyone the address,' said Betty seriously. 'Ever. It just looks like an ordinary house. That's the important thing. Just an ordinary house in an ordinary street.'

'Right-oh,' said Jack somewhat naively.

'Just drop me there and wait while I take in the soup. If you don't mind I mean.'

'Of course,' said Jack cheerfully. 'And then I'll take you home again.'

And so he was directed to an address in Church Street; it was, according to Betty, just an ordinary house in an ordinary street although all Jack could see, as he waited in the car for Betty's return, was a tall wooden fence, stained a reddish-brown, into which was set a matching gate and a letter box, and over the top of which he could see no more than the peak of a concrete-tiled roof.

# 5

IN THE MIDDLE of the next afternoon – an afternoon as fine and cool as the one it followed – Jack Landseer was again in his front garden attending to his roses. He had almost completed the annual task and was standing at the house end of the long row adjacent to the drive; his wheelbarrow was standing at his side almost full with the viciously barbed woody cuttings from his dormant roses.

When he wasn't bent to his work he stood as straight and tall as usual; the bright whiteness of his thick wavy hair made his face look more flushed than it really was and emphasised the bright blueness of his eyes behind his rimless spectacles. Despite his eighty-five years he looked as he always did, even in the garden: handsome, prosperous and well-groomed.

Such a lovely old chap, was the general opinion of the lady members of the Combined Club – some of whom were as old as he – of which he had been a member since his arrival in the town. Such a gentleman, they all said.

'He's decent old bloke alright,' said his fellow gentlemen members who were generally younger than he.

'A lot smarter than he lets on,' said others.

'Got a bit of dough too, I reckon,' said one.

'Plenty,' said others.

'But keeps himself to himself,' was the consensus.

And now, as he straightened from his work, and dropped another thorny stick into his wheelbarrow, the man in question noticed a familiar female figure in the street about to pass by. Her white hair was up, as usual, and on this occasion she was dressed in a bulky ankle-length dress in brown corduroy with a short jacket in orange paisley. He lifted his right arm, secateurs in gloved hand, in what was intended as a wave, and was about to call out, but both wave and call were aborted when he realized that Betty Krilich was either unaware of where in the street she was — perhaps absent-minded and preoccupied and so not connecting her position with his house or the broken shopping trundler event of the previous day — or was consciously avoiding him and any form of intercourse.

I think she's avoiding me, he decided. Well, too bloody bad, Betty. Plenty of time. Now it's time for my afternoon tea.

The roses were pruned, compact and naked, and now looked — at least to an enthusiastic and knowledgeable rose-grower which Jack Landseer was — right ready for spring. The pruned wood had been carried away to the back yard to be burned but inevitably a line of debris ran along the lawn on both sides of the roses row spoiling the neat appearance of the smooth green lawn. And that was the excuse Jack needed to spend another hour in the front garden in the darkling of that winter's day.

Setting the lawnmower high – to gather up, mulch and catch the rose pruning debris rather than actually cut the lawn which didn't need it – it required only two or three runs up and down each side of the rose row to return the lawn to its unsullied green smoothness. And it was as he was finishing with the mower, having switched it off, and as he was tipping and shaking the contents of the catcher into the wheelbarrow, he again caught sight of the familiar figure of old Betty Krilich stepping determinedly along the pavement, her brown corduroy maxi-skirt swirling and swishing around over her bright white sneakers, presumably on her return journey.

Undeterred by her dogged determination to ignore his presence only a few metres away, Jack stepped nimbly over the low wall which separated him in his front garden from her on the public pavement, a little ahead of her progress, so that after two or three more steps she was forced to stop and acknowledge him given that the alternative was to detour around him, completely ignoring him, which rudeness he knew she would not, could not, entertain.

'Betty,' he said. 'Jack. Remember?'

The old woman stopped and looked directly at the old man.

'Course I remember,' she said curtly. 'I'm not stupid.'

'No,' said Jack. He was somewhat taken aback. 'I saw you before.'

'When?'

'After lunch some time. I can't remember exactly.'

'I've been at choir practice,' she said.

'Where?'

'At Saint Peter's,' said Betty. 'Every Thursday afternoon if you must know.'

Jack knew the church; the Anglican church in Church Street, just two or three streets closer to town. They would have passed it on the way to the women's refuge the previous day.

'Oh. I see,' said Jack. 'Well, I wanted to ring you up.'

'Why?' she asked with curiosity mixed with suspicion.

'I couldn't find your number in the book,' said Jack.

'No. You wouldn't.'

'Why not?'

'I haven't got a phone,' she said.

'Oh,' said Jack. 'Why not?'

'Why not what?'

'Why haven't you got a phone?'

'Bloody people ring you up.'

'Tell me about it.'

'Why did you want to ring me up anyway?'

'Well, how are you?' asked Jack. 'Are you alright?'

'Of course I'm alright. Is that why you wanted to ring me up?'

'Not only that,' said Jack. 'How's your trundler?'

'Stupid question,' said Betty. Jack knew it was a stupid question even as he asked it. 'It's fine. Thank you. Now is that all? I'm busy. I have to get home. Things to do. Always things to do.'

And so at last Jack managed to ask the question that was the real reason for his interception.

'Do you want to go out to tea?' he blurted out.

'What?'

'Tomorrow night.'

'What?'

'I said do you—'

'I heard what you said,' said Betty. 'I'm not bloody deaf. But what do you mean, tea?'

Jack could see that she was genuinely puzzled although he didn't know why she should be.

'Dinner. An evening meal. At night. They cook a beaut steak, egg and chips at the Combined,' he said, adding: 'and pav for pudding, good as home-made, with all the cream you want. Caramel sauce too. And hundreds and thousands.'

'What's the Combined?'

'It's a club. My club. The Combined Club. Like a Cossie club. It's nice for oldies like us.'

'No,' said Betty.

'What?'

'I said no,' said Betty again. 'Thank you, but no.'

Jack was getting used to her plain speaking but he was still surprised by the bluntness of her reply.

'But why? Friday nights. They have old-time dancing. Good orchestra. Well, a band really. Pool. Darts. Big meat raffles. A good bar and a great feed. And nice people just like us.'

'Look at me, Jack,' she said. She raised her hands pointed them back at herself. He noticed that it was the first time she had spontaneously called him Jack. 'I'm not a going-out-to-tea person. I'm not a club person. I don't like crowds. I don't like mixing with strangers. And I don't like going out at night.'

'You weren't always like that,' said Jack although he immediately wished he hadn't.

'What do you mean?' snapped Betty with a hint of anger.

'Well, Catherine, my wife, late wife, she used to read about you,' said Jack quickly; recovering. 'In the social pages and that. You were famous in Karapuke. Famous in Wellington too.' He took a breath and noticed that his audience looked astonished. He suddenly felt foolish. 'You know what I mean,' he added lamely.

'No I don't,' said Betty.

'Look, forget it shall we. The thing is I was asking you out on a date,' said Jack with a smile.

'A date!' Betty Krilich looked disgusted. 'Don't make me sick,' she said.

'It's a *joke*, Betty. A joke. You and me. A date.'

'Why are you even talking to me? No one talks to me. At least not on the street. Not people I don't know.'

'Well I know you. And you know *me* don't you?'

'No.'

Yes you do, thought Jack. But he ignored her reply.

'What about a cup of tea then? Or coffee?' he asked hopefully. 'Next time you go to town. I'll walk with you and we can talk.'

'What about?'

Jack didn't reply. He just looked at her smilingly. Daring her to respond. Which she did. At last.

'I'm going to Saint Peter's again tomorrow morning,' she said. 'To do the flowers. There's a wedding on Saturday and four services on Sunday.'

'What time?' he asked although he knew well enough; she passed his house at the same time every Friday morning.

'I'll be coming past here – your place – about half past ten,' she said.

She obviously considered the conversation over and was ready to set off home.

'Right-oh, Betty,' said Jack as he stepped aside to let her pass. 'Half past ten. I'll be raring to go.'

He noticed that she looked at him quizzically — wonderingly — and he felt foolish again. And so she passed around him without saying goodbye. Without saying anything.

But after just a few steps she stopped, turned half around, and said: 'You can help me with the flowers if you like. And then we can have a cup of tea and a biscuit with Mr Widdop.'

'Who's Mr Widdop?'

'Reverend Widdop. The vicar,' said Betty.

And then she was gone. And Jack was left on the pavement watching her walking away, tall and elegant in her long brown dress and short paisley jacket set off by bright white sneakers with neon-green laces.

'Goodbye, Betty Henderson-Krilich,' he said. To himself. 'You *do* know me you know. You really do.'

✿

He was almost back at the house, at the front door, when he heard the phone ring.

'Bloody phone,' he said. To himself. 'Let it ring.'

It stopped ringing but started again as soon he reached the kitchen.

'Hullo?'

'Dad, it's me.'

'Alan.'

'Where were you? I rang a minute ago.'

'I couldn't get to the phone that quick. Outside. You should let it ring longer.'

'Sorry. But listen, dad, it's Michael.'

'What? Has something happened?'

'I'm home. Miriam had to call the ambulance. She's gone with him. It's bad this time, dad. Real bad. Probably *it* if you know what I mean.'

'Oh dear,' said Jack sadly.

'I'm going up to the hospital now,' said Alan. 'Do you want me to pick you up? Do you want to come? To see him? It's a long trip to Auckland.'

'Of course. I'll be ready.'

'He won't know we're there you know.'

'I know,' said Jack resignedly. 'I know that. But I want to go.'

Suddenly he felt sad and old and empty; as empty as his big house. He went to the garage for his jacket and scarf. And then to the workshop to check that it was locked. Checked the back door. He got his wallet from the bedroom, opened the front door, and then sat in his favourite arm-chair in the living room, by the window, where he could see the drive. There, in the company of the two Braithwaites, the Steele, the McCahon, the Lindauer and some of the others, he waited and thought about Michael.

And Alan.

Alan was the steady one. Always had been.

He's such a joy, Catherine used to say.

These days, though, Jack found him impatient and often cross. But he couldn't argue that as a boy Alan was a good child, obedient and cooperative, always wanting to please. A good student. Good at sports. And now, evidently, a kind and considerate husband, father and grandfather if somewhat over-bearing as an adult son.

'Don't worry, dad,' Alan had said when his mother died. 'I'll look after the business now.'

And he did. Took it over and grew it in a way that Jack knew *he* never would have; never *could* have; wouldn't even have wanted to. Now it was bigger and more successful than ever. So many trucks. Vast storage depots and branches all over the country. Meanwhile he was clever enough to marry well: Miriam was a remarkable wife, mother, grandmother and daughter-in-law – poor Catherine had loved her so much, and the twins, David and Dianne – and then to willingly take on nursing her husband's degenerate younger brother.

Miriam was an angel whom Alan didn't deserve; and nor did Michael.

Poor Michael. A young genius. A polymath. Schooled at home by private tutors who were recommended by the university and paid for by Jack somewhat reluctantly but under pressure from Catherine. By then he, Jack, was managing director of the increasingly successful and wealthy Town & Country Carriers Limited.

'Why can't he go to Boys' High like I did? Like Alan did? Like other boys do?' protested Jack each time he was asked to write a cheque to one of Michael's tutors.

'Don't you get it, Jack' said Catherine. 'He's not like other boys.'

'Tell me about it,' said Jack who had no idea how to deal with his younger son; a boy who looked like a child but thought and conversed like an adult. 'It'd be a lot cheaper if he was.'

And then university degrees in subjects that Jack didn't understand. Two masters. And then off to Oxford. A doctorate. A brilliant mathematician, they said, they being the big-wigs of his Oxford college. And a physicist.

'We should go and see him at Oxford,' said Catherine.

'England!' said Jack. 'Bugger that for a joke.'

He didn't go. But Catherine did. She was so proud of the photos she took. He looked up: they were still there, on the mantelpiece. What a dag, he thought.

'How will he ever earn a living,' he said to Catherine when she got back. He didn't know what mathematicians did; or physicists.

But he *did* earn a living; a good living. He was recruited directly from Oxford by British military intelligence.

'Does that mean he's a spy?' Jack used to ask Catherine and Alan. 'Like that James Bond or something?'

But they didn't know.

In fact for the more than twenty-five years that Michael worked for British military intelligence – MI5 first and then, later, MI6 – nobody but his immediate superiors knew exactly what he did. Even Sharon – his wife, who was also an operative although in a different branch – didn't know what he did although she knew enough not to ask. On the other hand Michael didn't know what *she* did.

'How can they live like that?' Jack used to ask. 'That's not a marriage.'

Indeed, for three years – during the late nineteen-nineties – Michael was working for the American CIA in Langley, Virginia; for those three years Sharon didn't even know if he were alive.

But in the end that very clever little boy who became a very clever young man wasn't clever enough. And now, age sixty, with nothing to call his own, childless, disowned by his English wife, and now entirely dependent on the financial support of the family business (which he had always claimed to despise), his older brother and the tender nursing of his sister-in-law, he lay in a coma, the vital organs of his body corrupted by alcohol, his brain being overwhelmed by a tumour, now evidently only hours away from death.

A car horn sounded; Jack looked up from his reverie, looked out the window, confirmed that it was Alan's big Range Rover in the drive, sighed deeply, stood up, adjusted his scarf and jacket.

Bloody kids, eh, he said. To himself. Bloody kids.

6

JACK WAITED FOR Betty at his front gate; but he didn't have to wait long. So straight and flat was Northumberland Road that he saw her leave her property – at one-seven-two – and set off towards him. He knew it was her from her height, from the way she walked, and from the bright whiteness of the hair on her head and the shoes on her feet.

She can probably see me here waiting, he thought.

It was a pleasant day. Not too cold. There was no wind. And the unwarm sun was sharing the pale sky with thin and milky clouds.

Betty arrived before long. Jack noticed that she was wearing the same widely-flared blue jeans she was wearing on Monday, when he helped her with her broken shopping trundler, with a matching and heavy-duty denim jacket – almost white with age – with metal buttons and pockets elaborately embroidered with what he took to be dragons although it was hard to tell as the once-bright embroidery threads were faded.

'No shopping trundler?'

Betty smiled and Jack was glad. 'Not today,' she said pleasantly enough. 'Not on Fridays.'

She didn't stop walking and so Jack fell into step beside her.

'Do you do the flowers every Friday?' he asked.

'Pretty much,' said Betty. 'Except on Good Friday and days like that. Got to be flexible.'

'How long have you been doing it? The flowers?'

'Ever since I moved back.'

'To Karapuke? Here?'

'Yes.'

'That's thirty-three years ago,' Jack said.

Betty was astonished. She looked at him suspiciously.

'How do you know *that*?' she asked accusingly. 'The years. Exactly?'

'Well, about,' said Jack evasively. 'It's a long time. Doing the same thing every Friday.'

He was trying to change the subject and it worked.

'I've always got something to do,' said Betty. 'Every day. Something different. I can't stand being idle can you? So much to do. Here we are,' she added, turning right into Church Street.

There was very little motor- or foot-traffic on the quiet suburban streets of Karapuke, especially off Northumberland Road, but Jack noticed that each pedestrian who passed, whether male or female, young or old, acknowledged Betty (and him incidentally) with a friendly nod or a 'morning, Betty'; and the drivers of most of the cars which passed them on the street, whether going to or from town, sounded their horn in a manner that was unmistakeably friendly.

I never noticed that before, he thought; that a car horn can sound friendly.

And he noticed that Betty wasn't at all surprised by the nods and greetings and friendly car horns but routinely acknowledged every salutation with a little wave, a faint smile or a nod.

They arrived at Saint Peter's which was a pretty little wooden church – typical of its age – painted a bright white with a steep roof of grey-painted corrugated iron, a squat and pathetic-looking steeple housing one small bell, and doors and windows in a pointed Gothic style; the window and door frames were painted dark green as were the doors themselves.

The church was set close to the street with a wide spread of lawn to the right in the centre of which stood a single, old and naked oak tree. In front of the tree, close to the unfenced boundary, stood a large notice board on two sturdy white wooden posts. ST PETER'S ANGLICAN CHURCH, KARAPUKE it announced with the scriptural quote below: *"I am the way the truth and the life"*. The office phone number was painted in small letters together with the website address: www.stpeterskarapuke.org.nz. And across the top of the board was a crawling electric sign announcing the times of four Sunday services (7.45 am, 9.00 am, 10.45 am and 7.00 pm) and one on Wednesdays (11.00 am). Jack saw everything at a glance and once again wondered – as he did so often lately – what the website address business was all about. He knew that Town & Country Carriers Limited had a website but he'd never looked at it – he didn't know how – and he knew that Alan and Miriam and the children and just about everyone he knew, including his friends and acquaintances at the Combined

Club, had an email address but he didn't – he didn't even have a computer – and didn't think he ever would. Not now. And he was sure Betty wouldn't have one. He knew she didn't have a telephone and he was pretty sure she didn't even have electricity.

Beside and attached to the church, although set back slightly, was what was obviously an all-purpose hall. What was not obvious was that it was a rather new building, at least compared with the church to which it belonged, and Jack couldn't help admiring the way the unknown architect had cleverly designed it to complement the church's traditional design and blend naturally into the mature ecclesiastical landscape.

And at the very back of that churchly landscape, at the end of a long and curving Macadam drive, stood the old vicarage wherein no doubt, thought Jack, dwells Mr Widdop and, perhaps, a Mrs Widdop and some little Anglican Widdops.

There was just one wide concrete step up to the church's heavy double doors; Jack followed Betty who pushed open one of them and entered the church porch. The door closed loudly and jarringly behind them, rattling the old door hardware, and Jack noticed that the ambient noise of the outdoors was immediately muffled; the small church, which opened out beyond the porch, lined with wood that was darkened with age, its pale light coloured by a stained-glass window above the alter, was empty and utterly silent.

'Good old Valerie,' said Betty suddenly, her voice echoing around the small building; it seemed loud and irreverent to Jack.

'What?' he whispered.

'You don't have to whisper, Jack,' said Betty. 'There's no one here but us.'

'But what did you say?' He forced himself to ask the question in a normal voice in which respect he was not entirely successful.

'Valerie O'Davies,' said Betty. She was taking off her denim jacket and hanging it on one of a row of antique hooks there for the purpose. Under the coat she was wearing a loose white t-shirt tie-dyed pink and blue and purple; Jack remembered that Catherine often wore one just like it.

'She delivers the flowers early in the morning,' said Betty pointing to a huge pile of white chrysanthemums, with their lacy foliage and over-length stems, lying wetly and heavily across a small table in front of the parish notice board. 'She's a florist and she buys the flowers for the church every week,' said Betty. 'At the market in Auckland. Donates them. Every week,' she said, adding: 'Generous. She's a professional florist but she's hopeless at big arrangements. Funny, eh.'

'Has she got that little florist shop in town?' asked Jack. 'Val's Flowers or something like that?'

'Val's Flower Pot,' said Betty.

'I know her husband,' said Jack. 'At the club.'

'Steve. Her husband's name is Steve,' said Betty. 'I've met him once or twice.'

'That's him. He's a builder,' said Jack. 'Big outfit too. O'Davies Brothers Construction. He's a friend of Alan's. I think they went to school together.'

'Nice chap,' said Betty. 'Now, could you bring them Jack? The flowers.'

'Good-oh,' said Jack.

'Right. Let's get on with it then.'

And so for almost an hour a willing and obedient Jack Landseer followed the firm and clear instructions of Betty Krilich, flower arranger.

'Go to the kitchen in the hall, there, and through the kitchen outside to the compost,' she said, 'but don't go into the hall itself.'

'Why not?' asked Jack. Naturally.

'It's ante-natal class this morning,' said Betty.

'Oh,' said Jack who didn't want to know more.

And so he took the old flowers from the church into the kitchen of the adjacent church hall – ensuring that the door into the hall proper was firmly shut – where he emptied the tall and heavy vases of their putrid water and left them rinsing in the sink while he went out the kitchen's side door and around to the back of the hall to dump the wilting old flowers in the compost bin. Back in the kitchen he washed out the vases with hot water and then cold, as instructed by Betty, while she, in the church, was dressing the foliage of the fresh chrysanthemums and trimming their stems to a suitable length. Finally Jack was asked to make another trip to the compost bin with the unwanted foliage and stems.

Betty was still busy when he returned to the church; she was half-way up a step-ladder, stretching out in the process of making some petty adjustment to her arrangement.

'Are you safe up there like that?' he asked.

'Oh, you're back,' she said without turning around or looking down at him, and ignoring his question and his implied concern.

'Yes. Are you safe?'

'I'm nearly finished here,' she said. 'Go and wait in the kitchen and we'll have a cup of tea in a minute. Won't be long.'

She seemed affable now and he was glad. Perhaps she appreciated his company. Perhaps she appreciated his help. Evidently she didn't appreciate or need his concern. And so, assuming she had been putting herself in danger up the church ladder every Friday for thirty-odd years, Jack decided to leave her to it.

7

THERE WERE A few square Formica tables and unmatched old wooden chairs – four chairs per table – in the kitchen so Jack sat at one of them, choosing the one nearest the bench where he assumed Betty would stand to make the tea. He'd only just sat down when a delicate-looking young man with wispy blond hair, dressed casually in blue jeans and a cream polo-neck sweater, came in through the outside door.

'Ah, no Betty,' he said.

'She's in the church,' said Jack. 'I'm waiting for her. Cup of tea.'

'I see. Yes. Flowers,' said the young man. 'Vance Widdop,' he said stretching out his right hand to the seated Jack.

Jack was surprised to see a priest dressed so informally; he stood up. 'The vicar I assume,' he said taking the hand. 'Jack Landseer.'

'Ah,' said the vicar, 'Of course. The jolly big carrying firm I take it. Trucks and things.'

'Exactly,' said Jack.

'Let's sit down,' said the vicar pulling out a chair opposite to Jack's and sitting down. Jack resumed his seat. 'I met your son I expect,' said the vicar. 'He moved us here from Hamilton. Not him personally of course. Nice chap.'

Jack nodded.

'It's a growing business I'm told,' said the vicar.

'Tell me about it,' said Jack.

'You don't approve?' The young vicar sounded surprised.

'Let's just say I'm glad I'm not running it anymore.'

'I understand,' said the vicar nodding wisely. He then leaned forward in order to speak quietly. 'So you're an old friend of Betty's,' he said rather than asked. It was almost a whisper.

'Yes,' said Jack quietly. He didn't know why the vicar felt it necessary to speak quietly but he felt compelled to follow his lead. 'We've known each other an awfully long time.'

'So you know,' said the vicar.

'Of course,' said Jack who didn't really know what the vicar was talking about.

'About the hall and that? This hall?'

'Of course,' said Jack.

'And the mission?'

'Of course.'

It makes sense, thought Jack. Of course it does.

'She thinks we don't know but of course we do.'

'I suppose you do,' said Jack.

'Such a generous soul. She arranged it all you know. The hall. The architect. The builders. All the sub-contractors.

Paid for everything including a new roof on the church. Must have cost her a fortune. And we – not me, before my time – I mean the church and the parish committee and everyone didn't have to worry about a thing. The bishop? Well!'

'I don't know the details of course,' said Jack non-committedly. 'When was that again.'

'Ten years ago,' said the vicar, sounding surprised that Jack didn't know. 'Ten years this year. I wasn't here then of course but that's the point. Of remembering I mean.'

'That's it,' said Jack, as if suddenly remembering. 'Of course. Ten years. I remember it well.'

'And the old Reverend Cherrington, my predecessor you know, lovely chap, told me, when we arrived, that she'd also bought the old house in Victoria Street for the mission. Bought it outright, cash, and just gave it to the church. Just like that.'

'I didn't know *that*,' said Jack. 'When was that I wonder?'

'I don't know exactly,' said Widdop. 'A long time ago I think.'

'Mmmmm,' said Jack. He was thinking. Calculating dates. But his thoughts were interrupted by the young vicar.

'Has she always been so secretive?' he asked.

'She does like to do things on the QT,' said Jack, tapping the side of his nose. 'Keeps herself to herself as they say.'

'A true Christian lady,' said the vicar.

'That's her way I suppose.'

At which point Betty entered the kitchen from the church and the two men sat upright with fright.

'This is Mr Widdop,' said Betty as she joined them at the table. 'The vicar.'

'We've met,' said Jack.

'Vance,' said the vicar.

'Vance,' said Jack although he sensed that Betty didn't quite approve of his using the vicar's first name.

'We've been chatting,' said the vicar guiltily.

'I'll make the tea,' said Betty.

'Thank you, Betty,' said Widdop.

And so the busy and efficient flower lady immediately became the busy and efficient tea lady taking three cups and saucers to the table, and a carton of milk – duly sniffed at as a fresh check – from the small under-counter fridge, as she waited impatiently for the tea to infuse in a big catering-size teapot.

Before long she was sitting with the men at the table where she poured a little milk into each of the three cups – without asking – and filled them with strong and scalding tea.

'Thank you, Betty,' said Mr Widdop again.

'My son died yesterday,' said Jack suddenly before any of them had lifted a cup from its saucer. 'Last night.'

He didn't know why he said it; not there and then. But he did – say it that is – and now it couldn't be unsaid.

'Oh, my son,' said Mr Widdop as he reached across the small table and covered Jack's hand with his own. 'Not the businessman I met?'

Jack pulled his hand away; he was annoyed by the unfamiliar intimacy and professional sympathy.

'I'm not your son,' he said sharply. 'No. Not Alan. His younger brother Michael.'

'I *am* sorry,' said the well-meaning clergyman, contrite and embarrassed.

'What on earth happened?' asked Betty.

'Brain tumour,' said Jack plainly. He was staring across the hall at nothing.

'Oh dear,' said Betty. 'How truly awful. How old was he?'

'Not that old,' said Jack. 'Sixty.'

'It's tragic when a child dies before his parents,' said Betty.

Jack shrugged. Mr Widdop chose to say nothing.

'Children are so precious,' continued Betty. 'At any age. So precious.'

Jack shifted his gaze and looked directly at her; quizzically. 'Children are a pain in the arse,' he said and looked away.

'We better go,' said Betty quickly, pushing back her chair.

'But my tea,' protested Jack.

Mr Widdop coughed and looked embarrassed again and pushed his own chair back. 'Yes, I understand,' he said. 'A splendid job, by the way, Betty. The bride's mother you know. I spoke to her. She's there now. In the church. Her words. So white. Splendid. She's delighted.'

'That's good,' said Betty as she stood up. 'I hope they're very happy. Now, come on, Jack, we'll get you home, eh.' And she cupped her hand under the old man's elbow to urge him to stand.

'What about my tea?'

'Never mind that now. Come on.'

'I am sorry, old chap,' said Mr Widdop. 'I really am.'

✿

'Why did you say that to poor Mr Widdop?' asked Betty.

They were outside. Betty was on the step buttoning her jacket. That done, she turned and closed the church door. Jack was waiting on the pavement below.

'Why didn't we stop and have our tea?' asked Jack. 'I was looking forward to it.'

'Because you embarrassed Mr Widdop,' said Betty. 'And me. What you said.'

'What in particular?'

'Well, everything. Saying arse like that. I know you must be upset but you were quite rude to the poor young man.'

'Well, his type annoys me.'

'What type is that?'

'He's a smug professional nice joker. His sincerity is so insincere. It annoyed me.'

'I know what you mean but, believe me, Jack, he *is* sincere.'

'I doubt it,' said Jack.

'He *is*,' insisted Betty. 'Anyway, we better get you home. Come on.'

And so they set off together, retracing their steps to Northumberland Road.

They didn't speak until they reached the end of Church Street when Jack stopped – and so Betty stopped – and Jack said: 'I shouldn't have said that. I admit it. I'm sorry.'

'What shouldn't you have said?'

'About my son. Michael. About him dying last night. It was horrible. I shouldn't have imposed that on you and that smug young vicar.'

'Why did you come with me today, Jack?'

'I wanted to. I did. We arranged it yesterday, didn't we, and I wanted to.'

'And you didn't know about your son when we arranged it yesterday?'

'No. Of course not. That was later. Last night. Late. We were sitting with him. In the bloody hospital it was.'

'I see,' said Betty. 'How awful for you. When's the funeral?'

'I don't know,' said Jack dismissively. 'His brother – that's Alan, my eldest – and his wife Miriam, they're arranging it all. I couldn't. I don't know why. I just couldn't.'

'I know. I understand,' said Betty kindly. 'Let's keep going, eh.'

And so they set off again along Northumberland Road and didn't speak again until they arrived at one-three-six. But half way there – between Church Street and Jack's house – Betty Krilich quietly slipped her right arm between Jack's left arm and his body and Jack didn't object. Her arm felt warm to him and his body felt warm to her. It was nice.

They stopped together at Jack's house; Betty withdrew her arm – slowly and perhaps even reluctantly – and Jack felt vaguely disappointed. They stepped apart.

'I'll come to the funeral with you if you like,' said Betty.

'Funeral?' Jack felt confused.

'Your son's funeral,' said Betty. 'If you'd like me to. What's his name again?'

'Was,' said Jack. 'Michael.'

'Yes. Michael. Well, would you like me to come? To the funeral? To keep you company?'

Jack hesitated before saying: 'I don't know.'

'Oh, well, if you're not sure–'

'No, no,' said Jack quickly. 'I don't mean that. I mean I don't know about it. The funeral. I don't know anything about it yet. Alan, you see. And Miriam.'

Betty patted Jack's arm in genuine sympathy and understanding. 'It's Friday today. It'll be Monday or Tuesday I should think.'

'Yes,' said Jack thoughtfully.

'Well, you let me know,' said Betty. 'I'll pop in tomorrow morning. About ten. You should know about it by then shouldn't you? I'll pop in then and you can tell me. That's if you want me to. Come that is.'

'Yes,' said Jack. Just 'Yes.'

Once inside the house Jack sat quietly in his favourite arm-chair in the living room, with some of his paintings, and thought. Why did I blurt that out, about Michael, in front of that young vicar? he thought. Why did I have to blurt it out at all? Betty doesn't need to know about that; about stupid bloody Michael. And Alan. About my family rubbish. About the funeral about which, by the way, old man, he said to himself, you know nothing. Yet. But one thing nice, he thought, Betty said she'd come to the funeral with me. That'd be nice. But what the hell will Alan think? Miriam won't mind, but Alan? And why did she say – what was it? – that it's tragic when a child dies before his parent. And that children are so precious. At any age, she said. Why'd she say that? And, anyway, I didn't think she had any children so how would she know?

And there sat old Jack Landseer, aged eighty-five, sad, lonely and alone, thinking. No cup of tea followed by no lunch. Then no dinner. And when he realized that the living room was dark and cold, that another day was over, that Michael really *was* dead, he went to the kitchen, toasted two crumpets which he spread with butter and Vegemite and ate hungrily, standing at the bench, before going to bed.

Meanwhile Betty Krilich, aged eighty-eight, sat on the edge of her cot, lonely but not entirely alone, and thought her thoughts about the past while Duchess sat on her lap,

Mittens slept curled up at her side and Norman sat patiently at the empty food bowls by the door.

For some reason she began thinking about Vibes McKenzie and the others – but especially Vibes – and those late nights in smoky Wellington clubs and how much she enjoyed playing with those brilliant boys for hours on end to knowing and appreciative audiences in back-alley places that were truly late-fifties early-sixties cool; and, more especially, how she relished the free improvisation that they could do – could share – when the clubs were shutting and the sun was coming up.

We played some cool shit in those days, she thought. Just the four of us. Sometimes five. Hot and so cool. And poor Gus, innocent and trusting, didn't suspect a thing.

And it wasn't until Norman ran out of patience and jumped up onto the bed that Betty roused herself enough to see that the customary feline feeding hour had passed and that the room was cold and dark.

'What a waste of time,' she said. To herself. 'Sitting here in the dark thinking about all that. Where will that lead? A complete waste of time.'

8

IT OCCURRED TO Jack the next morning that Betty might come to the front door. About ten she said. But he didn't want to – couldn't, mustn't – open the front door. Not to her. Not now.

Perhaps not ever.

No, that won't work, he thought. Not long term. I'll have to do something about that long term. Meanwhile, now, I'll send her round the back. It's a bit rude but that's what she did to me.

She arrived at ten as she said she would. Jack was waiting anxiously in the living room, watching and waiting, and saw her arrive. His plan was to go to the closed front door and ask her – from the inside, without opening the door, without letting her see into the hall – to go to the back door just as she had asked him when he had called to *her* front door. But perhaps because she didn't ever use her own front door she didn't think to use his and so he was relieved when he saw her go unswervingly down the side path to the back of the house. He was waiting for her at the open door of his workshop.

'It's Tuesday,' he said as she rounded the corner of the house. 'The funeral'.

She laughed. He was glad to see her and hear her laugh.

'You were waiting for me,' she said.

He stepped out of the workshop and stopped. It was a fine morning and he noticed that Betty was again wearing her old and faded flared jeans – evidently her favourites – this time with an olive-green polo-neck sweater and a large coloured stone of something or other hanging around her neck on a leather thong.

'Sort of,' said Jack.

'Are you alright?' she asked. 'About your son and the funeral and everything.'

'Michael? I'm alright,' said Jack perhaps a little too casually.

Betty noticed but didn't comment. Instead she said: 'I'm off to the hospice shop. Saturday you see.'

Jack nodded and stepped a little closer to her. 'It's Tuesday,' he said again looking at her face, watching for her reaction. 'The funeral. Will you come?'

'I said I would didn't I. That's why I'm here.'

'Absolutely. Of course,' said Jack. Relieved. 'Eleven o'clock it is. At Knight's in town. He's in Rotary with Alan.'

'Who is?'

'Knight. Barry Knight. The funeral director.'

Betty nodded.

'Can I pick you up? In the Zephyr. I'll honk.' And then, suddenly, he added: 'That's definitely alright isn't it? You're not doing anything else are you?'

'Tuesdays I'm at the mission. Food parcels and that. But it doesn't matter. There are others. People I mean.'

'Oh, good-oh,' said Jack. He was truly relieved that she would be there with him on Tuesday. Betty saw the relief on his face and heard it in his voice.

But then neither of them knew what to say or do next.

'Hospice shop,' said Betty at last. Awkwardly. She kicked at nothing with her white sneakered right foot and indicated vaguely with her left arm and nodded to the drive behind her. 'Better go.'

'Yes, of course, right-oh,' said Jack who wanted to say so much more.

He wanted to tell her – warn her perhaps – about Alan. He'll be there, he wanted to say. And his wife Miriam. Alan's a bit stand-offish. A bit superior. But Miriam's nice. You'll like Miriam. And the twins of course. David and Dianne. Kids? They're not kids any more. Forty I think. Dianne's married. To Fred. Got her own kids. Two. Can't remember their names now. Makes me a great-grandfather. Can you believe it? I can't. Actually I just remembered David won't be there. He's not married or anything. Not that I know of. Don't know what he does really. Poet or something. Or is it an artist? Long hair. Beard and that. A bit queer if you know what I mean. A mystery to me really. He's in London anyway. He's got a wife in London. Michael I mean. Not David. Sharon. Divorced. But he never had many friends. Not in New Zealand anyway. Michael I mean. Don't think there'll be anyone else.

That's what he *wanted* to say. But he didn't. Instead he said: 'I'll honk. Tuesday. About quarter to eleven.'

✿

But it wasn't the Zephyr he backed out of the garage the next morning, Sunday morning, but the Rolls-Royce. On the fourth Sunday of every month, in the morning when he knew Betty Krilich would be at Saint Peter's for the duration of three morning services – she'd always been a musician and now she was the church organist – he drove the Rolls down Northumberland Road to the State Highway and then to the Southern Motorway along which he cruised smoothly and silently north as far as Manukau calling on only a fraction of the great machine's superfluous power. Once there he retraced his motorway journey but turned off before the State Highway and took the Main Line to the northern fringe of Karapuke where he turned into Landseer Farm, the family property which was not and had never been a farm. It was there, in the old homestead built by his grandfather, that he was born eighty-five years earlier.

But the old house was no more; Alan had lately replaced it with what Jack considered a grand and ostentatious mansion. Beside the modern house – the mansion – but separated by a vast truck park and two truck-and-trailer washing bays, was a complex of garages, workshops and offices which together constituted the modern headquarters of Town & Country Carriers Limited.

As it was a Sunday some of the company's Karapuke-based trucks and trailers were at the base being washed down and cleaned, inside and out, one by one, by a crew especially employed for the purpose. As each was finished it was parked, its green and yellow livery gleaming in the watery sun, in one of a long line of parking bays where Alan Landseer could survey them – and the lush green fields of the Landseer Farm beyond – from the broad window at the end of the company's boardroom. It was there, in the boardroom on the building's upper floor, that on the fourth Sunday of each month the firm's directors, Jack and Alan, Miriam – whose sound judgement and opinion were valued by father and son – and Michael when he was alive and if he were in New Zealand, sat to review both the company's affairs and the personal affairs of the three shareholders: John Alan Landseer, Alan John Landseer and the late Michael James Landseer.

On this particular Sunday the formal meeting was brief: one item dominated the agenda although it commanded little in the way of time.

'Michael's shares will be allocated equally between you and Alan,' said Miriam to her father-in-law.

'I know,' said Jack quietly; he knew because he was instrumental, with *his* father, in drawing up and occasionally revising the company's constitution.

'But since he's been home, here with us, he's had no expenses,' continued Miriam. 'None at all. And so he has accumulated an awful lot of cash. An awful lot.'

'Tell me about it,' said Jack. He knew that as directors he, Michael and Miriam received the same monthly remuneration – hugely and unnecessarily generous, in his opinion, and far more than he could ever use which meant he was kept busy seeking and maintaining sound investments – while Alan received somewhat more as the active managing director and Miriam received an extra stipend for her duties as company secretary. Jack knew that thanks to Alan (and Miriam) the company was now wildly successful, and rich with cash which it passed on to its directors.

'It's a stinking lot of dough, dad,' said Alan. 'Really is.'

'Do you want to see?' asked Miriam across the table, glancing down at her laptop and then up at her father-in-law with a questioning expression as if wanting to show him something; she held the laptop screen ready to turn it in his direction.

But Jack didn't want to look at a computer screen. And he trusted Miriam completely.

'No, not really,' he said. 'I know.'

'The thing of it is, dad,' said Alan, 'Michael's left all his cash – every last cent of it – to bloody Sharon.'

'I know that too,' said Jack. 'Michael told us ages ago. Don't you remember?'

'I remember, of course,' said Alan. 'I just wondered if you did.'

'Of course I did.'

'Well–'

Miriam interrupted by saying: 'So, Jack, if it's alright with you I'll arrange to transfer all Michael's money to England. To Sharon. That's what he wanted.'

'After funeral expenses,' said Alan. 'That's in the will.'

'Of course, Miriam,' said Jack who was beginning to find the conversation somewhat distasteful. 'Do whatever you have to do.'

'I'll take care of everything,' said Miriam. 'Don't worry. I know it's hard but it'll be alright.'

After the meeting they went to the house for lunch. But while the official meeting was brief the lunch which followed was long; or rather the discussion which followed the lunch was long and intense. And it was naturally all about Michael.

'You know your mother understood him much better than me,' said Jack.

Alan nodded in agreement.

'Why was that do you think?' asked Miriam of the two men.

'I don't really remember,' said Alan.

'I don't know,' said Jack. 'All I know is that I didn't have a clue.'

'Mum kept everything you know,' said Alan. 'In the attic. Did you know that, dad?'

Jack nodded. He didn't enjoy remembering.

'I found it when we were clearing out the old house.'

'I know,' said Jack. 'I didn't want all that old stuff.'

'I kept it all,' said Alan leaning across to an adjacent bench to fetch an envelope that was lying there. 'And I found this. A letter.'

'Who from?' asked Jack.

'You should read it, Jack,' said Miriam.

'It's from a mathematician at Auckland university,' said Alan as he opened the envelope, unfolded the heavily creased and yellowing letter, and handed it to Jack who looked at it oddly. 'A professor. Read it,' he urged.

*I long ago discovered,* read the letter in old-fashioned typewriting, *that a subtle testing of a child's general knowledge provides a more accurate guide to his intelligence than specialist academic knowledge which can merely be the result of a prodigious memory. Young Michael's answers, by way of conversation, not knowing he was being tested, tell me that he is without doubt an exceedingly clever child. A young genius. A rare child prodigy in fact.*

'I've never seen this,' said Jack looking up accusingly, and adjusting his spectacles.

'It's addressed to mum,' said Alan. 'Maybe—'

'Maybe she never showed it to me,' said Jack. He looked at the date at the top of the page. 'He was only just ten.'

He returned to the letter:

*He has specific academic knowledge too,* it read. *A depth and breadth that often tests and stretches his tutors who find him exceptionally and mysteriously knowledgeable in mathematics (including calculus – differential and integral – algebra and trigonometry), science (including physics and chemistry) and astronomy. He also seems well-acquainted even with the arts: literature, music and art, ancient and modern, and their creators.*

Jack put the letter down on the table. He didn't want to read any more.

'How did he get so bloody smart-arsed?' he asked. 'I hardly ever saw him reading or studying or anything like that.'

Alan could only shrug in reply.

They spent the rest of the time discussing the funeral. Alan had arranged it all – with Miriam's help – with his Rotary friend Barry Knight, the funeral director.

'It'll be really simple,' said Alan. 'Barry understands. He knows we'll be the only ones there.'

Jack nodded.

'Do you want to say anything, dad?'

'Nothing to say,' said Jack.

'Barry is going to say a prayer,' said Alan.

'Michael wasn't religious,' protested Jack.

'None of us are, dad,' said Alan, 'but we've got to say something. Don't you think? Closure and that.'

'I suppose so,' said Jack who nodded; he remembered he had agreed to leave everything to Alan.

'Barry is going to arrange the cremation,' added Miriam.

Jack nodded again. He was glad he hadn't been party to the organization.

'David's in London,' said Miriam. 'He's going to Sharon's flat. We're going to Skype them so they'll see and hear everything. Just like being there. Except for them it'll be the middle of the night.'

Jack nodded again although he had no idea what they were talking about. And, he admitted, he didn't care.

'Betty Henderson is coming with me,' he said suddenly. 'To the funeral.'

Alan and Miriam looked at each other and then at Jack.

'Who's Betty Henderson?' asked Alan.

'I mean Betty Krilich,' said Jack. 'Betty Krilich.'

'Who's Betty Krilich?' asked Miriam.

'Oh, she's just a friend of mine,' said Jack. 'An old friend of mine.'

'Is she the lady you mentioned? You mended something for her.'

'That's her,' said Jack. 'I fixed the wheel on her shopping trundler. Both wheels actually. She uses it all the time.'

'Oh, that's nice,' said Miriam with a romantic smile, her head tipped to the side. 'Don't you think so, Alan?'

Alan nodded but he didn't think it was especially nice. He was naturally suspicious of what this old woman – Jack had said she was eighty-eight or something – or any woman would want from his father. Except his money.

'What's her name again?' Asked Miriam. 'Betty is it?'

'Betty,' said Jack. 'Betty Krilich.'

'And how do you know her again?' asked Alan.

Jack could sense the doubt in his son's voice but he decided he didn't care. 'She's a neighbour of mine for one thing,' he said. 'Lives a bit down Northumberland Road. Half way down.'

'And?'

'And what?'

'Well,' said Alan, 'you said for one thing. What's the other thing?'

'Oh, nothing. Don't know why I said that really.'

After the meeting, and the lunch which followed – which had itself turned into another meeting of sorts – Jack felt discomposed. He had loved Michael as a child, even as a teenager, despite not being able to comprehend his strange and extreme precocity. But they had been estranged for so long – for so many years – until he had come home: sick, sad, divorced, broken. A virtual stranger.

'You stupid bastard, Michael,' he said, to himself, as he drove slowly back to Karapuke late in the afternoon. 'Your mother would have hated what you became.'

Coming from Landseer Farm meant he drove through Karapuke township and came on to Northumberland Road from the north and so avoided driving past Betty's house.

And as he parked the Rolls in the garage, where it would remain, heavy and unmoving, until the fourth Sunday of the next month, August, and hit the switch to close the garage door, he was suddenly overcome with nausea. As a result he had to kneel where he was, on the garage floor of dirty concrete, to throw up the lunch so carefully and lovingly prepared by Miriam.

Such was the effect on the constitution of an old man of losing an adult child and the disturbing memories which forced themselves into his reluctant consciousness. And when it was over, as he knelt looking down at his own pool of lumpy and colourful vomit, he thought about poor Michael again and how, now that he was dead, he and Alan and Miriam had nothing else to discuss about him but the reallocation of his shares, and the remittance of his cash — his only asset — to his ex-wife in England, and inevitably, the disposal of his ashes.

That's it, he thought. The end of Michael Landseer. And that thought made him retch again, unproductively and painfully.

✿

At half-past six that evening Betty Krilich was hurrying through the dark along Northumberland Road on her way to Saint Peter's to play the organ for the evening service. As she passed the house at one-three-six, the home of her new friend Jack Landseer, glancing at it briefly and noting the yellow light glowing through the closed drapes of the living room window, she had no idea of what hung on the walls of that room and others in that house, nor of the presence of the vintage Rolls-Royce Silver Shadow which stood, cold now, behind the closed garage door. Nor did she know the trouble to which its owner went to conceal from her the very existence of both his car and his art.

# 9

ON THE TUESDAY morning of Michael Landseer's funeral Jack and Betty arrived at Knight's with only a few minutes to spare. Alan and Miriam were waiting outside for them. The other mourners – despite Alan's doubts there were a few – were already inside so there was time for only quick introductions before the four of them went in to the side-chapel which was used for small funerals.

Jack and Betty went ahead. Miriam pulled gently on her husband's arm to hold him back for a moment.

'What a strange woman,' she whispered when they were alone.

'Why? What do you mean?'

'Her clothes,' said Miriam quietly as they then entered the chapel to the sound of mournful recorded organ music. 'She looks like a Spanish matron out of an old black-and-white National Geographic magazine.'

On this sombre occasion Betty was wearing a long black linen skirt and a matching jacket with three-quarter length sleeves and large and shiny black buttons, over a white shirt and a thin black tie; on her hands she wore black kid gloves. A tortoiseshell *peineta* was holding up a black lace mantilla that covered her white hair and fell down her back. She was carrying a black leather handbag over her arm and instead of her white sneakers she was wearing long black boots. Both the handbag and the boots – of black leather – were dull and somewhat scuffed.

Alan looked at Betty ahead, then at Miriam, shrugged, and put a raised forefinger to his pursed lips as they reached the front of the chapel. And as they sat down, beside Jack and the black-robed Betty, and made themselves comfortable, the music faded and Barry Knight entered from a side door to stand beside the shiny coffin and begin the service.

Aside from Alan and Miriam, Jack and Betty, and Barry Knight the funeral director, the other mourners there, in that tiny, hushed and dimly lighted chapel on that gloomy Tuesday morning, were: Alan and Miriam's daughter Dianne with her husband Fred and their two teenaged children; two mechanics from Town & Country Carriers who had come to know and like Michael when he returned from England to live with Alan and Miriam; a male nurse from Auckland Hospital who had cared for him in his last few (unconscious) hours alive; and the Reverend Widdop, the vicar of Saint Peter's church. Miriam's laptop was sitting on a tall whatnot, to one side of the chapel, to capture and send what little was said and done there, that morning in that small chapel, across the world to Michael's ex-wife Sharon, and David – Alan and Miriam's son, Michael and Sharon's nephew – who were watching together, late at night, in Sharon's flat in Wandsworth, London.

There was little to be said but Alan made a small speech, a eulogy of sorts, in which he did his best to emphasise his younger brother's genius, maximize his successes and minimise his failings.

'Poor Michael seemed to find the hard things in life so easy and the easy things so hard,' he said while acknowledging that the tumour which was visited upon him, and which caused him so much suffering and pain before his inevitable death, was not something to which culpability could be assigned to him or anyone.

'He had his problems for sure,' Alan said, alluding to his addiction, 'but he didn't deserve to die like that.'

Meanwhile he avoided anything that might distress his innocent grandchildren who knew nothing of Michael's past and saw him as no more or less than an old and frail great-uncle who was often ill but generally kind towards them.

Finally – and properly thought Jack – Alan quietly praised and thanked his wife Miriam for the tender and loving nursing care she gave her increasingly infirm, ailing and undeserving brother-in-law in his last months, weeks, days and hours.

It was while Alan was speaking, quietly in that tiny chapel, that Jack sensed that Betty, sitting on his right, was weeping. Not crying or sobbing – her shoulders were still and she wasn't sniffing or breathing oddly – but nevertheless he guessed she was weeping silently and he wondered why. And his guess was confirmed when he saw her discreetly push a black silk handkerchief up and under her blue and pointed spectacles – with a black-gloved hand – to dab softly at her eyes; it was something Alan, standing at the front of the small chapel, in front of his brother's coffin, also noticed.

Like his father, late mother, ex-wife, brother and sister-in-law, the deceased Michael Landseer had subscribed to no religion; indeed, as far as Alan and Jack knew he was utterly atheistic if not mildly anti-religious. But none in that tiny congregation objected when, once Alan had resumed his seat, the funeral director acknowledged the presence of Vance Widdop – he knew the young clergyman from the many funerals he had conducted at Knight's – whom he asked to lead them in a final prayer. And so the Reverend Widdop, whose only connection to the deceased and his family was a slender one through Betty Krilich, his organist, stepped forward to stand beside the coffin where he extemporised a sensibly appropriate and comforting but not especially religious prayer. And as he surveyed those before him he too noticed that his old friend, parishioner and organist Betty Krilich had been crying.

Afterwards, outside, when Miriam came out of the chapel, having talked to David and Sharon in London, she joined Vance Widdop, Jack and Betty who were huddled together in the chill, she noticed that Betty's eyes were red, a little swollen, and that there was a moistness on her remarkably unwrinkled cheeks.

But she didn't remark. Instead she said cheerfully: 'Won't you all come home and have some lunch?'

She didn't know why Betty – she couldn't remember her last name – she didn't know why she should have been crying at Michael's funeral but she felt kindly disposed towards the sad and strangely dressed old lady who was evidently Jack's new friend.

'Fred's got to get back to work but Dianne and the children will be there,' she said. 'And me and Alan of course.'

'Thank you but I'm going to go back to Saint Peter's with Mr Widdop,' said Betty with a gentle touch to Miriam's arm.

'Oh, I see,' said Miriam. She was mildly disappointed by Betty's declination as she was intrigued by the strange – and strangely- dressed – old lady and would have liked the chance to get to know her better.

For her part Betty could sense Miriam's disappointment without understanding it.

'I *am* sorry but I usually spend Tuesdays at the mission you see,' she said quickly. 'I'd like to go there for the rest of the afternoon. The afternoon shift.'

Miriam wanted to ask Betty what she did at the mission but Betty spoke again before she could. 'Have you properly met Mr Widdop?' she asked.

And so Miriam and Vance Widdop shook hands, and Miriam said something complimentary about the clergyman's prayer while he in turn acknowledged Miriam's nursing of her late brother-in-law.

'So strong and kind,' he said, 'in the face of so much tragedy and sadness.'

'What about you, Jack?' asked Miriam of Jack while virtually ignoring Mr Widdop.

'Eh?'

'Come back home for lunch?'

'Oh, it's too far out for me today, love,' he said. 'I think I'll go back to Saint Peter's and have a cuppa with Betty, if that's alright with you, Betty,' he said as an aside, 'before you go to the mission, and then I'll just have a quiet afternoon at home.'

'That's alright, Jack,' said Miriam with a smile. 'Probably wise.'

'Yes. It's been quite a morning,' said Jack. 'Poor Michael, eh.'

'I know,' said Miriam kindly.

'What happens now?' asked Jack.

'Don't worry, Jack,' said Miriam. 'Barry's going to take care of everything. The cremation and that.'

Jack nodded sadly.

'You take care of each other now,' said Miriam to the old pair standing before her. It seemed appropriate to consider them together.

'Where's Alan?' asked Jack.

'He's in the chapel talking to David and Sharon,' said Miriam. 'On Skype.'

Jack nodded knowingly but he didn't know at all. 'Tell him we've gone,' he said.

✿

'This really *is* a nice old car,' said Betty from the passenger side of the Zephyr's bench seat. 'Such style.'

'So you said last time,' said Jack.

'Well, it is. So, the yoga's probably started by now,' she said, changing the subject as she removed her gloves, pulling at the fingertips one at a time; then she drew the high *peineta* from her hair and put it, the rolled-up mantilla and the gloves into her floppy old black handbag. 'In the hall I mean. But the kitchen will be free. We'll have a cuppa there.'

She clipped the handbag closed and held it on her lap.

'Aren't you hungry?' asked Jack as he turned into Main Street.

'Not really,' said Betty. 'We can have a biscuit or two if you like.'

'What about Vance?' asked Jack. 'Mr Widdop,' he added. The young vicar had gone ahead in his own car.

'What about him?'

'Will he have a cuppa with us? In the kitchen?'

'Heavens no,' said Betty. 'Mrs Widdop will have his lunch ready and waiting.'

Jack nodded. He was somewhat relieved that Widdop wouldn't be joining them in the hall kitchen. He had something to ask Betty and he didn't want to ask it in front of the young vicar.

'She's such a girl, you know, but a terribly devoted wife,' said Betty. 'And mother. Two dear little kiddies. At school now of course. Such little dears they are.'

'Which school do they go to?' asked Jack. 'Primary school I suppose.' He rightly assumed that the young vicar would have children of primary school age.

'Karapuke North Primary of course,' said Betty. 'Same school I went to. Isn't that funny. Oh, here we are, Church Street.'

'Me too,' said Jack.

'You too what?' asked Betty.

'I went to there too,' said Jack as he stopped and parked the car on the street at the church door. 'Karapuke North.'

He looked at Betty to gauge her reaction but it seemed she wasn't listening.

'That's nice,' she said casually, without interest, as she looped her bulky handbag over her arm and got out of the car. 'Now, don't forget, there's ladies' yoga on in the hall at the minute so we'll go in the side door.'

And so they did. And while Betty busied herself at the sink and bench and the cupboards – methodically turning on the Zip urn, choosing a suitably small (and somewhat dented) aluminium teapot and adding the dry tea leaves, getting a small carton of milk from the fridge, taking down cups and saucers from the cupboard, opening a tin of chocolate biscuits, waiting for the urn to boil and whistle – Jack sat at one of the tables, with her handbag, and waited. Eventually, when they were both sitting down, once they had sipped tentatively at the hot tea, chosen a biscuit and taken a bite, Jack asked Betty's permission to ask her the question which he had been anxious to ask since they had left Knight's chapel.

'Can I ask you something, Betty?' he asked.

'Of course,' replied Betty off-handedly, evidently incurious about the pending question.

'Well, what I want to know is,' said Jack, looking intently at his companion through his rimless spectacles, 'why were you crying at Michael's funeral?'

Betty stiffened; she quickly abandoned her relaxed attitude and returned Jack's curious stare with an unmistakeable look of defiance.

'I wasn't,' she said sharply. 'I didn't cry at all.'

'Oh yes you did,' said Jack. 'I saw you and I wasn't the only one.'

At that the old woman's shoulders slumped as her weak defence collapsed in the face of Jack's gentle insistence.

'Oh, but it was so sad,' she said. 'To lose a child so young.'

'But Michael wasn't young,' said a puzzled Jack. 'I know he wasn't all that old but he wasn't young. He wasn't a child.'

'He was *your* child. It's terrible to lose a child of any age. Any age. Terrible.'

'Of course, but–'

'Children are *precious*, Jack,' said Betty with a surprising passion. '*All* children. Every single one of them. Precious little human beings.'

'But surely,' said Jack, 'they might be precious little people as you say, children, but most children grow up to be very ordinary and unprecious adults. Murderers, thieves, criminals, violent husbands and fathers some of them – that's what your women's refuge is all about isn't it – they were all children once.'

'So was Jesus.'

'That's not fair,' said Jack. 'You must know what I mean.'

'Children *are* special,' insisted Betty. 'I don't care what you say, they *are*. Every single last one of them.'

They both finished their biscuit; sipped again at their tea; thought.

'I'll tell you something,' said Jack as they put down their cups. 'About Michael. He *was* special as you say. Really special. Once, when he was just thirteen, his mother – Catherine – enrolled him in the chess club. Here in town. She wanted to find something that would keep him stimulated in the hope that he'd meet more young people like him of his own age. But you know what? On only his second night – having learned the game on his first visit – he played a long table of adults and children, him on one side of the table playing all the others, making a move on one board before moving on to the next, until he had quickly won every game.'

Betty said nothing.

'You know what he said?' asked Jack rhetorically. 'He said that chess was boring and that people played it too slow.'

'He must have been a brilliant child,' said Betty. 'Exceptional, surely.'

'Yes. Brilliant at chess. Brilliant at everything. But what good was that to him? Or anyone?' Jack sounded bitter. 'My point don't you see. Look how he ended up. A mean and selfish drunk who cared about nobody, not his wife, not me, not Alan, not even himself in the end.'

'His poor mother.'

'Well,' said Jack as he was reminded of Catherine. 'I'm only glad she didn't live to see how he ended up. She thought he was a precious child too.'

'What about Alan?'

'He was a good boy,' said Jack, remembering. 'His mother adored him of course. But now, well, he's just a man isn't he. A decent man for sure but – the same as any other man – he's not perfect. Just ordinary. Good and bad. No better or worse than anyone else. A bit selfish maybe. A bit greedy for money probably.'

'I know *that* feeling,' said Betty.

'But to think that *all* children are so precious – even adult children – it doesn't make sense.'

'It makes sense to me,' said Betty.

'But for you to cry for Michael.'

'It wasn't just Michael,' said Betty. 'The funeral. I was reminded of something. Something that made me sad. That's all. Nothing really.'

'Nothing?' insisted Jack.

They had finished their tea.

'Jack,' said Betty as she pushed aside her cup and saucer and leaned forward across the table to make her point with quiet insistence. 'It was nothing. Let's leave it, eh.'

'Are you sure?' said Jack leaning back in his chair.

'Well, it *was* something. Once,' said Betty. She straightened up, took up her handbag and made ready to leave. 'Of course. A long time ago. But nothing important. Not now.'

'You don't want to tell me I suppose.'

'It's not important, Jack,' said Betty brusquely. 'Something that happened a long time ago. I got reminded that's all. Funerals do that you know. To people.'

Jack shrugged. 'If you ever want to tell me,' he said.

But Betty merely smiled. 'I better put this stuff away and get back to the mission,' she said. 'I'll do the afternoon shift see.'

'I'll give you a lift,' said Jack.

# 10

IT WAS DURING the short ride from Saint Peter's to the mission in nearby Victoria Street that Betty asked Jack for a favour. But before she did – before she had the chance – Jack asked her about the mission and about her work there on Tuesdays.

'It's only a branch really,' she said. 'Of the big mission in Auckland I mean. We tell them what we need and they send down emergency food parcels, great big Kleensaks actually, full of stuff, and leave it to us to distribute them here.'

'I never knew anything about that,' said Jack. 'Never knew there was a need. Not in Karapuke. Not these days.'

'It's not in town so much,' said Betty. 'A bit. But it's in the backblocks mostly. Rent is cheap in the country. Old run-down derelict houses. Farmers build new houses and rent out their old ones. They're terrible some of them. Damp and draughty. But they're all some people can afford. So they rent them and then get stuck out there in the boo-eye without a car or anything, and there's no jobs and no buses and they've got no money and they go hungry. And cold. Sometimes they get free firewood but they can't afford coal. And the power's too expensive. It's bloody terrible sometimes, Jack. You've got no idea.'

'I've got *some* idea,' said Jack. 'I grew up out there don't forget. 'Thirties and forties. Plenty of rural poverty then. Even into the fifties. But no mission. No food parcels or anything like that. Not then. We had to fend for ourselves back then.'

'Where did you live then?'

'It's called Landseer Farm,' said Jack wondering again why she didn't remember. 'Out on Main Line. But it's not a farm really. A carrying business started by my grandfather in the good old year of nineteen hundred and nothing. A horse and cart. Imagine that. But it's huge now.'

'Oh,' said Betty who wasn't really interested. 'Well, it's the kiddies I worry about most,' she said. 'I hate the idea of poor little children living out there in poverty. Cold and hungry. And some of the parents are so bloody useless. Not all of them but some.'

'So what do you do?'

'We go out there once a week and take the food parcels they send down from Auckland.'

'Who? You and who else?'

'Oh, I don't always go. Sometimes but not always. Some of the young women, volunteers, they've got cars you know. Not like this though. Big truck things for rough roads and farm tracks. But there's plenty for me to do at the mission house. Some of our town clients call in. For food. Or advice. Sometimes just for a chat. Or to help them fill out a WINZ form or something like that. And we have classes for reading and writing and the internet and emailing and that sort of thing.'

'I could go to one of those,' said Jack.

'One of what?'

'Those classes about the internet and emailing,' said Jack. 'It's all a mystery to me.'

'It's a mystery to me too,' said Betty with a laugh. 'I don't care. I'm too old to worry about it. But they're quite popular with some people, those classes, so that's good. So where exactly did you grow up again?'

'Landseer Farm,' said Jack again. 'Not quite in the boo-eye. On Main Line. Half way between town and country.'

'Town & Country Carriers Limited,' said Betty. 'Of course. So that's what Alan runs.'

'That's it,' said Jack. 'Jack Landseer at your service.'

'So you went to Karapuke North Primary. Like me.'

Jack didn't reply at once. 'Victoria Street,' he said.

He had to wait for the traffic to clear before turning right.

'I could have gone to the country school,' he said when the old Zephyr had cleared the intersection. 'But there was only one old lady teacher there and my mother thought I'd be better off at Karapuke North.'

'And were you?'

'I don't know,' said Jack. 'How could I. I just did what I was told. Kids did that then. Could have got the school bus to the other school – the country school – but no bus to Karapuke North. I had to walk to school, there and back, all the way, every day.'

'Why didn't your parents take you to school? And pick you up?'

Jack laughed. It wasn't irony; he was genuinely amused at the thought of his father taking time to drive him to school in the firm's one and only precious van.

'We were pretty poor when I was a kid,' he said. 'Went hungry sometimes even. But dad always found work. Something. Worked like a nigger too, his whole life.'

'You can't say *that*, Jack,' said Betty. 'Not these days.'

'Well, sorry, but he did. He had horses and a cart then, in the beginning. It was *his* father, my grandfather, started the business. But the horses were gone by the time I was going to school. Some of the Maori kids still went to school by horse. Gave me a ride on the back sometimes. Bareback. Remember that?'

'Not really,' said Betty grimly. 'My nanny used to take me to and from school in the car. Until I was in standard four I think. I didn't have a nanny after that because of the war.'

'That's when it happened,' said Jack. 'Don't you remember?'

'No. When what happened?'

'You don't remember anything then?' said Jack. 'One day after school. I remember it like it was yesterday.'

'I don't know what you're talking about,' said Betty. 'I really don't.'

'Don't you remember me at school? I was John then. John Landseer.'

Betty shook her head slowly. 'No. Sorry, Jack,' she said. 'What happened anyway?'

'Never mind,' said Jack as he pulled up outside the mission. 'Here we are. I'll tell you one day.'

A woman was sitting on the front steps of the old bungalow that was owned and used by the mission. She was smoking as she watched an unsteady toddler plucking at a daisy bush growing wild beside the porch steps; he or she was shredding the daisies and throwing the debris ineptly onto the unmown lawn. The woman looked up as the Zephyr stopped at the kerb and waved when she recognized Betty.

'Before you go though, Jack,' said Betty as she waved in reply to the woman on the steps and made ready to get out of the Zephyr, 'I wanted to ask you something. About Thursday. A favour.'

'Ask away,' said Jack.

✿

'I thought you weren't coming back to the house,' said Miriam. 'You've just missed Dianne and the kids. They've been here since the funeral. Just left a couple of minutes ago.'

'I forgot about them,' said Jack. 'Anyway, I changed my mind. I hope that's okay.'

'Of course it is, Jack,' said Miriam. They were at the back door of the big Landseer Farm house. 'But the Rolls? On a Tuesday?'

Miriam had seen the old limousine arrive.

'There's a reason for that,' said Jack.

'Oh. Well come in. Come in. Alan's in the office.'

'Don't bother him right now,' said Jack.

'I was going to buzz him. We have afternoon tea about now.'

'That'd be nice.'

And so Miriam called Alan on the intercom fixed to the wall beside the door: 'Your father's here.'

'I know.' Jack heard Alan's detached and distorted reply. 'I can see the car. I'll be right there'.

'I'm not interrupting anything I hope,' said Jack as he stepped up into the kitchen and shut the door behind him.

'Honestly, Jack, no,' said Miriam. 'It's been such a day hasn't it. Awful really. You must have found it hard.'

'You must have too.'

Miriam smiled weakly and nodded.

'Anyway, sit down,' she said. 'I'll make the tea.'

And so Jack sat at the kitchen table and watched his kind, gentle and generous daughter-in-law fuss about at the kitchen bench, making tea in a large brown and shiny teapot, setting cups, saucers and plates on the table and cutting what looked like a Battenberg cake which he had no doubt she had made herself.

How does she find the time? he wondered, as he often did.

Before long Alan came into the kitchen. Like Jack he was still wearing the clothes he wore at the funeral although he had shed the suit coat, loosened his black tie and undone the top button of his white shirt. He was trying to look calm and welcoming, smiling, but in fact he looked somewhat harassed and preoccupied.

He wishes I weren't here, thought Jack. Already wasted so much time at the funeral. And now me. He looks more like an accountant than a truckie. He probably *is* more of an accountant. Never drives the trucks. Can't stand livestock. All that piss and shit. Or farmers. Bit bloody useless as a truckie. But, I have to admit, I couldn't even begin to run the business today. Wouldn't even want to.

'Dad,' said the son brightly. 'Busting for that cuppa, love.'

'Is everything alright?' asked Miriam.

'Yes and no,' said Alan. 'Usual stuff. Don't worry about that now. Tea, eh. How are you, dad? Now?'

'I'm alright,' said Jack. 'You? After the funeral and that?'

'Yeah, yeah,' said Alan with a dismissive wave of his hand. He pulled out a chair and sat down. 'So what are you doing here with the Rolls anyway? We're not having a special meeting or anything?' he asked jokingly. 'Something I don't know about?'

Miriam sat down at the table, poured the milk and tea without ceremony and slid a cup and saucer and a plate of cake across the table to each of the men.

'No, of course not,' said Jack humourlessly. 'So, no Michael, eh.' He looked across at Miriam before taking a sip of tea.

'He was a lot of work in the end,' said Miriam. 'That's for sure. But I will miss him you know.'

'It was awful this morning wasn't it,' said Jack. 'Just us lot. The nurse. The boys from the garage. No friends. No Sharon.'

'He burned off his friends a long time ago,' said Alan bitterly. 'And Sharon.'

They all took tea and cake as an excuse to pause.

'Poor Sharon,' said Miriam at last. 'She was so upset. And David.'

'How do you know?' asked Jack.

'They saw the funeral, remember,' said Miriam. 'And I was talking to them later. So was Alan.'

'Oh,' said Jack. 'I forgot.'

'I'm so glad they were together,' said Miriam. 'Sharon and David. Must have been some comfort to each other.'

'I suppose so,' said Jack who had never met Sharon; she had never bothered to come to New Zealand and he had never been to England; never been out of New Zealand. And David – the painter or poet or something, bearded and queer – he had never understood. He's not a

Landseer man, he used to say to his friends by way of an uncalled-for excuse. Not even sure if he's a man at all.

'I like your friend Betty,' said Miriam brightly. 'She's nice, isn't she, Alan?'

Alan's mouth was full of cake but he nodded dutifully.

'Tell me about it,' said Jack. 'I've known her for years you know. We went to school together. Karapuke North.'

'That's a long time ago,' said Miriam. 'To know someone that long.'

'Well, to tell you the truth she doesn't actually remember me,' said Jack. 'But I remember her.'

'She's nice I think,' said Miriam. 'Seems kind.'

'She's *very* kind,' said Jack. 'Too kind and generous for her own good sometimes I think.'

They were all quietly glad they weren't talking about Michael's funeral any more. They were enjoying their tea in the warm kitchen. And so they were silent until their cake was gone and Miriam reached across to top up their tea. Only then did Jack explain, or at least partly explain, the reason for his unscheduled visit.

'I want to leave the Rolls here for a while,' he said.

'No problem,' said Alan. 'I saw you arrive. She's looking great.'

'She *is* great,' said Jack.

'So there's nothing wrong is there?' asked Alan who loved the Rolls-Royce as much as his father did but was perhaps more conscious of its advancing age and the need for constant maintenance.

'She's fine,' said Jack.

'So?'

'I need room in the garage,' said Jack. 'Space. There's a bit of rust in the Zephyr — in the front doors — so I'm going to take them off.'

'Can you manage that, dad?' asked Alan. 'They're bloody heavy those doors.'

Jack wanted to remind Alan that he, Jack, had restored the old Zephyr from scratch, on his own, without help. But he didn't. He simply said (insisted): 'I know *that.*'

'Your ticker still alright?'

'It's fine,' said Jack.

'Good. You've got the medicine if you need it, eh.'

'I've *never* needed it,' said Jack. 'Bloody doctor.'

'Well, you never know,' said Alan. 'I can help if you like. With the doors I mean. Or I can send one of the boys.'

'I'll be fine,' said Jack.

'You only have to ask.'

'I know,' said Jack sounding more patient that he felt. 'But it'll be fine. I'll enjoy it. A project.'

'Well, we'll put the Rolls in the home garage. Next to Miriam's Vee-Dub. Well away from the trucks.'

'That'll be fine,' said Jack. 'She needs a bit of work but I'll worry about that later.'

'What sort of work?' asked Alan, concerned.

'Not mechanical,' said Jack. 'A few parts. I'll get the Zephyr fixed first.'

'Nothing serious? Really?' Alan couldn't hide his concern and Jack couldn't miss it.

'No,' said Jack wishing he'd never raised the subject. He'd bought the Rolls forty years ago, when it was only eight years old, for its sentimental value which was the reason he continued to maintain it so carefully; he secretly wished Alan didn't value it only as a good investment to be realized at a later date.

'That's good,' said Alan. 'So you'll need a ride home.'

'Not in the Rolls,' said Jack.

'But I was going to enjoy giving her a run,' said Alan.

'Any time you like,' said Jack. 'She'll be yours one day anyway. But not today, eh. Not around Karapuke.'

'Whatever you say, dad,' said Alan who glanced questioningly across the table at Miriam who merely shrugged; she was as puzzled as Alan by Jack's mysterious demurral.

11

'ARE YOU SURE you don't mind?'

'Of course I'm sure,' said Jack. 'Now are you going to get in or what?'

It was half past eight on the Thursday morning following Michael Landseer's funeral. After the funeral Betty had asked Jack for a favour which Jack had happily agreed to provide. But Betty had not waited at home to be picked up as agreed; she was already standing beside Jack's garage door as he backed out the Zephyr. He was glad therefore that the old Zephyr was now the garage's only resident.

I've got to be there about ten, Betty had said, but I wouldn't leave Karapuke too early. She said the traffic on the motorway would probably be too heavy. Jack said he wouldn't know about that. Never go on the motorway at that time, he had said. She said she didn't either but she could see the slow traffic from the train. And so they had agreed that leaving about half past eight should be about right.

'I have to put the trundler in the boot first,' said Betty.

She was standing patiently at the edge of the drive, beside one of Jack's heavily-pruned and naked rose bushes, with the familiar-looking tartan trolley at her side. She was wearing a not-quite mini-length dress, high at the neck with a lace collar, with a matching unbuttoned jacket which had long flaring sleeves. They were both made of a heavy fabric printed in a bold pattern of large bright purple and orange swirls. The bright purple was repeated in her tights.

She'll scare the living daylights out of the kids in that outfit, thought Jack as he got out of the car to open the boot.

'I didn't know you had a trundler load,' he said.

'Of course,' said Betty. 'That's why I need the lift. I told you. Otherwise I'd get the train like I usually do.'

'So you do this every Thursday?' asked Jack as he heaved the heavy trundler into the boot and laid it on its side ensuring that the contents – a collection of toys and board games – wouldn't fall out.

'Every Thursday,' said Betty. 'But taking this in is just once a year.'

'Where do you get all this stuff?'

'Oh, the hospice shop puts these aside for me. Good quality clean stuff for the toy library.'

'What's the toy library?'

'It's a special sort of storage room for all the toys and games and things,' said Betty. 'It's run by wonderful lady volunteers. People can be so nice, Jack, you know that? Of course they have to clean and sterilise every single thing before and after they get used. A lot of work.'

'Sounds like it,' said Jack. 'And you get the train every week?'

'Of course.'

'And you get off at Newmarket?'

'Yes.'

'But it's a long walk from Newmarket station up to the hospital.'

'Not that far,' said Betty. 'Up Carlton Gore Road and I'm there.'

'What if it's raining?'

Betty shrugged. 'It's only water,' she said. 'Raincoat. Umbrella. Galoshes.'

'Right-oh,' said Jack as he slammed down the boot lid and pulled up on the handle to check that it was securely shut. 'Let's go.'

By the time he was settled Betty was sitting and belted beside him on the Zephyr's bench seat.

'You *do* know where to go don't you?' she asked.

'Roughly,' said Jack. 'I know where the hospital is. I was there last week remember. *Last* Thursday. A week ago today.'

'Oh, yes, I'm sorry,' said Betty. 'Actually I would have been there that morning.'

'It was late at night when I was there.'

'I remember,' said Betty. 'I *am* sorry, Jack. It must have been awful.'

'That's alright,' said Jack. 'But you'll have to show me where the Starship bit is when we get there.'

'It's a big separate building,' said Betty. 'Not hard to find. And there's a big parking building.'

'Expensive I bet,' said Jack.

'I don't know.'

They came to the end of Northumberland Road and Jack turned right onto the State Highway.

It started to rain.

'Bugger,' said Jack.

'What's the matter?'

'Oh, the rain,' said Jack as he turned on the windscreen wipers. 'The windscreen wipers in this old thing are useless. Always have been.'

'Will we be alright?' Betty sounded anxious.

'We'll manage,' said Jack although he knew the rain meant he would have to concentrate on his driving, even more than usual, especially on the motorway to which they were heading.

'So you go all the way to Auckland Hospital, to Starship, just to play games with sick kids,' he asked.

'It's not just playing games,' said Betty. 'Sometimes we just talk. Sometimes it's just a wee mite who needs a cuddle. Or a feed. Or a worried and distressed mother who needs a break. Those poor mothers. So it depends what's needed. We just do whatever's needed.'

'Who's we?'

'I'm a Starship grandmother, Jack. There's a few of us. Grandfathers too although not enough of them.'

'So how do you know what to do? What's needed?'

'The nurses know what's needed, what the little ones need, or the parents, and they tell Brenda – she organizes us, the volunteers – and she sends us off to the wards to provide whatever help is needed. We do whatever we're told. Whatever's required.'

'Must be hard,' said Jack. 'Emotionally, I mean.'

'Oh, some of those poor wee tots, Jack. It'd break your heart. And they're so brave. Braver that their mothers sometimes. Or so it seems.'

'Really?' Jack was impressed.

'Oh, Jack, sometimes it just so sad,' said Betty. 'Some of them are so sick. So frail and fragile. And so brave. Last week I—'

But Jack interrupted her. 'I don't really want to know the details,' he said.

'And the poor mothers. Some of them are there with their babies all day and all night. The selfless love and dedication of mothers for their sick and vulnerable children is unbelievable you know. Absolutely unbelievable.'

At that point they entered the motorway on-ramp. The rain had stopped but the road was wet and potentially greasy; Jack loved his Zephyr but he wasn't blind to its faults and shortcomings and as he had been personally maintaining it for the last twenty-five years he was well aware of its limitations: its lack of power, somewhat sluggish acceleration, old braking system, and now its slow and ineffective windscreen wipers. And so he went quiet then; he needed to concentrate if he were to properly and safely navigate the old car onto the motorway. Betty too fell silent as she sensed Jack's anxiety. Indeed, he didn't relax until he was settled in the slow lane pointing the elegant sixty-three-year-old blue Ford north towards Auckland.

'Right-oh,' he said. 'Like Gough we're off to the smoke.'

And so began the long motorway journey to Auckland.

Nothing was said between them for half an hour or more although they each had their own secret thoughts which they each wished they could share with the other but couldn't. They were each thinking of the past as the old mostly do when they ruminate. And, as the old mostly do when they think of the past, they thought not of how good things once were but of how much better they might have been if not for their unkind words which could never be unsaid or their regrettable deeds which could never be undone. It was sad – they each thought, as old people think – that the people they may once have hurt or offended by their unkind words and regrettable deeds, innocent people, friends and family, even casual acquaintances, were now dead and so would never know how much they longed to apologise. Indeed, Jack thought often and ruefully of the apologies he wished he could make while Betty often cried herself to sleep – with only her three feline friends for company – thinking of what she had said and done and what might otherwise have been. Perhaps the only consolation she and her motoring companion had – the only consolation available to *all* old people – was that while their sins may not have been forgiven they were certainly forgotten as they who once may have remembered and judged them could judge them no more. Indeed, sensible old people – Betty Krilich and Jack Landseer included – get to a point where they care not what living people think of them; the only people they ever cared for, whose opinion they once valued, are dead.

And so they drove on steadily on the busy motorway, being passed on the right by a constant stream of seemingly frantic and impatient drivers.

Betty was thinking how awful she had been to Gus. And about that horrid day in Toradh Street, Surry Hills. She hated thinking about that day but it entered her consciousness without warning; and more often lately. And so, to make the thought go away, she said brightly: 'It's a nice car though. It really is.'

Jack was thinking about a young secretary – Catherine Winstanley was her name – with whom he fell in love too easily and who became his wife too quickly when they were both too young. Did she ever regret it as he did, he wondered, although he knew he'd now never know. And he thought of their two children, one of whom was decent, honest, reliable, well-meaning and hard-working but somewhat calculating and ambitious, with a wonderful wife he didn't deserve, while the other – once so clever but lazy and so easily seduced by temptation – was dead leaving a childless widow in England whom he, Jack, had never met and now never would.

'Tell me about it,' he said in response to Betty's comment which, he recalled, she had made before. 'It's English of course. I like old English cars.'

Although I wish the brakes were a bit better, he thought; and that the windscreen wipers worked. God I hope it doesn't rain hard while I'm on the damn motorway. Bloody useless old thing.

'Gus liked English cars too,' said Betty. 'He really did.'

'What was he like, your Gus?' asked Jack; he really wanted to know. 'I never knew him. Never met him.'

'How could you?' said Betty. 'You were in Karapuke all the time weren't you. He was a Wellingtonian through and through.'

'Well, I won't hold that against him,' said Jack with a smile and a glance across to his companion. 'But, seriously, what was he like?'

'A proper bloody gentleman if you really want to know,' said Betty. 'I never deserved him and that's a fact.'

'Really?' Jack was doubtful. Surely the Betty he knew – so kind and generous to everyone and everything, always had been as far as he knew – must have *deserved* a proper gentleman like Gus Krilich for a husband.

'Took him for granted,' said Betty. 'And then when he died it was too late.'

'Too late for what?'

'To appreciate him properly of course.'

'He was a bit older than you wasn't he?'

'Fifteen years,' said Betty. 'But how do you know?' She was more curious than offended.

'I told you. Catherine, my wife, you know,' said Jack quickly. 'She followed the gossip columns in all the magazines and papers, *Weekly News* and that. All the latest goings-on in Wellington. And Auckland. All the big dos. Like the races and that. Who's going where on what ship when. Debutante balls; she loved them. The bishop and the governor-general. Posh weddings and engagements. The honours list.' He glanced sideways, quickly, to see Betty's reaction to his answer but there was none. But she did appear to be listening, paying attention. 'All that gossipy stuff,' he continued blithely. 'You two were quite famous in little Karapuke.'

'Really?'

'Oh, yes,' said Jack. 'Quite famous.'

'I don't know about that,' said Betty with an embarrassed laugh. 'It's all over now though. Anyway, poor Gus, he was only sixty-three you know. That's not old. Not really.'

'Tell me about it. Michael was only sixty,' said Jack. Then he dutifully asked the predictable question although he already knew the answer. 'So that's when you came back to Karapuke?'

'No, no,' said Betty. 'I stayed in Wellington then. I had to take care of everything. All Gus's affairs, you've got no idea. Took quite a while actually.'

Actually I've got quite a good idea, thought Jack. A far better idea than you can imagine, he thought. But he said only: 'I see.'

'So much to do,' added Betty.

'I can imagine,' said Jack. 'So when *did* you come back to Karapuke?'

It was the next obvious question and once again the questioner knew the answer.

'I came back when mummy died,' said Betty. 'That was in nineteen eighty-five. She was ninety you know.'

'Really,' said Jack with feigned surprise. 'Ninety.'

'I sold the Karori house then. She left me the house you see, in Northumberland Road, where I live now.'

'Oh, I see,' said Jack feigning surprise again.

'I'm going to leave it to the women's refuge,' said Betty.

'What? Leave what?'

'My house. In Northumberland Road. It'll be a women's refuge one day. A safe house, you know.'

*That* was something Jack didn't know. 'Really!' he said.

'It's a bit of a mess but I'll get it done up one day. For the refuge.'

'I see,' said Jack. Take a good bit of doing up though, he thought.

'I've got no one any more, Jack,' said Betty. 'No children, nothing.'

Jack again glanced quickly across the car at Betty – smiled, raised his eyebrows to convey the irony he felt – and then, as he returned his attention to the road, he said what he felt: 'I had children. So what?'

'So what?' Betty sounded shocked.

'Grandies too, and great-grandies now.'

'Jack, you're so lucky.'

'Lucky?'

'Yes,' insisted Betty. 'Lucky.'

'Lucky to get a life-time of worry,' said Jack. 'God, this motorway's a nightmare,' he added as an articulated petrol tanker thundered past the Zephyr followed closely – too closely, thought Jack – by a huge red Mack hauling two long containers.

I'll be glad to get off this motorway, he thought. But at least it hasn't rained any more. The windscreen wipers are bloody useless. Doesn't matter around Karapuke, in the country, but here. My God, I forgot how bad they were in traffic. Not just the rain. The road grime.

But Betty ignored his motoring concerns; she was more concerned by his attitude.

'What do you mean worry?' she asked accusingly.

'Well, you worry when they're babies,' he answered. 'You worry when they get a cold, a sore throat – will they get some awful disease? – when they have nightmares, when they come off their bike on the road, when they go to school, will they get bullied?, when they break an arm playing rugby, when they leave school, when they start driving, girls, going to parties and getting drunk, when they're grown up, when they start work, when they work too hard, get greedy for money and success, when they take their wife for granted, when they go overseas, when they divorce, become alcoholics, get a brain tumour. Shall I go on? And then you start worrying about *their* kids. And then their kids' kids. It's a lifetime of worry.'

'That's a bit cynical,' said Betty. 'More than a bit.'

'No it's not,' said Jack. 'It's true. I worry all the time. A lifetime of worry. Ask anyone. For what?'

'Well I think children are precious. Big or small, young or old, you're bloody lucky to have them all. If you could see what I see in Starship.'

Jack was as glad to leave the conversation as he was to leave the motorway at Khyber Pass Road; from there, past the domain, they were at the hospital in a matter of minutes. Betty guided him through the hospital roads to the main Starship entrance where he stopped – illegally, but only for a minute or two – while he lifted the shopping trundler of toys and games from the boot and stood it on the road beside the waiting Betty.

'Thanks, Jack,' said Betty. 'Now if you insist on taking me home, which by the way is completely unnecessary–'

'I'll definitely wait and take you home,' interrupted Jack.

'Yes, well, if you do, I'll finish a bit after twelve. Half-past the latest. So you go and park the car and then ask one of the Bluecoats to show you where the volunteer centre is, on level four, and wait there for me.'

And so Jack closed the boot, checked it, and returned to the car where he sat for a minute to watch Betty – looking bizarre in her gaudy orange-and-purple ensemble, purple tights set off by bright white sneakers with neon green laces – enter the building with her little tartan trundler. Smiling at her apparent indifference to how she might look to others, he set off for the parking building.

A bit after twelve she said, he thought. Bet it'll cost a bloody fortune in that car park. Always does.

But it didn't. Because as a volunteer Betty was entitled to a parking voucher.

# 12

'SO YOU'RE WAITING for Betty?' asked Brenda, the Starship volunteer coordinator. She was standing in front of Jack who was sitting in a soft arm-chair which was a little too low and a little too comfortable.

'Yes,' said Jack looking up awkwardly. 'She said it would be alright for me to wait here.'

'Of course,' said Brenda kindly. 'Would you like a coffee? It's instant I'm afraid. Or tea?'

'Oh, no thanks,' said Jack. 'But I don't think I should sit here too long. Could go to sleep.'

And so he stood up and moved to a hard and upright chair.

'Are you a friend of Betty's?'

'Yes,' said Jack as he sat down. 'Just a friend. Jack Landseer.'

'Pleased to meet you, Jack,' said Brenda, holding out her hand expectantly. Jack took it in his own hand, large and rough, and shook it gently. But not immediately; he had never gotten used to shaking hands with women. 'I'm Brenda.'

After that Jack sat alone in his chair, reading the *Herald*. He noticed that the air conditioner was noisy – old probably, probably needed attention, Alan would get someone onto that – but like all constant background noises it seemed to fade away and then, for no particular reason, suddenly become noticeable again. People – other volunteers he supposed, mostly women – came and went. Some went to a bank of steel lockers to deposit or retrieve some personal item; some came in and went to the kitchen bench where they made a mug of tea or coffee which they took to a large table in the middle of the room where they sat, idly paging through an old magazine, helping themselves to a plastic box of biscuits which sat in the middle of the table; others, looking busy and important, holding papers or a folder or a clip-board, knocked and went into Brenda's office without waiting where, he could see through the glass walls, they chatted with Brenda about something, or looked frowningly at a computer screen, before leaving as hurriedly as they had arrived. Whoever they were, though, they all greeted Jack politely and kindly, one way or another, by saying hello or good morning or just smiling and nodding. Brenda herself left the centre two or three times, to go somewhere and do something in the line of duty, but she always acknowledged the seated Jack with a smile as she passed him on the way out and when she returned after ten or so minutes.

After an hour or so the traffic through the room seemed to stop and there was nothing to hear in the quiet and soundproof room but the vibrating and rattling air conditioner. When Brenda returned from what was evidently her last errand of the morning she stopped and sat on a hard chair beside Jack who had long ago consumed the entire contents of the day's paper and was slowly being overcome by drowsiness brought on by boredom not exertion. And so he welcomed Brenda's company and apparent desire to converse.

'You alright, Jack, waiting here all morning?' she asked.

'Good as gold,' said Jack in reply, quickly adding: 'I'm sorry, I don't remember your name. I know you told me but–'

'Brenda,' said Brenda.

'Right,' said Jack. 'Brenda.'

'You been friends with Betty long?'

'It all depends,' said Jack. 'But, yes, a long time I suppose. A long time.'

'She's such a dear,' said Brenda. 'Loves the children. And so good with them. They all love her you know. The mothers too. They love her.'

'Tell me about it,' said Jack. 'I know.'

Strictly speaking though it was something he had assumed rather than something he knew.

'And *so* generous,' said Brenda. She looked around suspiciously, conspiratorially, unnecessarily, to make sure they were alone. 'She thinks we don't know,' she whispered. 'But of course we do.'

'I suppose you do,' said Jack.

'You know,' she continued, her voice returning to its natural conversational level, 'I don't know what we would have done without those ventilators. They're the absolute cornerstone of intensive care.'

'Are they?'

'*Are they?*' Brenda sounded astonished at Jack's apparent ignorance. 'Jack,' she stressed, 'Betty outfitted Starship, when it was new – that was in nineteen ninety-four you know – with the latest neo-natal ventilators. Such specialist equipment you know. Specially imported. All we needed for our tiny, sick and fragile little babies. And so *expensive*. It must have cost her a fortune.'

'It did,' said Jack only half-knowing the truth; or rather guessing at it.

'I don't know how many lives those things must have saved over the years. And even now she replaces them whenever necessary. Without question.'

Jack said nothing. He didn't know what to say. And so he waited.

'And then only last year,' said Brenda. 'We couldn't believe it. We're not supposed to know but, you know, the foundation and that. Hard to keep that sort of secret.'

'The foundation?'

'There's a foundation. The Starship Foundation. Raises all the money. They do a fantastic job.'

'I've heard of them,' said Jack.

'Betty's still a big supporter,' said Brenda. 'Financial I mean. You must know that.'

Jack nodded sagely; knowingly.

'Like last year we refurbished an entire ward *and* one of the theatres with donations like ______'s.'

She didn't actually speak Betty's name but mouthed it silently, with an exaggerated expression, as if it were a word too sacred to be uttered aloud.

'We're not supposed to know,' she continued quietly. 'But you can't keep that sort of thing secret can you.'

'You can in Karapuke,' said Jack. 'She's very active at home but most people think she's just an eccentric old lady. Poor but busy and well meaning.'

'I don't think she's poor,' said Brenda raising her eyebrows and shaking her head very slowly. 'I don't know the details but I don't think she's poor. I know how it looks, but no.'

'She's been coming here for a while,' said Jack. 'That's no secret. She loves it here.'

'Since we opened,' said Brenda. 'I was still at university then.'

Jack looked directly at Brenda and smiled benignly at her confession of youth.

Suddenly though she looked worried.

'You won't say anything, will you,' she said. 'That we know who she is and what she's done.'

'Of course not,' said Jack tapping at the side of his nose.

And of course he didn't – say anything that is – although he didn't know exactly what he was not supposed to be saying anything about. Not exactly.

On the way home Betty did most – all – of the talking. Jack could see she was excited by her morning's work and enjoyed having someone to talk to about it. He realized that usually, in fact for as long she'd been a Starship grandmother, she would travel home alone on the train.

She told him about the little girl she'd been minding all morning.

'She must have been only about, I don't know, five or six months old maybe,' she said. 'She was recovering from major heart surgery – oh, Jack, you should have seen the wee pet with her scar and tubes and everything – but she was so bright and inquisitive. She looked awfully pale and delicate but the look in her eyes told me that she's a real fighter. I saw her last week and she's improved so much. Her name's Jewel. Isn't that nice? Jewel. I had to relieve her poor mum whose been basically living at the hospital and sleeping in the room with her baby. They have a fold-down bed in the rooms. It's marvellous what they do.'

And so Betty went on for most of the journey. And although he was hungry for lunch, and perhaps – he admitted it to himself – a little bored by Betty's enthusiasm, Jack let her talk.

She went quiet for a while once they left the motorway but then, out of the blue as it were, at least that's how it seemed to Jack, she said: 'I used to know the man who named Starship.'

'Did you?' said Jack more from politeness than interest.

'Yes, of course,' said Betty. 'It's a funny story. Bob Harvey was his name. He was a friend of Gus's. Seemed to know a lot about New Zealand art and literature and things like that. He was in Wellington a lot in those days. For the Labour Party I think. He and Gus always had awful lot to talk about. About Labour and politics and that. I don't know what. He was just nice Bob Harvey then, I remember, but he's a Sir now.'

'Never heard of him,' said Jack.

'You should have,' said Betty. 'Most people have. He was a mayor or something.'

'Anyway, we'll be home soon. Are you hungry? I am.'

'Not really,' said Betty. 'Just drop me at church if you wouldn't mind.'

'At Saint Peter's again?'

'There's ladies' choir practice this afternoon. I play for them see. Piano. They're practising for a competition.'

'But aren't you hungry?' Jack was very hungry and couldn't imagine why Betty wasn't.

'I'll get something to eat in the hall.'

'Are you sure?'

'Quite sure, Jack. Just drop me at the church if you wouldn't mind.'

'Right-oh,' said Jack. 'The church it is.'

'And flowers tomorrow,' said Betty. 'You want to help again?'

'Why not,' said Jack. 'I'll pick you up this time. Half past ten, right?'

'Right.'

And I'll ask you again then, thought Jack. About the Combined. I know what you'll say, he thought, but it doesn't matter because I know what I'll say after that. And then I think you'll accept. Which means Zelnick. I must sort things out with Zelnick. This afternoon. After lunch. I'll do it. I better do it before she says yes.

☼

'Everything?'

'Everything,' said Jack.

'On Saturday? You want Saturday?'

'It *must* be Saturday, Mort. Must be.'

'But the hurry, my friend,' said Zelnick. 'On Saturday. My new van. My men. Overtime. Is very expensive.'

'That's alright, Mort. I don't mind,' said Jack.

'But why? Zelnick must know.'

'I don't think they're safe here anymore,' said Jack. 'And my son thinks – well, never mind that – the thing is, Mort, there's not enough security. And there's something else worrying me. I can't explain. It's complicated. But I want you to take care of everything for me. Saturday. Everything. You understand?'

'Of course, of course, my friend Jack,' said Zelnick. 'Am I stupid? Zelnick understands everything.'

'You'll take care of it then?' asked Jack seeking reassurance. 'Everything into storage. Full security, insurance, the works.'

'The works he says. But of course,' said Zelnick. 'The works as you say. But, my friend Jack, there is the matter of, may I say it? So crude. Money you see. Not just Saturday, overtime for the men, but a monthly fee you understand. Storage. Security. Insurance. Everything is the works.'

'Yes, Mort, I understand. Everything,' said Jack. 'But, one more thing,' he added.

'Yes, my friend?'

'Your new van. The van you'll come in with your men.'

'What about it, the new van, my friend?'

'Well, it hasn't got your name on it or anything has it? M. A. Zelnick, Fine Art Gallery and Auctioneers, and all that bullshit? Like the gallery sign.'

'I am stupid? A fool?' said Zelnick. He sounded hurt; insulted. 'Zelnick is always the highest discretion. A white van is all. Plain white van. No words. No nothing.'

'Good,' said Jack, satisfied. Experience had taught him to trust Mordecai Zelnick.

'Now, forgive me, my friend,' said Zelnick, 'I have much to organize. Do you have anything else for me? Zelnick is always your servant.'

'Nothing else, mate. I'll see you Saturday morning. Eleven o'clock.'

'Eleven o'clock Saturday,' confirmed Zelnick.

'Better allow a couple of hours.'

'A couple of hours he says,' said Zelnick. 'Maybe more. Who knows?'

# 13

'YOU'RE A JOLLY quick learner, Jack,' said Betty.

'Always was,' said Jack who had come prepared with his gardening gloves in his back pocket.

Betty was wearing a denim bib-overall – not a real workman's overall but a once-fashionable imitation with widely-flared legs, shoulder straps trimmed with lace, and metal buttons mostly for show – over the same purple tie-dyed t-shirt she wore the previous Friday. Jack assumed it was her flower-arranging outfit. Her bleached-out denim jacket – the one with dull copper buttons and pockets embroidered with faded dragons – was hanging in the church porch.

They were sitting together at one of the tables in the church hall's kitchen. Betty had made tea which she had brought to the table on a tray and which they were now enjoying together. She had put a biscuit tin between them and they were helping themselves to the stale round-wine biscuits it contained. They could hear the muffled sound of a woman speaking to the ante-natal class which was being held in the hall proper.

And just as he had a week earlier the young vicar Vance Widdop bounced jollily into the kitchen from the side door.

'Morning, Betty,' he called cheerfully across the room. 'And Jack. Good morning to you too.'

Jack turned and nodded his acknowledgement while Betty called out: 'A cuppa, Mr Widdop?' as she readied herself to get up and fetch another cup and saucer.

'Love to, Betty,' said the vicar, 'but can't stop. Flowers all done?'

'Of course,' said Betty.

'Oh, good,' said the vicar. 'Mrs Reliable, eh. And Jack Reliable too.' He came across to the table, stood between the seated tea drinkers, and rested his right hand on Jack's left shoulder. 'Another funeral soon you see. One o'clock.'

'I know,' said Betty.

'Yes, of course,' said the vicar. 'And, Jack, how are you? And your family? Such a sad time.'

'I'm alright, Vance,' said Jack whose unreasonable antipathy to the young vicar was fading. He looked around and up. 'But thanks for asking,' he added.

'An awful time, I know. Well, enjoy your tea. Must dash.' And off he went across the kitchen and through the door into the adjacent church.

Only when Jack saw that the church door was shut and that the vicar was unlikely to return to the kitchen, at least in the next little while, did he move to ask Betty the question to which he anticipated a negative response for which reason he had prepared a second question which he expected would stimulate an interesting debate if not an answer in the affirmative.

And so he took a sip of milky tea, put down his cup, and asked permission to ask what was to be the preliminary question: 'Can I ask you something, Betty?'

Betty, who was also sipping at her tea, put down her cup and answered: 'Of course, Jack.'

'The thing is it's Friday,' said Jack.

'I know that, Jack,' said Betty sarcastically. 'Flowers day.'

'Tell me about it,' said Jack. He picked up his cup and took some more tea before continuing. 'Well, the thing is, I usually go to the Combined on Friday nights. Have steak and chips and that with some friends. Good steak.'

'That's nice,' said Betty. 'What's the Combined?'

'I told you before,' said Jack. 'It's my club. A club for oldies like me. Like us. Like a Cossie club.'

Betty frowned and shook her head. Slowly. Her lack of interest – indeed, her contempt for even the idea of such a club – could not be mistaken.

'But I thought you might like to come along with me tomorrow night,' said Jack.

It wasn't exactly a question but it was meant to be and it was taken as such by Betty who, in response, toyed absentmindedly with her almost empty teacup, using the tip of her forefinger on its handle to turn it in its saucer. 'I told you before, Jack,' she said, 'I'm not a club sort of person. People I don't know.' She shook her head slowly again. 'No thanks.'

'But you like to dance don't you?'

'I *used* to like to dance,' said Betty, remembering. Remembering the after-hours parties in Wellington. The balls in season. Friends in Toorak. Nights at Gus's club in Sydney. Dancing on the ships to and from Sydney and

San Francisco. And even guesting once or twice with the ship's orchestra. 'But not anymore, Jack. Not now.'

'Why not?'

'Look at me. I'm eighty-eight years old.'

'That doesn't matter,' said Jack. 'You're as fit as a flea.'

'No, Jack,' said Betty with a slow head shake.

'But it's a club for oldies. Just like us. Older even. And plenty of them like to dance. You'd love the old music. And a really good band.'

Oh, the bands I remember, thought Betty. I wish I could tell you. Vibes and the others. The Capital Jazz Quartct. Quintet sometimes. And you know what? Gus and I met Sinatra once. He was singing with Nelson Riddle in Reno. We went backstage. Dean wasn't there but Sammy Davis was – I liked him – and so was Joey Bishop but I didn't really know him. Gus had met him before and didn't like him. Wouldn't introduce me. Can you believe that, Jack? Can you? I can hardly believe it myself.

'No, Jack,' she said aloud but not unkindly. 'Thanks, but no. Not my thing.'

'Right-oh,' said Jack brightly. 'Actually, I knew you'd say that.'

'Did you?'

'Of course.'

'How? Did you know, I mean.'

'Well, you turned me down once didn't you? Only logical.'

'I see.'

'So, I'll go alone tonight. I usually do. Lots of old mates there.' He paused. There was obviously more to come so Betty waited. At last he said: 'And so to my next question.'

'What's that?'

'Well, will you come to my place tomorrow night, Saturday night, or any night for that matter, and let me cook tea for us both? Anything you like.'

'You cook?'

'Of course I cook. I'm a pretty good cook actually.'

Betty closed the biscuit tin and poured them more tea. Jack added milk. Betty didn't. But she did look across the table at Jack as he added his milk, stirred it in, took a drink and pulled a face.

'Nearly cold,' he said.

'Oh, sorry,' said Betty. 'But why.'

'Too much milk didn't help.'

'No, Jack,' said Betty. 'Not the tea. Why do you want me to come to your place tomorrow night or any night for that matter you said? What's it all about?'

'We're friends aren't we?'

'I suppose we are,' said Betty sounding a little surprised at the realization. 'Here let me clear the table.'

And so she stood up, collected the cups, saucers and teaspoons, the biscuit tin, the carton of milk, the Vegemite jar holding the little paper tubes of sugar, and the by-now cool pot of tea, loaded them all onto the tray and took them across to the kitchen bench where she busied herself putting away the biscuits, milk and sugar, emptying the teapot, and rinsing the crockery and cutlery under hot water and leaving them in a wire dish rack to dry.

'But I don't quite know how or why we're suddenly friends,' she said over her shoulder as she worked. 'Do you?'

'Does it matter,' said Jack who did know. 'We're old fogies. I don't know about you but most of my old friends are either bedridden or in a rest home that stinks of cabbage and piss, completely ga-ga. Or they're pushing up daisies.'

Betty returned to her place at the now-cleared table. She was wiping her hands on a tea-towel.

'I know what you mean,' she said. 'But you talk about your Combined Club and the friends you have there. What about them?'

'They're not really friends,' said Jack. 'Acquaintances more like. And, to tell you the truth, even though it's a club for oldies, I think I'm the oldest one there.'

'You just said there were people older than us even.'

'I made that up.'

'Why?'

'To make you feel better.'

'Silly bugger,' said Betty with a smile as she flicked the tea towel at him across the table. 'Anyway, why do you go there then? If they're not *really* your friends?'

'We all need a social life,' said Jack. 'People to talk to, have a drink and a joke with. Dance. Play pool. Darts. Talk about the rugby and that.'

Betty grimaced. 'Bloody hell, Jack,' she said. 'Not my sort of thing at all.'

'But you must need friends and family as much as anyone. They help keep us alive and kicking. Don't tell me you don't.'

'Of course I do,' said Betty. 'I don't have family though. Not anymore. But you're lucky to have children and grandchildren, Jack.'

'We've been through that.'

'Well, you *are*. Lucky I mean.'

'There's only Alan now, of course,' said Jack. 'And Miriam. And grand-children and great-grandchildren too. Don't really know them though.'

'Well, you *are* lucky,' said Betty although she didn't miss the apparently involuntary rolling of Jack's eyes. 'You *are*,' she insisted. 'But as for me, I *do* have plenty of friends.'

'You mean here, at Saint Peter's? And at the mission and hospice shop and Starship and all the other things you do?'

'Exactly,' said Betty. 'Good friends. Friends who really care. Who share *my* interests. Not rugby and darts but *my* interests.'

'That's good,' said Jack.

'People to talk to, as you say. We're human beings, social animals.'

'But are they enough?' asked Jack. Seriously. 'They're not *real* friends are they.' It was meant as a statement of fact, not a question.

And then, at that moment, when the conversation was getting interesting – at least from Jack's point of view – the door from the hall was flung open and three vivacious and very pregnant young women, dressed in gaudy Lycra gym-wear not necessarily fit for purpose, burst laughing and talking into the kitchen, evidently intent on making refreshments for the members of the ante-natal class. They hardly noticed, and certainly didn't acknowledge, the presence of the white-haired old man and the old lady in funny clothes sitting together at one of the tables, chatting quietly.

'I think it's time for us to go,' said Betty.

And a mildly embarrassed Jack didn't disagree.

# 14

BY THREE O'CLOCK the next afternoon – after more than the expected couple of hours – Mordacai Zelnick and his men – two of his senior curators and two security guards – were gone from one-three-six Northumberland Road taking with them the old owner's collection of cherished and now exceedingly valuable paintings, large and small, old and modern, including of course the Lindauer which he had owned for only eighteen months. They, the paintings, were destined for Zelnick's own art, antiques and precious metals security vault in a secret underground location in the industrial Wairau valley.

'Completely safe even in nuclear war,' was Zelnick's claim. 'Built by the Mormons but then too small. They said it. They need bigger. So Zelnick buys it. A bargain maybe but not easy to bargain with them the Mormons. Not easy, even for Zelnick.'

For more than three hours Jack Landseer had watched as Zelnick's young experts, supervised by Mordacai Zelnick himself – dressed and bejewelled for a Saturday trip to rural Karapuke as flamboyantly as for a weekday's work in urban Parnell – carefully inspected his paintings, which he knew had rarely been seen by anyone but him and their few former owners, before wrapping them in soft blankets, securing them in rigid and steel-reinforced wooden crates built for the purpose, and moving them uprightly to Zelnick's plain white van parked in his driveway. Together with the two grim and hefty-looking security guards he looked on but didn't help.

'Is for experts only to handle,' said the busy Zelnick with a dismissive wave. 'No other peoples.'

Then, later, as he sat alone in his living room, in the soft light of the weak and watery afternoon sun which was filtering through the room's net curtains from its distant source in the west, he looked at the rectangles of unfaded wallpaper, large and small – there were others like it in the hall and in his bedroom – and saw the ghosts of what he had once bought joylessly, to satisfy an obsession, for a calculated reason, but had unexpectedly come to love with an unreasonable passion.

Now, suddenly, he felt empty and melancholy; as empty and melancholy as the room in which he sat.

The room was not really empty – of course not – but without the paintings it seemed empty. And sad. And so he felt empty and sad with it in sympathy. There was the lounge suite of course – he had bought that new when he bought the house and was sitting now in one of its arm-chairs – and the old China cabinet of lead-light panels full of what? bric-a-brac he supposed, Catherine's bric-a-brac. Bits and bobs. Not his. Some of it, perhaps, valuable. Can bric-a-brac be valuable? he wondered idly. Don't know really. Don't care for that matter. Mostly rubbish. Silly worthless ornaments saved by Catherine for sentimental reasons known only to her. I'll give them to Alan and

Miriam. And there were the photos on the mantelpiece, above the unused fireplace, crammed together, overlapping, with Catherine's antique carriage clock for company. They were mostly black-and-white, the photos, in dusty unmatched frames of uneven quality; and they all, separately and together, made him depressed despite their portrayal of ever-smiling never-ageing faces on always-sunny days: he and Catherine on their wedding day; a smiling Catherine, looking up, half-in and half-out of the white Jaguar that was their wedding car; Alan being christened; Michael being christened. Why did I agree to that? he thought. I don't believe in God. I just went along with it for Catherine's sake. Alan in his rugby gear; first fifteen. I got player of the day, dad, he said. I was proud that day, thought Jack. I really was. He went on to play rep footy, at least until he met Miriam. Michael in Oxford in his funny floppy hat. Catherine took that. I didn't go. England. Bugger that. But she was so proud. Can't blame her of course. I should have been there too but I wasn't. I never really got Michael and he knew it. Catherine did. From the beginning. Thank Christ she didn't see how he ended up. Then him and Sharon on their wedding day in England. In the street outside some Pommie registry office somewhere. Not a wedding dress. Not a real proper wedding. Sharon's holding her hat; must have been windy. Alan and Miriam of course. Their wedding. At Miriam's church in Cambridge. Presbyterian from memory. Or was it? And their kids. And their grandkids. Kids. Little kids. Big kids. All staring into the camera. Looking directly at the looker. All smiling. Laughing. Teeth everywhere. Crinkled-up eyes. Laughing and smiling. Always happy. Always happy families. Always happy sunny summer days. Never a worry in the world.

What a lot of bullshit, he thought. I think I'll give all the photos to Alan and Miriam too. Miriam'll appreciate them all. She'll look after them.

That decided, he looked away from the photos and around again at the empty walls. I suppose Alan'll be glad now, he thought. No security worries any more. Save a bit on insurance but I'll have Zelnick's fee. That won't be small. But now I don't have to worry about Betty any more. Now I can get on without worrying about Alan or the paintings or security or Betty or anything like that.

He had a plan of course.

Yes. A plan. Got to have a plan. A long term plan. And when I'm ready, when the time is right, I'll do it. It'll be terrific. I'll get Zelnick to take care of everything. I know him. He'll do it all with complete discretion. No one will know. I know that. I know that for sure. Complete anonymity. When I'm ready. When the time is right. When the time is right, Betty Henderson, he thought. When the time is right, you just watch out.

Now, though, I better think about tomorrow. Lunch tomorrow.

✿

Betty had declined Jack's invitation to dinner at his place on Saturday night. They were in the Zephyr, outside the church on Friday, their privacy in the church hall kitchen having been invaded by three young, chattering and excited mothers-to-be; Jack was about to drive Betty home. She said she really didn't go out anywhere at night. No offence.

'Except Sunday nights,' she said. 'I play the organ on Sunday nights.'

'Oh,' said Jack.

'That's the only night I go out,' she said. 'Otherwise, no.'

'Oh,' said Jack. 'Why's that?'

'I don't have electricity.'

Jack had guessed that.

'Oh,' he said again, feigning surprise. 'So how do you see at night?'

'Candles. But I go to bed early, get up early, so it doesn't matter.'

'And what about keeping warm?'

'If I get too cold I go to bed. The cats keep me warm.'

'Cats?'

'I've got three cats.'

'Of course. Yes. So no telly. No radio?'

'I've got a radio. Little transistor thing. Batteries. Listen to talk-back sometimes. If I can't sleep.'

'And no phone.'

'No need for one.'

'What about cooking?'

'I've got gas,' said Betty. 'And, I've just remembered, I've got a gas heater if I want it. But I hardly ever use it. It's expensive, gas.'

'I see,' said Jack who didn't see much at all.

And so, without saying more, he turned on the ignition and reached to press the starter. But his unspoken confusion, sympathy, affection and disappointment all showed on his face and in his manner. Betty saw them all and was touched by Jack's artlessness.

'Wait,' she said.

And so Jack didn't start the car but sat back on the bench seat, his hands resting on the somewhat cracked and crazed old steering wheel, and waited.

'I'll tell you what I *could* do,' said Betty.

'What's that?' Jack wasn't even sure what she was talking about any more; but he was nevertheless intrigued.

'I could come for *lunch* on Sunday if you like,' said Betty. 'After the eleven o'clock at Saint Peter's. I usually stop and help Mr Widdop sweep out the church and generally tidy up, after three services you know, put everything away, but he won't mind if I dash off. That'd be a bit after twelve at your place. How would that be?'

'That'd be absolutely corker,' said Jack with a smile of satisfaction. 'What a dag, eh.'

And just as Betty had so easily sensed Jack's disappointment she now easily sensed the genuine pleasure in his simple response and was somehow glad; flattered; but puzzled.

'Let's get you home,' said Jack.

# 15

BETTY ARRIVED AS promised a little after twelve on the Sunday afternoon having come straight from church.

She was wearing her camelhair coat and red mohair scarf – Jack was familiar with them both – but when she removed them he was surprised to see that her long black dress, longer than her coat, almost floor-length, with long sleeves and a high collar, looked especially formal; it was an elegant but somewhat inappropriate look for a winter's Sunday lunch in rural Karapuke. But any suggestion that the wearer might be guilty of showy pretention was quashed by the bright white sneakers with neon green laces.

Jack steered his guest into the dining room which was furnished with a large table of polished mahogany, set with eight matching chairs, which Jack had brought with him from Landseer Farm.

'Catherine loved to entertain,' said Jack by way of explanation.

He had set the table for two with a small cream tablecloth at one corner of the large table, the corner nearest the kitchen.

'We used to entertain a lot too,' said Betty. 'Me and Gus. In Wellington I mean. And elsewhere.'

Jack wanted to say I know but didn't. But Betty's thoughts had flown to the house – a mansion really – in Karori and the big flat in Double Bay and years of fun and laughter and gaiety in both and–

'You're not a vegetarian are you?' asked Jack suddenly, diverting Betty's thought train, because the frightening possibility suddenly occurred to him.

'A vegetarian? No. Why do you ask that?'

'Well, people like you often are aren't they.'

'What do you mean, people like me?'

Jack now wished he hadn't asked the question; or at least hadn't referred to people like you.

'I mean, you're a nice kind person. I've noticed that. Gentle. Kind. And I've noticed that kind and thoughtful people like you are often vegetarians. People who do charities and that.'

'Well I'm not and that's that,' said Betty gently. 'So don't worry.'

Jack sighed with relief and said: 'Just as well. I wouldn't have a clue what to give one of them.'

Betty, who had sat herself at the table and was unfolding a carefully-ironed cream linen serviette, merely smiled benignly, not unkindly, and asked the standing Jack: 'Well, what have you got then?'

'I was going to roast a chicken but I thought–'

Betty laughed loudly as she spread the serviette across her lap.

'You *thought*. You silly old bugger. Perhaps you just think too much, Jack Landseer,' she said. 'I do eat chicken, you know. My chickens. When they get old and stop producing. Give them away sometimes but they're a bit tough and gamey by the time they're egged out and old. I don't mind but some people do. Anyway, whatever you think I might be I'm also practical. Have to be.'

It was true: Jack had thought of roasting a chicken but had changed his mind for precisely the reason guessed by Betty. Instead he prepared a plain old-fashioned lunch of grilled fish fingers with buttered and minted potatoes, and tinned peas.

'That was just perfect,' said Betty as her host got up and took her plate and cutlery. 'Simple. And not too much. I don't eat much these days. Not like I used to.'

Once again she remembered Karori. The banquets they used to hold in the ballroom. Who were they? she wondered. Those cooks and kitchen maids? Their names? There was a Barbara, a Mary, a Maud; she thought she remembered a Hannah, a Lizzie, a Kate, an Esme, and a Dulcie. Did they do everything on their own? All those great meals for so many people? I thought they were important, those guests, now I can't even remember who they were. Not even one of them. I don't eat much these days, she said. Not like I used to. Even the breakfasts we had together – me and Gus – were such ridiculously lavish affairs.

'Neither do I,' said Jack. 'I've got quite a small appetite really. Compared with what I used to be like. When I was working. A man gets an appetite when he's working hard.'

He went to the kitchen with the empty plates leaving Betty alone at the table.

We had maids then, she thought, to wait at table. To take away the plates and things. And do the dishes I suppose. Even when there was just me and Gus. Maids. I can hardly believe it now. And a housekeeper.

And then for some reason she thought of her little tartan shopping trundler which had broken outside Jack's house – the event which led to her to now being *inside* Jack's house – and remembered that Gus had once bought the cook, whoever she was in those long-ago days, a shopping trundler of sorts. An unpainted wicker-work thing made by blind people somewhere. Did she, the cook, use it for shopping? I have no idea, she thought. Weren't most of the groceries delivered by those awful Four Square people? That horrible man in a grubby white apron and a black eye patch. He had a blurred tattoo on his hairy forearm. I remember that. I suppose all those staff – our staff – went on to get married and have children and have a full life. I hope they were all happy but I have no idea. I have no idea even who they were. Isn't that terrible.

Jack returned then with two deep dessert dishes each with a scoop of vanilla ice-cream and a spoonful each of a red jelly and a green jelly.

'Oh, Jack,' said Betty with what Jack thought was a girlish giggle. 'That is so sweet and old-fashioned. I haven't had jelly and ice-cream since I don't know when.'

Immediately after lunch the talk was small and the activity domestic as the old pair worked together in the kitchen to clean the grill tray and wash and dry the few pots and dishes, knives, forks and spoons, and put them all away. Betty sometimes had to ask Jack where this, that or the other should go, but generally Jack was impressed with how harmoniously they worked together and how his friend seemed so at ease in his kitchen; so confident and competent.

And he said so: 'You're obviously perfectly at home in the kitchen.'

'Thank you,' said Betty.

'Really domesticated.'

If only you knew, thought Betty. If only you knew.

'A lot of oldies like us give up on cooking and eating,' Jack continued. 'Too lazy. Can't be bothered. Then they wonder why they get ill.'

'I eat well enough, Jack,' said Betty. 'I've got my own garden don't forget. I know all about health and nutrition and that.'

'There was an old bloke at the club, lived alone, found dead after a week,' said Jack. 'Died of malnutrition they said. Absolutely no food in the house. No bread, milk, nothing. Just a half-empty bottle of Scotch and a full ash tray.'

'That's terrible,' said Betty.

'He never turned up for bowls so his partner went round. His pairs partner. Asked a neighbour. She said she hadn't seen him for ages. They called the police. Broke in and found him.'

'So sad,' said Betty.

'That can happen when you're old and you've got no one,' said Jack.

'At least you've got children looking out for you,' said Betty. 'I've got no one.'

'You've got me,' said Jack brightly. 'Now.'

Betty smiled.

Suddenly Jack had a thought; a thought he thought was important.

'You should give me a key to your house,' he said. 'You know, in case of an emergency.'

But Betty looked shocked. Horrified even. 'Absolutely NOT!' she said.

Her fierce resistance to Jack's innocent – and to him sensible – suggestion chilled the warm atmosphere which had prevailed during their lunch together. Betty's mood was now anxious and brittle which made Jack regret ever having made the suggestion. And he remembered again how once before she had been anxious to keep him from seeing inside her house.

'I'm sorry,' he said not really knowing what he was apologising for; he had no idea why she should object so strongly to what he thought was a reasonable and practicable idea. But his apology was nevertheless sincere and Betty not only sensed that it was but realized that her negative reaction had been extreme.

And so she smiled and said: 'It's alright, Jack. I'm being silly.'

But she didn't agree to give him a key.

She did give him one later though but for a different reason.

The warmth between them gradually returned and when everything was washed, dried and put away, and when the sink was emptied and swirled out, and the bench tops all wiped down, they shared a towel to dry their hands and Jack allowed Betty to make a pot of tea – something she seemed good at – while he took down two of Catherine's good cups and saucers from his "best" cupboard, and they sat together to enjoy their tea at the kitchen table.

After their tea Betty visited the toilet.

She had to go into the hall to get to the little room and apparently – to Jack's relief – she hadn't noticed the ghostly outlines of what for years had hung on the walls of the hall; or if she had she didn't comment on them when she returned to the kitchen.

Thank you, Zelnick, said Jack. To himself. Thank you.

16

'BUT WE *ARE* old friends,' insisted a puzzled Jack. 'Don't you remember?'

The cups and saucers had been pushed aside and although the diners were still at the table the Sunday lunch *rendezvous* was drawing to its natural conclusion. Betty was set to go home insisting that she didn't need a lift for such a short distance and that an after-lunch walk would do her good.

'I'll have a wee rest,' she said. 'Then I've got a lot do in the garden before church tonight.'

But now there was a completely new line of conversation. It began with a question – Betty had asked it – about how the two of them, no more than distant neighbours for more years than she knew, had lately become friends so quickly and easily.

'Just because you helped me when the wheel came off my trundler,' she said. 'Just a couple of weeks ago.'

'Well, what's odd about that?'

'Jack, my new friend, I have lived in my house in Northumberland Road, down the road, since mummy died there in nineteen eighty-five. More than thirty years. Gus died seven years before that so I was already used to being on my own. I came back here. I inherited the house you see. In all that time alone, in Wellington and here, I have kept myself busy, kept myself to myself, made good and loyal friends here in Karapuke, at the mission, Saint Peter's, the choir, Starship, the refuge, the hospice shop, everywhere. But never have I been to anyone's house or had anyone to mine. *And–*' and here she paused for emphasis '–Jack, I'm eighty-eight years old and I've never in that time, since I lost Gus, never have I been out alone with a man. Anywhere. Let alone in his house. And here we are, you and me, having lunch together on a Sunday afternoon, chatting away like old friends.'

'But we *are* old friends,' insisted a puzzled Jack. 'Don't you remember?'

'No, Jack,' said Betty who was getting somewhat annoyed by Jack's mysterious allusions. 'I honestly don't know what you're talking about.'

'Well it *didn't* just start with your broken trundler.'

'Tell me,' said a puzzled-looking Betty. 'Please.'

'You don't remember? Yet you were so nice to me.'

'Really?'

'Yes. Really,' said Jack. 'I've never forgotten it.'

'Forgotten what?'

'I fell over – actually, if you remember, no, you don't do you, I was pushed – and cut my knees really bad. And my hands. Bleeding. You were there. You helped me.'

Betty shook her head slowly. Her expression and the slow shaking of her head told Jack that she was genuinely trying but failing to remember the event.

'Where was this?' she asked.

'In Anzac Street,' said Jack. 'Right on the corner of Showgrounds Road. You really don't remember?'

Betty shook her head again. Slowly. Thinking. Thinking hard.

'But you were so *nice* to me,' said Jack. 'You helped me. So kind. Like you've always been.'

Betty looked frustrated. 'When was this exactly, Jack?' she asked. 'I really don't remember anything about it at all. How long ago?'

'It was in nineteen forty-one. February nineteen forty-one.'

'What!'

'After school.'

'What!'

Betty was both shocked and annoyed. Shocked that Jack should remember something so unimportant from so long ago, and annoyed that he had led her — or so she thought — to think that he was referring to a recent event and that her memory was therefore faulty or even failing.

'Don't you remember it at all?'

Jack couldn't understand why something so important to him — well-remembered after even, what? getting on for eighty years — wasn't equally as important to and well-remembered by her. Indeed, for a long time he had taken it for granted that she would have remembered.

Betty shook her head slowly. 'Not at all,' she said with a sigh.

But Jack remembered. He remembered an eight-year-old motherless boy — he was called John then — walking home from school. A long walk every afternoon from Karapuke North primary school in Anzac Street to the corner and then along Showgrounds Road to the Shell station, where

Main Street becomes Main Line, north of the town, where the Macadam ended and the country road became and remained unsealed all the way home and beyond. He remembered, every day, the long walk home in the heat of summer, the cold and wet of winter, home to a grieving and preoccupied father who was too fretful to imagine how an eight year old boy was coping without his mother; a mother who, when she was alive and loving, would always be waiting with a piece of cake and a glass of cool milk in the summer, Vegemite toast and hot Milo in the winter; a father too busy with a business that was struggling under wartime restrictions on fuel and oil and tyres, and truck licensing; an inadequate businessman who needed help but couldn't afford it even if there were any young men available to employ which there weren't due to the army and the war; a man who should have been in the prime of his life but was burdened by the early death of his wife, a son he didn't want, and an inherited business he hadn't asked for, didn't want, and now worried him sick.

He remembered that particular after-school afternoon in February nineteen forty-one when, on the corner of Showgrounds Road, those three big boys – who always mocked him about his father's old truck, and about being poor, and having eczema, and having old clothes and no shoes and always needing a haircut – taunted him and teased him and chased him when he tried to run away until they caught him and shoved him over, and sent him flying onto the road. And so he fell, his hands stretched forward to save himself, and so grazed not only his knees on the hard sharp stones set into the seal of the hot road but the heels of his hands. And he remembered how, as he heard the bullies laughing as they ran away, his spelling book and the precious banana he was saving to eat on the way home both spilled from his schoolbag and skidded away. So he sat up, retrieved his grimy spelling book and bruised banana, returned them to his schoolbag, and limped, sore and bleeding, to the side of the road where he sat on the soft coolness of the grass verge, picking small pieces of sharp gravel from his torn and bleeding knees, while the tiny and taut muscles of his chin quivered uncontrollably as he fought the shameful urge to cry.

And then, suddenly, she was there: big Betty Henderson.

'I got pushed over after school by some bullies and you were there and you helped me. Don't you remember?'

'Sorry, Jack,' said Betty. 'I really don't.'

But *he* remembered. He remembered *everything*: how Betty Henderson, one of the big girls from standard five, kneeled at his side, on the grass, and put her hand under his underarm to help him stand – he didn't need help to stand but he liked it that she wanted to help – and said those horrid boys, I hate them all. And he remembered how he limped along with her such a long way down Main Street to Northumberland Road and to her home at one hundred and seventy-two – he never forgot the number – where, once inside the house (which was so large and luxurious compared to the Landseers' old and unkempt property in the country, on the pretentiously-named Landseer Farm) Betty's mother bathed his knees and hands in warm water laced with Dettol, carefully easing out the fine gravel with soft pads of cotton wool, and then daubing the four sites with mercurochrome which left his skin stained bright yellow which he didn't mind.

And then, most remarkably of all, he remembered sitting with Betty in the back seat of the Henderson's brand new dark blue Ford Prefect while Mrs Henderson drove him all the way home. And, grateful as he was, he didn't know how to express his thanks partly because of his natural shyness but more because, when Mrs Henderson drove up the muddy and pot-holed drive of Landseer Farm, and parked beside the old and large corrugated-iron shed that was Town & Country Carriers Limited, adjacent to the almost derelict house, and his overalled father came out of the shed wiping his hands on a greasy rag, he was desperately ashamed of everything that was his.

'Your mother bathed my hands and knees in warm water and then drove me all the way home with you.'

'Did she?' asked Betty who was genuinely surprised and amazed that Jack remembered an event from so long ago while she remembered nothing about it. 'It does sound like her I suppose. But, honestly, I don't remember.'

But the boy John Landseer never forgot. And for that year of nineteen forty-one, and all the year which followed, he secretly adored Betty Henderson even though she was three years his senior. It was an innocent and honest school-boy love. He thought she was the prettiest girl in the world – and she *was* pretty – and so he spent hours dreamily staring at her across the playground. He loved to look at her pretty face. He loved the way her shiny nut-brown hair fell in ringlets down her back and how she – actually it was her mother – tied the ringlets on the side in pink (or blue or yellow or red or green) shiny satin ribbons to keep them out of her pretty face. He admired the way she dressed, her clothes, without knowing why, without realizing that he was unconsciously recognizing both the quality and style that only money could buy and the refined good taste which money could not. He admired even her ankles and thought her bright white ankle socks and black slip-on shoes – which looked as soft as slippers – were, well, he didn't know what they were but he liked how they looked. He innocently longed to touch her bare arms; they were lightly-tanned with a faint covering of soft hair which looked golden when it caught the sunlight. In the playground, at playtime and lunchtime, he would sit alone and look at her wistfully as she sat with her friends in the shade of the monkey-apple trees – unaware of his longing looks – perhaps eating a sandwich or biting into an apple, talking and laughing; or on the playground skipping a long and heavy rope, running in and out of its sweeping circle, and chanting the skipping songs which only girls seemed to know. And at night he would lie in bed, sighing frequently, thinking only of her until he fell asleep. Yet not once in those two years – until she left Karapuke to go to a boarding school somewhere, he didn't know where – did he ever speak to her again or even get to stand- or sit near her.

Only then, on that Sunday afternoon in his kitchen, did Jack Landseer finally come to realize that old Betty Krilich, his neighbour for so long, had always ignored him not because she was shy and eccentric and odd – which she was anyway – or rude, which she wasn't, but because she simply didn't remember him. He saw now that because kindness seemed to come so naturally to her – then as a girl, now as an old woman – an act of caring kindness that was so important and memorable to the vulnerable him in nineteen forty-one, an unforgettable event, was in fact routinely normal and utterly forgettable to her.

'I'm sorry, Jack, but I really don't remember.'

'It doesn't matter,' said a disappointed Jack as he helped her put on her old camelhair coat.

17

WINTER IN KARAPUKE is not harsh. It rains a lot but it's not especially cold. But old bodies, like those which had been carried through life for so long by Jack Landseer and Betty Krilich, feel the cold more than young, even in a mild climate, and even more as they get even older. And rain is more than just a nuisance to those whose determination to remain active is challenged by their reliance on Shanks's Pony.

So even though Betty Krilich's pony had been lately semi-retired – thanks to Jack Landseer and his willingness to exercise his vintage Zephyr Six – she was perhaps more pleased than most when she noted the sudden bright greening of her *pittosporum* hedge and the white and delicate-pink flush of apple, peach and nectarine blossoms which signalled the awakening of the trees and the promise of long summer days in which to ripen their heavy and fleshy fruit. Even her cats, with their internal and oh-so-sensitive thermostats, stopped curling up in the soft-edged spotlights of winter's weak and gentle sun, on the comfort of her cot, in the shelter of the sun-porch, and began unfurling themselves, slowly at first, until at last they were lying outstretched – long and lean and vulnerable – on the cool wooden floor. And outside, her hens, whether in their run or in the garden under the tractor, also sensed change; they seemed to become more alert, perhaps a little more aggressive in their scratching and pecking searches, and absolutely more argumentative, fighting mercilessly and noisily over a tender lizard or especially over a juicy weta come out into the new warmth. And perhaps they wondered, in their own way, inherited from their jungle forebears, why they didn't have a big proud rooster to protect and serve them in this the most important season of the year.

So winter ended in Karapuke and spring began and Betty sowed her summer vegetables in the seed trays which sat on the long wooden slatted benches in her glasshouse. There, with no help from her but a misty spray of water, and encouraged by the embracing warmth of the medium and the humidity of the enclosed air, the lives hibernating in the tiny seeds miraculously stirred and flexed and burst through their protective carapaces to squirm blindly up through the dark into the life-giving light and there spread their little green arms with heavenly joy and the promise, the certainty, that before long they would produce the vegetables of summer – whether leaves, stems and stalks, roots, pods and seeds or fruit – which, together with the harvest from her mini orchard, would nourish not only Betty, and now her friend Jack Landseer, but, amongst others on her list, those few sometimes desperate and malnourished mothers and innocent children who passed through the Karapuke women's refuge in their escape from harm and then on – so was the hope – to safety and a full and happy life. There were also a few rural families with young children who, in Betty's opinion, but contrary to the opinion of mission officials, were deserving of her fruit and vegetables; she knew who they were and they knew to come to her house in Northumberland Road rather than be humiliated by a polite refusal at the mission.

For Betty Krilich, then, spring was the guarantee of longer days, warmer weather, and a continuing abundance of natural, fresh and nutritious fruit and vegetables all through the months of summer and autumn, together with a small but reliable supply of eggs, with which she could continue to help the otherwise forsaken women and children of her community to whose welfare she was dedicated with an unreasonable and seemingly irrational love.

But for the first time since she returned to Karapuke, to assume the life she now lived and had lived for more than thirty years, the balmy warmth of spring and the coming bright summer were darkened and chilled by two gloomy clouds of worry. They were worries she did her best to set aside but like all such worries they couldn't long be denied, nor ever be completely dismissed, and so she knew they would each one day – soon but separately – have to be confronted. The first – her desire to invite her friend Jack Landseer into her home and so return the open-hearted hospitality he had given her over the last few winter months – she saw as impossible to satisfy without an embarrassing and horrible explanation she was loath to furnish. And the second: a matter of money, or rather a lack of money, which she couldn't bring herself to face. She knew she would have to. One day. Soon even. But she also knew it was a problem she couldn't solve alone and that the only person she now knew she could turn to in complete confidence was the same Jack

Landseer. And yet given the daunting size of the problem she couldn't imagine how such a pleasant and unassuming old man – so kind and generous and willing but almost as old and perhaps more frail than she, with evidently few resources – could help her in what she couldn't deny was looming poverty if not destitution.

There was a third threat to Betty Krilich's contentment and wellbeing that spring but it was lurking unknown, unfelt, ominously silent, and therefore did not contribute to her nagging anxiety which was just as well. She was worried enough.

Farther up Northumberland Road old Jack Landseer too noted the coming of spring. But unlike the days of Betty Krilich his spring days were free of nagging worries since he had managed to conceal the awkward possession of his beloved Rolls-Royce and his artworks (some of which were, in the words of Mordacai Zelnick, virtually priceless). In fact he had grown accustomed to the bare walls of his front living room, and the walls of the hall and bedroom, although the large rectangles of faintly-brighter wallpaper were a constant reminder of the paintings which had hung there, some of them for many years. And there was still only one car in the garage – the blue Ford Zephyr Six – although the work he said he would have to do to arrest the hidden rust on its doors, and repair the damage, had not been started simply because it had not been necessary. Wanting room to remove the Zephyr's doors had been merely the excuse he needed to house the Roll-Royce anywhere but in his own garage in Northumberland Road. Meanwhile he had decided to give it, the Rolls-Royce, to Alan. It'll be his one day anyway, he reasoned.

And so the old man's mind was in a positive frame as he happily put aside his winter clothes and welcomed the warmth of spring. He was not a vegetable grower, nor a particularly keen gardener, but he did love his roses; he knew them well, knew them all by name, and watched them daily as they sent out the tender purple and fleshy shoots which were destined by nature to grow into long and strong canes and carry the buds and then the blooms of some of the world's most famous roses including his favourites; among others: *Josephine Bruce, Graham Thomas* and his favourite old favourite, *Peace.*

Their sudden coming to life in spring brought him unalloyed joy; and their long and productive growth throughout the summer and well into the mild autumn ensured that the joy of roses would be his every day of the long months ahead. The petty but essential tasks imposed on the enthusiast – of weeding, feeding, spraying, judicious pruning and ruthless dead-heading – were undertaken with pleasure as every act contributed more to the overall beauty of his front garden, the individual shape and beauty of each plant, and ultimately, to the exquisite beauty of every bloom, whether with or without a strong scent, which he could choose to leave, to cut for himself, or cut and bunch to give to a friend, notably this coming summer to Betty Krilich, to bring inestimable if not enduring pleasure. Not least of his rose-growing pleasures were the many compliments volunteered by admiring passers-by.

In the meantime the friendship between the two old people of Northumberland Road had warmed and matured with the warming and maturing of the year. Their having Sunday lunch together in Jack's kitchen, after the eleven o'clock service at Saint Peter's, had become a regular appointment to which they both looked forward. Indeed, important as it seemed to them both, it was in fact the physical expression of an emotional need – a need that was more profound than mere companionship – being regularly and most satisfactorily satisfied.

Marked by mutual caring and consideration, it was a bonded friendship which over the months they had both come to treasure, to rely on. Betty – now beset by worries that wouldn't go away – nevertheless followed her established weekly and daily routines conscientiously but now assisted by Jack; occasionally at first but eventually as a matter of course. He happily drove her in his trusty old Zephyr wherever she needed or wanted to go. He liked being useful, and the mechanic-engineer in him thought the Zephyr's engine, which he had so carefully maintained for twenty-five years, was running better and smoother thanks to the more frequent and longer journeys it was now experiencing; for her part Betty appreciated the speed and comfort of the transportation her friend Jack so willingly provided using what she considered his lovely old English car.

In the process he, old Jack Landseer, gradually became interested in *her* interests, coming to understand her motives, learning if not to share but at least appreciate her concerns, especially her concern for the poor and more especially still for vulnerable children and their mothers.

Above all he came increasingly to simply enjoy Betty's company. Indeed, he even took to attending Saint Peter's of a Sunday, usually the evening service. He said he liked the hymns, and the fact that there was no preaching, although in the process he even came to like the young vicar, Vance Widdop, and to sympathise with his thankless task amongst people to whom his religion, its rituals, beliefs and scriptures, were utterly irrelevant. His increased engagement with Betty and her activities meant he went less often to the Combined Club which was once his principal source of society.

But such was the nature of the Jack-and-Betty relationship that while it somewhat curtailed Jack's attendance at his club it didn't end it altogether and the woman who once declined his invitation to share a meal there, saying she was not a club sort of person or some-such protest, agreed to accompany him – once or twice at first – but then regularly. Once there she discovered that she enjoyed meeting new people and the company of Jack's male friends; she enjoyed the old-fashioned food and the old-time dance music (although she declined any invitation to take the floor). And she discovered – much to her surprise – that she was in fact well known in the town, by sight and reputation, and that many of the club's members – men and women both – felt quietly pleased, even privileged, to make the acquaintance of famous Old Betty.

And as spring turned to summer the discovery the old pair had made together in Jack's kitchen on that Sunday afternoon late in July – that what Jack had thought so important for so long was not even remembered by Betty – had been set aside by them both as a silly misunderstanding. Jack accepted that he had been foolish to have obsessively remembered (although he didn't admit to Betty the strange consequences of his obsession) while Betty felt sorry to have forgotten.

But the trivial event in question, of that fateful day in February nineteen forty-one – whether remembered or forgotten – had set off a sequence of events which would not and could not be undone and which would continue to affect not only he who had remembered and she who had forgotten but many more men and women, and children as yet unborn, for as far into the future as anyone could then imagine.

# 18

BY THE END of October Betty Krilich could no longer pretend, to herself or anyone else. Indeed she had spent a good few weeks not exactly pretending but at least hoping that something would turn up – as something always had in the past – to relieve her fiscal problem. But nothing had. And now she knew nothing would. Because there was nothing left.

She knew that to have no money was a commonplace condition, a problem she had helped many others face since she had left the cocoon of safety and security into which she had been born and which was her later life in Wellington. And so while she was familiar with the nature of the condition, and its debilitating effect on its victim, such familiarity bred not contempt but trepidation. It was a problem, a state, a condition, which she had never in her long life had to face for herself. But now it was hers and so it had to be faced.

'Sorry, declined,' the girl had said.

'What? What do you mean?'

The Four Square girl pointed to the terminal. 'The bank's declined your card,' she said.

'What does that mean?'

'Don't you know, Betty?' asked the girl tilting her head quizzically; sympathetically; not wanting to explain to Old Betty; not wanting to embarrass her in front of other customers.

'No I don't,' said Betty indignantly.

'Sorry, Betty,' said the girl. 'It means the bank—'

'Yes, I know what it means,' interrupted Betty who suddenly *did* know what it meant.

But while she now knew what it meant she had no idea what to do about it.

'What do I do with all this?' she asked no one in particular.

'Don't worry, Betty,' said the assistant manager with a familiarity she didn't understand. He had hurried across to waylay her much to the relief of the young and embarrassed checkout girl. 'I'll take care of them.'

He meant he'd return all her unpaid items – a week of grocery shopping – to the shelves. She looked at the name-badge on his bright white shirt and said thank you, Derek, and left him to it and went, with her empty little tartan shopping trundler, to sit on the uncomfortable backless and cold aluminium form that stood to one side of the supermarket's main door. It was a Monday afternoon, fine and warm, so she was wearing only a limp and faded red t-shirt, with the head of Che Guevara printed in black and white, as well as her familiar flared jeans and bright white sneakers with neon-green laces. She had happily walked to the Four Square in the warmth of the sun after spending most of the day with her friends at the Karapuke women's refuge.

'The children do love it when you read to them,' said Kate, the trust's manager. 'Some of them have never had a story read to them before. You can see the pleasure on their little faces as the story unfolds.'

So I could, thought Betty, her hands resting on the empty shopping trundler's handle. Sitting on that comfortable couch in that cosy lounge, which was furnished just like a happy home anywhere, I could look up from reading the words and read the innocent pleasure on their dear little faces. They were sitting on the carpeted floor, grouped around me, some cuddling a favourite doll or a scruffy teddy bear, looking up at me with their eyes and mouths wide open, listening intently. What could be more pleasurable than giving pleasure to the sad and stressed little ones? But now what? They depend on me. A bit, anyway.

And then the hospice. How could I turn them down? They needed those special beds so badly. And all that equipment. And the overdraft; they never should have gotten into debt like that. Bloody bad management if you ask me. But how could I refuse? I couldn't.

Now they're not broke but I am. Not even enough money in the bank for all those groceries. Must be *some* there. It's pension day. But not enough I suppose. I'll just go back and get, what? Some toilet paper. I'll need that. And some Whiskas. Tea. Some water crackers. A *Listener*. That'll do. There'll be enough for that. But I'll do it tomorrow. Not now. Not after that performance in there. But I'll need that toilet paper by tomorrow. The rest doesn't matter much. Except the Whiskas. I hope I've got enough for tonight and tomorrow morning. I could probably get something cheaper, some cheap mince or something, but they do like Whiskas the best. And I've got eggs for tea. They'll eat raw eggs too at a pinch. Actually, now that I think of it, Norman loves a raw egg. Not sure about the others. We'll see. At least the girls will eat anything and keep giving. Must remember to move the tractor.

The sun's nice, she thought. I like the warmth of the sun. Funny about the shopping I suppose. That poor bloke Derek having to put back all my stuff. Funny thing shopping though. Never did much when I was young. Mother did it all when I was a girl. And nanny. I can remember going with them sometimes. To Marriott's the grocers. On Main Street. I remember that. Gone now of course. And the butcher's. Mr Isherwood it was. Wonder what happened to him. I suppose I must have done some shopping when I was at Victoria. I was in that flat with those other girls. Can't remember their names but they were as young and stupid as me. A bit slutty I suppose now that I come to think of it. What on earth did we eat? Did we *ever* go shopping? I know we bought beer. And whisky sometimes. But I really can't remember anything much about those days. It was like another me. Another life. And after that, with Gus, I can remember a lot but I can't remember doing any shopping at all. Did I? I think *they* did it. Yes, they did it. I'm sure they did it. The cooks and housekeepers did all the shopping then. Leave them to it, Gus used to say. They're professionals. They know what they're doing.

There was of course a series of cooks, housekeepers and other servants. But she, the cook, whoever she was at the time, shopped for the food while the housekeeper shopped for everything else and did all the washing and ironing as well as unknown and unspeakable things to the toilets, bathrooms and wash house.

Who *were* they? What *were* their names?

She wished she could remember but she'd tried before – often – and she just couldn't. Not because of a faulty or failing memory but because the young Karori Betty had never been interested in, or even mildly curious about, the detailed nature of the work of her many unremembered cooks and servants let alone their names, private affairs and personal welfare. And as for their shopping duties.

It's not that she never went shopping; she did, and often, mostly to Kirk's. But clothes and shoes and hats and gloves and furs and jewellery and fine china and silverware were the objects of her shopping. And then there were the expeditions abroad. Expeditions she undertook, when young, with her not-so-young but handsome and dashing husband when he had to go to Sydney on business and so took her along for company; and shopping. Indeed, he (and by extension she) had an account at Mark Foy's, Grace Brothers and, of course, David Jones. And Myer in Melbourne. Oh, I loved that shop. Gus seemed to know the Myer family somehow. She wondered sometimes how that was. How did he know so many people? Was it religion? But he wasn't religious. Not really. How many times, she wondered, had she and Gus sailed to and from Sydney in those long-ago days, her return luggage heavily swollen by her expensive and fashionable purchases? How many times? She couldn't remember.

So much I can't remember, she thought.

And then *that*. The one thing I don't want to remember is the one thing I can't forget. And if it hadn't been so awful it would have been ridiculous. It *was* ridiculous. To call her Mrs X. That's what they called her. Mrs X. Go and see Mrs X, they said. She's an expert. No one will know. I can even remember the address. Twenty-one Toradh Street, Surry Hills. I remember the date too.

She shook her head sharply then in an attempt to clear her head. Then she set off for home with her little tartan shopping trundler. Empty.

19

'THE FACT IS, Jack,' she said to Jack the following Friday morning, 'I'm completely bloody broke.'

The fresh church flowers had been lovingly arranged – indeed the whole church smelled as damp and fresh, as sweet and spicy, as a flower shop before Mother's Day – and the old flowers, looking sad and limp, dropping their browning petals, their stems beginning to rot and smell in their stale water, had been unceremoniously disposed of in the compost bin. Now the honorary flower arranger and her willing assistant were sitting sharing a pot of tea, and picking out the best of the stale biscuits from the community biscuit tin, as was now their custom on a Friday morning. The perennially cheerful young Vance Widdop had come and gone, having inspected the fresh flower arrangements in the church, paid his courteous respects to the old pair in the kitchen, stolen a chocolate biscuit from the tin, and hurried out the door having said: 'Must dash. Meeting with the bish.'

Meanwhile the muffled sound of a woman lecturer lecturing, interspersed with the rhythmic bumps and thumps of the members of the ante-natal class doing their recommended exercises, provided a background to Betty's humiliating confession.

Jack was astonished. For good reason.

'But I thought—'

'You thought I was one of those eccentric rich old bitches didn't you,' said Betty. 'Eccentric but secretly rich.'

'Tell me about it,' said Jack. 'But I wouldn't have put it quite that way.'

'Well you must have thought something like that,' said Betty. 'You said your wife followed Gus and me in the social pages. What we were up to in Wellington.'

'But everybody in Karapuke did in those days,' said a protesting Jack. 'Not just her. You were a famous local. People around here were proud.'

'How stupid,' said Betty with contempt. 'But we *were* rich. It's true. I was rich. And a bit of a bitch with it to tell the truth.'

'So what happened?'

'I got old didn't I,' said Betty.

'So did I,' said Jack. 'But what's that got to do with it?'

'Well, my money, I never thought it would have to last so long did I.'

'You mean you spent it all too soon,' said Jack. 'Too quick.'

'Sort of,' said Betty.

'But you can't complain about living too long,' said Jack. 'I don't.'

'No. I suppose not,' said Betty. 'As long as I'm healthy.'

'Healthy. Oh, yes.'

'Don't want to be sick or ga-ga,' said Betty.

'Nor me,' said Jack. 'That Old-timers disease absolutely horrifies me.'

'But why did we d'you think?'

'What? Live so long?'

'Yes,' said Betty. 'Healthy in body and mind as they say.'

It was a question Jack had asked himself many times. And so he gave Betty the only answer he had ever been able to concoct: 'Bit of a raffle I think,' he said. 'Luck of the draw and all that.'

'Mmmmm,' said Betty. 'I've thought of that too. Could be genetic though.'

'Could be,' said Jack who had considered inheritance as perhaps part but not all of the answer. He still preferred the idea of a random lottery; getting old and staying healthy without dementia being a matter of chance. 'But my mother died when she was just thirty-three. Cancer.'

'You told me that,' said Betty. 'So sad.'

'My father was seventy-one,' added Jack. 'I'm eighty-five. Eighty-six next year. Doesn't make sense.'

'My mother was ninety,' said Betty. 'That makes sense.'

'What about your father?'

'He was seventy I think,' said Betty. 'That was considered old back then. Nineteen sixty-five.'

'But it's not only that,' said Jack. 'I haven't had any illnesses or diseases or anything. Had my appendix out just after I got married. Bit of angina the doctor reckons. Alan goes on about it but it's not much. And no heart attack. No stroke. I once saw a young bloke keel over from a brain aneurysm. In a restaurant.'

Betty shook her head slowly and grimly. 'Me too. I've seen it all.'

'So, we're lucky.'

'You've still got your teeth haven't you?'

'Couple of crowns,' said Jack. 'Cost a fortune.'

'Me too,' said Betty. 'I need my glasses and that's it.'

'I've had the same glasses for donkey's years,' said Jack.

'Me too.'

'No pills. Some people I know,' said Jack, shaking his head slowly in disbelief.

'I don't take any pills either.'

'My cholesterol's alright. And the water works. The angina pills if I need them. Never have. They're probably out of date. In fact I'm sure they are. Doesn't matter.'

'Don't like pills,' said Betty. 'Never been to hospital either.'

That was not quite true but Betty had always preferred to tell that little white lie – even to herself – than face the big black truth.

'It's just luck,' said Jack. 'I'm sure of it.'

'I used to smoke a bit when I was young,' said Betty. 'But that was just for show. Copying the people in the pictures. But I soon stopped when I met Gus. He didn't like smoking.'

'Can't say I blame him,' said Jack. 'I never did. Thank God for that. My father did. Horrible skinny little rolled-up things. Such a stink. But everyone smoked then didn't they. Men anyway. But all the smokers I used to know are dead. Every one of them.'

'I used to drink a lot though.'

'Me too,' said Jack. 'Still do. A bit. At the club. Just beer.'

'I've seen you,' said Betty with a smile. 'Anyway, maybe you're right.'

'About what?'

'Luck,' said Betty. 'Lucky genes. Lucky we didn't smoke.'

'Could've been an alcoholic like Michael,' said Jack.

'Where'd that come from?' asked Betty but she didn't expect an answer and didn't receive one.

'Most of my old friends are dead,' said Jack glumly. 'Or lying in a bed somewhere quite doolally. I'm the oldest bloke at the club you know.'

'I'm the oldest person I know,' said Betty.

'How old are you exactly?' asked Jack.

'Eighty-eight,' said Betty. 'You know that.'

'I mean when's your birthday?'

'Birthdays are ridiculous.' She almost spat out the epithet with a vehemence that surprised her companion.

'What do you mean?' he asked.

'I mean it's one thing to celebrate a kiddy's birthday,' said Betty. 'Every childhood birthday was once a milestone of survival. In the old days. Infant mortality and that. And kiddies love the fuss don't they. Cakes and lollies and presents and games. But for adults–' she made a noise which Jack interpreted as an expression of disgust '– bloody ridiculous.'

'Why?' Jack was genuinely curious.

'It's my birthday. Whoopee. The earth went round the sun three hundred and sixty-five and a bit times. What's to celebrate? One year nearer the grave as far as I'm concerned. Hooray for that I *don't* bloody think.'

Jack was again taken aback by Betty's attitude which seemed so cynical and uncompromising. But he didn't remark on that. Instead he simply said: 'Mine's on the twenty-fifth of January.'

'What is? Your birthday?'

'Yep. I'll be eighty-six next year.'

'I'll try not to remember,' said Betty with a smile which relieved the tension created by the subject of birthdays; Jack was glad.

'I just hope I go quick in the end,' said Betty. 'And painless. Some of the people I've seen die.'

'Tell me about it,' said Jack.

'Anyway,' said Betty with a sigh, 'I didn't plan things well did I?'

'What do you mean? Plan what things?'

'I told you. I've run out of money, Jack. Run out of money before I've run out of life.'

Jack nodded grimly.

'So what are you going to do?'

'I'll be alright I suppose,' said Betty. 'I've got my super. And the house. That's freehold. I need a few groceries but I grow so much in the garden you know, and the ladies – the chooks – and I haven't really got any expenses. Gas but that's not much. Biggest expense is the rates every year.'

'So you'll be alright then?' asked Jack.

'I'll be alright. I'll manage. Bit depressing though.'

'Why? Why depressing if you think you'll be alright?'

'I can't really explain, Jack,' said Betty. 'It's just that, well, people depend on me. I've made plans and promises. Always have. About money and that. And now?'

'You've given all your money away haven't you,' said Jack, and it wasn't a question.

At that Betty rested her elbow on the table, rested her chin on her clenched fist, looked across the table, directly into the eyes of her companion, and smiled bravely.

'What else could I do?' she said at last. She shook her head slowly, grimly. 'All that bloody money.'

✿

'Zelnick.'

'Mort. It's Jack Landseer here.'

'Ah, Jack, my clever old friend. How are you on this beautiful Friday afternoon? So warm and sunny, no?'

'I'm fine,' said Jack. He had driven Betty home from church and was now on the phone in his kitchen. Betty had given him half a dozen fresh eggs as they left the church hall; he had thanked her and told her that he'd have two of them for lunch with buttery soldiers of hot toast. Accordingly, two eggs were now rattling away in a pot of boiling water as he was speaking to Mordacai Zelnick. 'Just going to have my lunch.'

'Ah, you are so lucky, my friend,' said Zelnick. 'Zelnick is so busy. So very very busy. Is a nightmare, no? And lunch? Is a dream that will never come true.'

Jack couldn't help smiling. He knew that Zelnick dined and wined almost every day at the Parnell bistro owned by his fat cousin Maurice.

'Oh, I'm so sorry,' he said without concealing the sarcasm which Zelnick either didn't notice or intentionally ignored.

'Not to worry, my friend Jack. Is my problems. Now, what can I do you for this fine day?'

And so Jack outlined his plans to Zelnick. It took longer than expected – Zelnick had many questions, many suggestions – which meant that his lunch of Betty's soft-boiled eggs with buttery soldiers of hot toast was eventually consumed, with less pleasure than planned, as hard-boiled eggs with buttered soldiers of cold toast.

Never mind, he thought. It'll be worth it.

# 20

'THIS SUNDAY I want you to come to *my* place for lunch,' Betty had said. 'For a change.'

Jack was surprised by Betty's invitation. In the months since they had become good friends – in fact since that wintry July day he had returned her shopping trundler – she had withheld any suggestion of hospitality despite being welcome at his place any time; indeed, they now had lunch together there almost every Sunday.

Now it was Sunday again and Jack was at Betty's house, at her invitation, having driven her home after church.

On this day she was wearing a smart and timeless navy-blue suit comprised of a flared skirt of a modest length and a matching jacket with white lapels and wide white cuffs. The white shirt which showed under the jacket was plain cotton and was closed at the neck with a large oval brooch of polished pounamu set in gold; an antique.

Jack had been inside Betty's house only once before but that was in nineteen forty-one when he was just eight years old. Then – as Betty's mother had nursed his damaged hands and knees – he had been astonished by the size and grandness of the Henderson house, and the quality of its furnishings. Now, nearly eighty years later, he was there again and was astonished by what he saw in this once grand old house; it was now devoid of furniture, dirty and unkempt, falling into ruin.

'I don't understand,' he said. 'What's it all about?'

'There's more,' said Betty. They were standing together in the kitchen looking down the long hall to the front door. In the glare of the diffused light from the front door's eight panes of dirty dimpled glass he could see that each wall of the hall, all the wooden doors off it, their architraves and the deep skirting boards, were all covered with the same dusty–

What?

He didn't know what.

'Go down to the lounge,' said Betty, pressing him gently in the back. 'I'll get lunch ready.'

Jack walked alone, slowly, down the long hall, looking to the left and right as he went – so many rooms, all large, all empty of furniture, their windows dressed with dusty and disintegrating drapery – trying to understand. And once in the lounge he was overwhelmed by what he saw but still didn't understand.

What the bloody hell? he thought as he stood in the middle of the room looking around.

The noonday sun, filtered by thick, grubby and rotting lace curtains, did nothing to either warm or brighten the cold, gloomy and empty room. The floor – here and throughout the house – was covered with a dusty carpet of a vintage woven pattern, once modern and expensive but now faded and threadbare with visible joins, torn stitching and frayed edges. And on the walls there were pictures: of a lake somewhere, and old-fashioned hand-coloured photographs of two old people (Betty's parents? grandparents?) in elaborate oval wooden frames behind thin and brittle-looking convex glass. A wide bay window looked out onto Northumberland Road and a cast-iron fireplace was set into the internal wall opposite. Its wooden mantelpiece was home to a silent chiming clock set off by a few dead flies and half a dozen pieces of cheap and non-descript ornaments; an oval mirror on a rusty chain hung above the mantelpiece, set at a deep angle down into the room.

It was a strange and eerie sight; an unused room with everything in it covered in dust and draped with ancient and dusty cobwebs. But what puzzled the visitor more than anything were the room's dull and dusty decorations – if that's what they were – which, as he had seen in the hall, covered each of the walls, the door, the window frames, indeed all the woodwork including the decorative moulding around the fireplace and hearth. From floor to ceiling, from corner to corner, thousands of them, tiny things glued somehow to the wallpaper and wood and then painted over with a coat of once-clear but now-browning polyurethane, presumably as a sealing preservative. They were set close together, tier upon tier, row upon dull-coloured row, running around the pictures and photographs, covering every available space. And so dusty.

Suddenly he was aware of Betty standing beside him.

'Betty,' he said without looking at her. 'What is it? What are they? What's it all about?'

'All my babies,' said Betty.

'Babies?'

'Oh, Jack,' she said sadly and quietly. 'They really are little babies.'

Jack moved to one wall to have a closer look and saw that they really were babies: tiny coloured sweet jelly babies. Thousands of them.

'They're everywhere,' she said waving her arm about the room. 'All down the hall. The bedrooms. Lounge. Everywhere. See for yourself.'

Jack hesitated.

'Go on,' she insisted. 'You might as well get it over and done with.'

'All the bedrooms?'

'Yes,' Betty insisted. 'Go on. Have a look. All the other rooms except the kitchen, bathroom and toilet. And the sun-porch where I sleep. The only rooms I use.'

'I'll take your word for it if you don't mind,' said Jack.

'Over to you,' said Betty. 'At least you know now. Lunch?'

And so they returned to the kitchen, sat down at Betty's little table where she had set out a simple lunch of thinly-sliced ham, hard-boiled eggs and a salad.

'All mine, except the ham,' she said.

They ate in silence, although Jack once asked for the mustard, and then the salad cream, and later managed to compliment his hostess on the quality of the lunch she had prepared; but otherwise Jack's reservoir of cheerful and pleasant small-talk had been choked off by the oddly and eerily decorated walls in the rest of Betty's house.

Of course Betty noticed and understood.

'I wanted you to see, Jack,' she said at last. They had finished eating and were enjoying their tea. 'I didn't want to before but I need your help now and so I wanted you to see and understand.'

'I've seen,' said Jack. 'But I don't understand. I really don't.'

Betty reached behind her, to the bench, and fetched a thin black plastic binder which she handed to her puzzled companion who looked at it, took a draught of tea, put the cup down, and said: 'What is it?'

'Open it, Jack. Please.'

He opened the binder. There were papers in clear plastic sleeves. Letters. Nothing that made sense.

He looked at the first letter. He noted the deferential salutation but was not surprised. He looked across at Betty who looked back blankly; took a drink of tea. He went back to the letter. From the New Zealand Department of Statistics. He looked across at Betty again, questioningly, but her expression didn't change. And so he turned the flimsy page. Another letter from the same department. A list. Columns. Dates. Numbers. He flicked through the other pages. They all looked the same – they looked important – but to him they meant nothing.

He put down the binder and looked across at Betty who was now watching him carefully, evidently seeking a reaction.

He shrugged to show complete bewilderment.

'Abortions, Jack,' said Betty.

'What?'

'Abortions,' she said again. 'Thousands of wee ones.'

'You mean—'

'Yes, Jack,' she said, pointing to the open door which led to the hall. 'Every jelly baby in there. A New Zealand abortion.'

'How many?'

'Sixteen, seventeen, eighteen thousand a year, more or less.'

'That many?' Jack was obviously surprised.

'That many,' she confirmed. 'Just in our little New Zealand. Every year.'

'Since when?'

'Well, Jack, that's the point isn't it. I did it for ten years.'

'Ten years!' At first Jack was surprised but then, he thought, nothing surprises me about Betty Krilich. Nothing.

'The thing is, Jack, Gus and I didn't have children. My fault. A gynaecological abnormality they said. Gus said he never minded and neither did I. At least that's what I said. But, you know, when he was gone I did wish we had children together. Just one. It'd be nice to have someone to love, someone to love me. And ever since then I've thought of all those wee babies sucked from their uncaring mothers and thrown away. Like off-cuts of meat.'

Jack involuntarily looked away. But Betty wasn't finished. She picked up the closed binder which Jack had pushed to the middle of the table and held it forward, towards him.

'One hundred and seventy-six thousand, four hundred and seventy-nine babies killed in just ten years, Jack. A decent-sized city of people don't you think. And it's still going on. Every year.'

'I'm sorry, Betty,' said Jack. 'Perhaps I'm naïve. I didn't know.'

'Don't be sorry,' said Betty cheerfully. She dropped the binder on the table. 'It's not your fault.'

Jack didn't know what to say. He'd always wondered why Betty had never invited him into her home and now he wished she hadn't. He'd always been puzzled by her strange domestic arrangements – using only the sun-porch, kitchen and bathroom – and now, after what he had seen and heard, he was somewhat horrified; he'd never had strong feelings about abortion, one way or the other, didn't really know anything about it, but the graphic way she described it, and the bizarre and futile manner she had been driven to express her disgust, left him perturbed and, it must be said, sad. Sad for her.

'This is bloody hard for me, Jack, you realize that don't you?'

Jack nodded somewhat unconvincingly. 'I suppose it is,' he said, 'but I don't really get the point. Why are you telling me this now? Showing me?'

'That's why I asked you here, Jack,' said Betty as she poured them both more tea. 'I need your help.'

'What help? How?'

'Well, I'm going to give the house to the women's refuge you see. Leave it to them.'

'Eh?'

'The Karapuke Women's Refuge Trust. I'm going to give the house to the trust. I told you that before.'

'When?'

'I don't know. Ages ago.'

'No,' said Jack who really was confused by this meeting. 'When are you going to give them the house?'

'When I'm gone of course.'

'But where are you going?'

'When I'm dead, Jack. What do you think I mean?'

Jack nodded. 'Oh, I see,' he said. He hadn't really thought anything.

'It's in my will. Mr Widdop knows all about it. He'll arrange it.'

'Yes, yes,' said Jack. 'I think you told me that before. But they've got a house. The one in Church Street. I've been there with you.'

'That's an old Housing Corp house. They bought it,' said Betty. In fact, as Jack knew, she herself had long ago bought it for the trust. 'But it's too small,' she went on. 'They'll be able to sell it and use the money. And this place is bigger. Much bigger. And a huge back section for the kids to play in. And private too. It's perfect.'

Jack merely nodded to show he understood. But Betty wasn't finished.

'The thing is I realize now it was pretty stupid of me to buy all those bloody jelly babies and stick them everywhere.'

'It is a bit of a problem,' said Jack. 'I can see that.'

'Bit obsessive don't you think? A bit nutty. I admit it: a stupid obsession.'

Jack shrugged. He didn't know what to say. He himself had every reason to understand an obsession and he could see how hard it must be for Betty to admit hers.

'Don't you see, Jack?' Betty continued. 'I can't leave them there. The house is a bit of a mess anyway but I definitely can't leave it to the trust, to house vulnerable women and children and wee babies, with abortion jelly babies stuck all over the walls.'

Jack raised his eyebrows and nodded in understanding. Indeed, he thought, the jelly babies were only a small part of the problem; the whole house needed a major makeover.

'It *was* a stupid thing to do. I know that now. So I don't want anyone to see it. They all think I'm nutty around here anyway.'

'No they don't,' said Jack.

'Yes they do.'

'They don't,' insisted Jack. 'A bit eccentric, that's all. They think you're a bit eccentric.'

'To tell you the truth I'm a bit ashamed of myself really. And whatever anyone else thinks of me I don't want them seeing the mess I made of my house. My mother and father's beautiful house.'

'You let *me* see,' said Jack.

'You're the only person who ever has,' said Betty. 'The only one. Ever.'

☼

'So how long have they been here like this?' asked Jack.

'The first ones, these ones, I put up in two thousand and one,' said Betty. 'The last year was twenty-ten.'

They were in the hall, just outside the door which opened from the kitchen. Betty had finally persuaded Jack to closely inspect the glued and polyurethaned jelly babies and to advise how best they might be removed to return the walls and woodwork to a more conventional finish.

'Well the polyurethane will be totally cured and hard as hell,' said Jack. 'And God only knows what those little lollies will be like after all those years under it.'

And so he started pushing and pulling and prying at one of the little jelly babies, at eye level, with his thumb and forefinger before taking out his car keys and trying to get a metal key under the edge of one of the little things in order to lever it away from the wall.

'What on earth did you use? What sort of glue I mean?'

'I don't know. Don't remember,' said Betty.

'Hell's bells. Anyway, they *will* come away,' said Jack when he managed to get a purchase with his key, 'but it'll

173

take a lot of work and it'll rip away the old wallpaper in the process.'

'I see,' said Betty.

'And where they're stuck to the wood, well, the old varnish. The wood would need sanding back and that.'

'That won't matter,' said Betty, although she added, doubtfully, questioningly: 'Would it?'

'It'll make a hell of a mess,' said Jack. 'And then, when you get them all down, jelly babies and wallpaper and all that polyurethane, what the hell are you going to do with it all?'

Betty looked completely helpless. 'What do you think?' she asked hopefully.

'How many did you say there are?'

'A bit more than a hundred and seventy-six thousand.'

'Christ, Betty, they must have cost you a fortune. Like thousands.'

Betty looked embarrassed. She shrugged awkwardly and said: 'I don't know. I really don't.'

'And they must weigh – I don't know – about a tonne or more. Literally. I mean *literally*.'

Betty looked at her friend and grimaced with embarrassment.

Jack felt sorry for her. 'Don't worry, love,' he said reassuringly. 'We'll sort it out.'

'What a fool I was, Jack.'

'Well, you obviously felt passionate about it once,' said Jack.

'Oh, I still do,' said Betty. 'But this is a bit of problem isn't it. I feel so foolish and ashamed.'

'I better get going,' said Jack, looking at his watch. He was due, later, at Landseer Farm for the monthly meeting with Alan and Miriam. He had plenty of time but he didn't want to stay at Betty's house any longer. He wanted – needed – time to think. So he turned back to the kitchen and towards the back door.

Betty went with him. 'I'm glad I told you, Jack,' she said as they stood together at the back door. 'But don't tell anyone else will you.'

'Of course not.'

'Do you think you can help me get rid of the mess? Tidy up the house? Make it nice for the refuge?'

'There must be a way,' said Jack. 'There will be. I'll think about it.'

'Please do, Jack.'

'I will,' said Jack. 'I'll think about it. I've got to go to the farm now but I'll be back in time for church tonight. Then I'll bring you home and we can talk about it then.'

21

THE SUNDAY AFTERNOON meeting in the boardroom at Landseer Farm was remarkably routine and as usual Jack was surprised only by the success Alan continued to make of his great-grandfather's horse and cart business. He seemed to do it without the support of a management team although Jack knew enough about business — especially a business as big and successful as Town & Country Carriers now was — that such size and success wouldn't have come without management support staff. But Alan rarely talked about his support — except the big Auckland accounting firm he had engaged when Jack retired — and while he himself, Jack, was a director of the company, along with Miriam, he knew he was there only because he was still a large shareholder; he had no illusions about his paltry contributions to the company's affairs.

'To tell you the truth, most of the time I have no idea what Alan's talking about,' he once said to Miriam.

'Alan knows that, Jack,' Miriam had said gently. 'Don't worry about it.'

Jack also knew that his daughter-in-law – always so kind and gentle, patient and thoughtful, wifely, motherly and grandmotherly – was as clever or more than her husband; and he knew she was capable of steering Alan, manipulating him even, to do what she thought was best while cleverly allowing him to think it was his idea.

'Me and Miriam make a great team,' Alan always said.

And so at the meeting – for Jack's benefit – Alan laid out his new expansion plans which included the commissioning of vast storage facilities in Palmerston North and Christchurch, a new fleet of stock trucks for the South Island based in Oamaru, replacing two of the inter-island house removal trucks, and plans for the purchase of a small aeroplane.

'It'll take a couple of years to sort that out,' said Alan as he closed the meeting and Miriam closed her laptop into which she had been minuting, 'but it'll eventually make it easier for us to get around the branches. And it'll be able to carry a bit of freight.'

'But what about a pilot?' asked Jack.

'Me. I'm taking flying lessons at Ardmore,' said Alan. 'Didn't you know?'

'No,' said Jack. 'I didn't.'

'Tea, Jack,' asked Miriam lightly as if buying a plane was as routine as buying a bicycle. 'And I've made some fresh scones. In the house.'

'Yes, *please*,' said Jack. He knew from the beginning of the meeting that Miriam would have planned something special for afternoon tea.

'You go ahead,' said Alan. 'I've got a couple of things to do. I'll be over in a couple of minutes.'

And so, on the walk with Miriam across the wide yard and truck park to the house, Jack broached the subject

with the only young woman – or at least younger than he
– he knew and respected.

'I need to ask you a rather awkward question,' he said.
'A bit – I don't know – embarrassing I suppose.'

Miriam smiled. She was sixty-two and had known her
old father-in-law for forty or so years. She therefore knew
from experience that what he found embarrassing would
be pretty inoffensive to her or almost anyone else. But
even having known him so long she was often surprised
by his naivete, his endearing innocence. Indeed, she often
wished that his son, her husband Alan – tough,
uncompromising and ambitious, quite the opposite of
naïve and innocent – was more like his father. But she
remembered her mother-in-law Catherine – shrewd,
practical, unloving even (was she always like that? she
wondered) – and saw her in Alan. Like mother like son,
she thought. Perhaps poor Michael was more like Jack.
Perhaps the gentleness and naivete which were strengths
in the character of kind and uncomplicated Jack were
flaws in the otherwise brilliant Michael. Perhaps. Perhaps.
So many ifs and buts. Poor Michael, she thought. What a
life.

'Let's wait till we get inside,' she said – or rather shouted
– as a truck and trailer unit curled into the truck park and
the driver blasted his horns in greeting. Miriam waved
cheerfully in reply as she steered Jack by the arm to the
side of the yard and onto the path which led through the
cottage garden to the house.

'What's he doing working on a Sunday?' asked Jack as
the noise of the big diesel and its air brakes receded and
they reached the fenced quiet of the garden.

'More and more of the boys are out on a Sunday now, Jack,' said Miriam. 'Seven days a week these days. All over the country.'

'I thought the cleaning and maintenance crews came in on Sundays.'

'They do. And every other day of the week as well.'

'Really?'

'Things are booming, Jack.'

'So I've noticed,' said Jack without enthusiasm. 'But Sundays?'

He was vaguely puzzled by how things had changed. It was a sad and unsettling feeling. He had to admit that he didn't really like the way the business had grown. It didn't seem to bother Miriam. She seemed perfectly at ease with everything. She and Alan are it, he thought. I don't really know why Alan bothers consulting me once a month. He'll have my shares when I'm gone; he knows that. But it's good to see Miriam every now and then.

'Come on, Jack,' said Miriam cheerfully as they entered the house. 'Fresh scones, remember. With my own strawberry jam and fresh whipped cream.'

✹

The tea was cold before Alan eventually got to the house.

'I'll make a fresh pot,' said Miriam.

'That'll be beaut,' said Alan. 'And what have you two been talking about?'

Jack was sitting at the kitchen table – where they always sat after their Sunday meetings – with the detritus of the afternoon tea and scones he had shared with Miriam spread out untidily before him; Miriam was at the bench making a fresh pot of tea.

Jack, still somewhat unnerved by his conversation with Miriam, didn't know what to say. But Miriam did.

'About Dianne and Fred and the children,' she said brightly. 'They're all coming for dinner tonight. Di was telling me they're going to Disneyland at Christmas. They think the children are old enough now to appreciate it. I was just telling Jack, wasn't I, Jack.'

Jack nodded but he didn't know what Miriam was talking about.

'Why don't you stay, Jack? The kiddies would love to see you.'

'I'll stay for a while,' said Jack. 'But not for dinner.'

'You'd be very welcome you know,' said Miriam kindly.

'I know that, love,' said Jack. 'But I've got to get back to Saint Peter's.'

'You've never gone to church before, dad,' said Alan off-handedly as he sat down heavily opposite his father and reached across the table for a scone.

Jack could tell that Alan was thinking more about the new warehouses in Palmerston North and Christchurch and the rest of it, all those new trucks, his flying lessons and buying a plane, than he was about his father's church-going history.

'Mrs Krilich,' said Jack. 'She plays the organ. I like to drive her home on Sunday nights.'

'Oh, that reminds me,' said a suddenly attentive Alan as he buttered his scone and looked over the table for the jam. 'I meant to tell you.'

'Not now, Alan,' said Miriam sharply; she was standing at her husband's side as she poured him a fresh cup of tea. She too was preoccupied but not with the company's plans for expansion; she was thinking about the strange conversation she and Jack were engaged in before they were interrupted by Alan's arrival in the kitchen. And now Alan had to bring up *that*. I wish he wouldn't, she thought. Not *that*. Not now. Not after what we've been talking about.

Jack had asked her what she knew about abortion.

'Why on earth are you asking me about that?'

'I was just talking to someone,' said Jack. 'But I don't know anything about it.'

'Well, this someone you were talking to,' said Miriam who had a good idea who that someone was, 'were they for it or against it?'

'Do you have to be for or against it?'

'You don't have to be, Jack, but most people only talk about abortion because they're for it or against it.'

'I suppose she's against it,' said Jack, and Miriam noted the she. 'Yes,' he added, thinking about those thousands of little jelly babies he had promised to have removed from the walls of her house, 'definitely against it.'

'And what about you?'

'Well, I never thought about it, see,' said Jack. 'Never knew anything about it really.'

'But you must have read about it. Seen it on the telly. It's been a controversial subject for years.'

'I know that, love,' said Jack. 'But it didn't affect me and I didn't know what it was all about so I never took any notice.'

'But now?'

'Well, when she – it's Mrs Krilich I'm talking about; Betty – when she told me about the thousands and thousands of abortions every year. How it's like murder. Thousands of lives unlived. Little human bodies torn away from the safety of their mother's – you know, her womb – and thrown into the incinerator without another thought. It's horrible.'

'Is that what she said?'

'Yes. And she's got proof. From the government. Thousands and thousands of them every year. How can they do it? Mothers I mean. Or doctors? How could anyone do that?'

'It's covered by the law, Jack,' said Miriam. 'Two doctors have to agree – I think it's two doctors – they have to agree that it's necessary.'

'Why would it be necessary?'

'Could be the mother's got too many children already. Or she's too old. Could be risky. Could be for her health.'

'For the mother's health? To have an abortion?'

'Yes, Jack.'

'Seems a bit selfish to me,' said Jack. 'And what about the baby's health? It's murder isn't it? Don't you think?'

'They might know there's something wrong. With the baby I mean. Could be deformed or something. They can tell those things these days,' said Miriam who didn't really know what to say. 'Or it's got – what do you call it? – Down Syndrome or something like that. Some sort of awful handicap. Rape, that comes into it,' she said and she saw Jack wince at the use of such a word. She guessed rightly that he'd never had such an intimate conversation with anyone, man or woman, in his long life; he obviously found the subject distasteful and unsettling.

'Why do you want to talk about this, Jack?' she asked. 'It's not a pleasant subject is it.'

'I just didn't know anything about it,' said Jack. 'I had no idea. And it seems to upset Betty so much.'

'Is she a Catholic?'

'No,' said Jack. 'At least she didn't used to be. She goes to Saint Peter's. Anglican. No, she's definitely not. I'd definitely know if she was Catholic. Why?'

'Well, they're strictly against abortion aren't they,' said Miriam. 'And birth control. Homosexuality. Same-sex marriage. Masturbation. And plenty else along those lines.'

She noticed Jack wince at her frankness. Again.

And, unfortunately, that's when Alan came in.

# 22

'WHAT?' ASKED JACK innocently. He was glad Alan had arrived and so changed the subject. 'Meant to tell me what?'

Alan took a sip of his freshly poured tea, took a bite from his jam-and-cream scone, and wiped cream from his top lip with the back of his hand, before answering.

'I had the boys go over the Rolls,' said Alan when he was ready. 'Fine tooth comb and that.'

Jack nodded. He thought that was a good idea. But he wondered why Miriam looked ill at ease; embarrassed. She went to the bench with the teapot to avoid the conversation between the two men.

'It's in good nick alright,' said Alan. 'Mechanically and that.'

'Tell me about it,' said Jack with not a little pride. 'I've been looking after her.'

'I know that. But, anyway, they found a couple of things needed fixing or missing.'

'What sort of things?' Jack was surprised; a little hurt.

'Don't worry, dad,' said Alan. 'Little things. Broken light lens in the back. One of the door handles is a bit corroded. A little bit of flaking chrome. Some stone chips. That sort of thing. If you want to make it perfect.'

Jack shrugged. 'I knew about them,' he said. 'I was going to get around to them eventually.'

'But the thing is, dad, I got Vicky – she's the secretary in the engineering shop and she loves the old thing – I got her to ring up Rolls-Royce in Auckland to see if we could still get parts.'

'And? What did they say?'

At this point Miriam interrupted from the other side of the kitchen. 'Come on, Alan,' she said. 'This isn't important.'

But Alan brushed aside her protest. 'It's not *important*, I know,' he said. 'But it's interesting.'

'What is?' asked Jack who had no idea what was coming.

'Well, the bloke at Rolls asked Vicky which car she was talking about and she said – she loves the car, remember – she said it's a nineteen seventy Rolls-Royce Silver Shadow.'

'Exactly,' said Jack. 'And?'

'Well, you know what he said? The Rolls-Royce joker.'

Jack shook his head; he noticed that Miriam was also shaking her head in what looked like disappointment. Or disapproval.

'He said, which one?'

'Which one?'

'Yes. Which one *exactly*?' he said.

'Eh?'

'That's what I said,' said Alan. 'And Vicky. But apparently Rolls can identify each individual car, serial numbers and that, who built it, when, the parts that were used, the paint job, the source of leather, the woodwork, all that sort of stuff. But the joker said to Vicky well don't worry about that, just tell me the rego.'

Jack suddenly felt sick; and he noticed that Miriam looked plain uncomfortable.

'And you know what he said? The joker at Rolls?'

'Alan!' said Miriam in more than mild irritation. 'Must you?'

'No, love,' said Alan. 'It's interesting. I told you. Dad'll be amazed.'

'I don't think so,' said Jack in dismay.

But Alan didn't hear.

'Listen, dad,' insisted Alan. 'Apparently your Rolls-Royce was imported in nineteen seventy especially for Sir Augustus Ivan Krilich, MBE.'

✿

Jack didn't stop at Landseer Farm for dinner and so didn't get to see his granddaughter and her husband and their children before they went to Disneyland. Instead he went home to make himself a simple evening meal before setting off down Northumberland Road in the Zephyr to pick up Betty and take her to Saint Peter's. Indeed, he even enjoyed the service, telling the Reverend Widdop so afterwards. And although the hymns, their words and music, were still unfamiliar to him he enjoyed listening.

The venerable pipe organ at Saint Peter's was set at the back of the church – built into the choir – so he wasn't able to see Betty as she sat working at the broad keyboards; he couldn't see her hands confidently pressing out from memory the notes and chords of the ancient English hymns, or her brightly-white sneakered feet hovering over the bass pedals and automatically touching them on cue, or that she played and sung with her head back and her eyes closed most of the time. He couldn't see but he could hear her playing and singing and he observed, not for the first time, that the voices of the human congregation and the pipes of the old organ combined in the dark wooden atmosphere of old Saint Peter's, at end of the day in rural Karapuke, inevitably induced a feeling of peace and contemplative calm.

It was the perfect atmosphere to consider his situation.

'Did you know who you bought it off?' Alan had asked.

Now that Alan had raised the subject – when she had so wished and willed that he wouldn't – Miriam sat down at the table, between the men, determined not to let Alan badger his father.

'Of course I knew,' said Jack.

'So she's a Lady, your Old Betty. Lady Krilich.'

'Alan!' said Miriam.

'It's alright, love,' said Jack calmly; he knew the subject would come up one day. 'Yes, she's Lady Krilich,' he said. 'But that was a long time ago you know. Most people don't know. Or don't remember. And she doesn't want to remind them. She never does. And I won't say anything.'

'So she doesn't know you know?'

'I don't know. We never talk about it.'

'So you bought the Rolls off her husband, this Sir Augustus Ivan Krilich.'

'No,' said Jack. 'That's not quite right. He died. I heard about it, it was properly advertised, and I bought it off the estate. His lawyers managed it.'

'So Mrs Krilich didn't know it was you who bought it? Doesn't even know now?'

'No,' said Jack.

'Why?' asked Alan.

'Why what?'

'Why would she have sold it? To you or anyone? Surely she would have been rich as hell. He was.'

On this occasion Miriam was thinking the same thing. And, as she saw that her father-in-law was quite happy to answer his son's questions, she was becoming more relaxed. And more interested.

'She doesn't drive,' said Jack. 'Never has. Neither did he. They had a chauffeur. And after he died, her husband, according to the lawyers, she needed the money.'

'That's odd,' said Alan. 'I wonder why she needed money. How much did you pay again?'

Jack told Alan. 'But that was way back in nineteen seventy-eight don't forget. That was worth a lot more then than it is now.'

'You wouldn't get a fraction of that now,' said Alan. 'Rolls-Royce bloke reckons it's only worth about twenty grand. If that.'

Jack shrugged. He genuinely loved the old car and really didn't care what it was worth. And anyway he planned to give it to Alan. Now.

'I wonder what she needed the money for,' said Alan.

'It is funny,' said Miriam. 'Not that she sold it especially but that she said she needed the money. I wonder what she did with it.'

'I really don't know,' lied Jack. 'And I really don't care,' he added, lying again. 'It was for sale. I always loved the model. Always wanted one. So I bought it. You loved it too. Most people do.'

'I know. Fair enough, dad,' said Alan. 'She's a real beaut. Don't worry about it.'

'I'm not. I don't regret buying her,' said Jack. 'I've had years of pleasure, driving it *and* maintaining her. But the fact is, Al, I don't want her anymore.'

'Eh?'

'You can have her,' said Jack. 'Now. I'm giving it to you.'

'Oh, Jack,' said a delighted Miriam.

'You can't do that, dad,' said Alan. 'You love that car.'

'I was going to leave it you anyway,' said Jack. 'Obviously. You might as well have it now. It's getting a bit much for me to look after anyway. And I've got the Zephyr.'

'Wow. Okay, dad. Thanks,' said a genuinely thrilled and grateful Alan. 'I'll look after her, don't you worry.'

'Only one thing,' said Jack. 'One condition.'

'What's that?'

'If Betty ever sees it here, or anywhere, and recognizes it and figures out it belongs to you, don't tell her you got it from me.'

'When will I ever see her anyway?'

'I don't know,' said Jack. 'But just in case. Tell her anything but don't tell her that.'

'But in all these years hasn't she seen you driving it around town? She must have.'

'I don't know,' said Jack. 'She's never mentioned it. But I've never driven it around town much anyway as you know.'

✿

'I asked Miriam what she thought about abortion and that,' said Jack to Betty.

They were sitting in the dark in the Zephyr outside Betty's house. Jack had driven Betty home from Saint

Peter's after the Sunday evening service. She was still wearing her navy-blue suit.

'And what did she say?' Betty remembered Miriam from Michael's funeral and had liked her – and respected her – at once.

'Not much really,' said Jack. 'We got interrupted.'

'Oh,' said Betty.

'Tell me again,' said Jack.

'Tell you what again?'

'Well I get it that you think it's the murder of little babies – unborn babies who will grow into real people – but according to Miriam it's covered by law. And doctors have to agree and approve. And there are circumstances where it could be important for the mother's life. Or the baby might be deformed or handicapped or something horrible like that.'

'Jack, listen to me,' said Betty. She unclipped her seat belt and half turned in the car's bench seat to better see and face her interlocutor in the dim light of the car's cabin. 'What Miriam says is true. It's what most people think and say and it's true. In law. But it's not that simple to me.'

'Why?' asked Jack. He really wanted to know.

'Life is amazing,' said Betty. 'Don't you think? Amazing and miraculous. But mysterious. It's impossible for even the most brilliant scientific minds to understand it. What is it, Jack? The life that moves through "all things bright and beautiful, all creatures great and small"? Nobody knows. They don't know where it comes from when it arrives or where it goes when it leaves. They can recognize it – anyone can – when it's present. Whether it's a tree or tomato, a bird, a fish, a cat, a human or a cockroach, anything, they know it when they see it but they don't know what it is or how or why it works. They cannot understand it or explain it.

'They certainly can't create it. And yet they don't hesitate to destroy it when it's not wanted. Even in one of their own.

'Honestly, Jack, it breaks my heart. To do that or allow it to be done to a trusting and innocent little baby, pulsing with life, in the process of being formed in the womb. The head and eyes and nose and ears and mouth. Little toes and fingers. A tiny beating heart. A real living growing human being. Destroyed. Gone. Snuffed out. Never to be brought back. Never. It's horrible.'

Jack didn't know what to say and so he said nothing. Meanwhile Betty turned back to the door, opened it, and made ready to get out.

'So you can understand my obsession,' she said.

Jack had reason to understand obsessions and sympathise; but he couldn't help thinking, knowing, that Betty's sad and particularly bizarre obsession must have cost her a lot of money, time and effort, none of which she could afford, as well as testing her emotional resources, distorting her judgement, and turning her into the eccentric albeit harmless old woman so familiar to the citizens of Karapuke.

At least she's sincere in her opinion, he thought. And how can I condemn her for her innocent and well-meaning protest. At least she did something even if it was weird, strange and compulsive in the privacy of her own home that no one else will ever know about. Except me of course. And now it seems it's up to me to undo it so no one else will ever know.

Which means that after all that, she achieved nothing, he thought. Nothing at all.

'That reminds me,' said Betty as she opened the car door to make her exit. 'I'm at the refuge tomorrow. You haven't forgotten about, you know, my little problem.'

'I haven't forgotten,' said Jack with a sympathetic smile.

'Good,' said Betty. 'So, good night, Jack.'

'Good night,' said Jack. 'I'll be in touch.'

23

RORY ENNIS DRANK regularly – in fact almost every evening and almost always too much – at the Karapuke Combined Club, Inc., of which Jack Landseer was a life member. He, the young Ennis, was a familiar, popular and enthusiastically active member of the club and its committees; he was notable for the copper colour of his thinning hair, the ruddiness of his pudgy face, the roundness of his belly, the jolly generosity of his nature, and his propensity, on occasions, for singing mournful Hibernian ballads that reduced him (but no one else) to tears.

Jack preferred the company of men more his own age, and more inclined to sobriety and his own conservative comportment, and so knew Rory more by reputation than acquaintance. But he knew that Rory the storyteller, when not entertaining an audience in the club's main bar, worked at Waikato university and would therefore be able to help him take the first steps towards solving the matter of Betty's jelly babies which had somehow become his responsibility.

The promise of a whiskey was all it took to draw the cheerful and helpful young Irishman away from his place at the bar to a small table in a quiet corner of the room near the billiard tables.

'You're right there, Jack,' said Rory when he and Jack were sitting down and Jack had asked his simple question. 'Exams are over for the year by and large now. They're on vacation. Most of them that's for sure. Or soon will be.'

'And so how do I arrange it? What do I do?'

'It's called Student Job Search, Jack, don't you know? All over the internet now it is.'

'I don't know anything about the internet, Rory,' said Jack. 'I haven't got a computer.'

'Have you not now? Well somebody would help you with that surely.'

'I don't want anybody to help,' said Jack. 'It's a sort of secret. A surprise.'

'That's grand, Jack. I like that, so I do. A surprise. For someone special I'm thinking.'

'Sort of,' said Jack impatiently. He noticed that Rory's glass was empty. 'Another one?'

'Grand,' said Rory handing over his glass. 'And what about yourself now?'

'I'm fine,' said Jack who had hardly touched his beer. 'I'll be right back.'

And he was. He put Rory's glass on the low table.

'Oh, thanks a lot there, Jack.'

'So, Rory, no computer, no internet.'

'There's a phone number I'm sure, Jack. You've got a phone now?'

'Of course,' said Jack.

'Well, it'll be one of them oh-eight-hundred numbers. In the phone book for sure. Just ring them up, Jack. It'll be no problem there.'

'Student Job Search, you say?'

'That's it exactly, Jack. Student Job Search. Something like that anyway. In the phone book. Look there. You'll find it right enough.'

'Thanks, Rory,' said Jack as he took his beer glass in hand and stood up to leave.

'You going somewhere, Jack?'

'I thought–'

'You know what thought thought now, Jack,' said Rory whose glass was empty again. 'Now yourself, take the weight off your legs and I'll get you a what? – a Lion Red is it? – and it'll be another Jameson for meself.'

And so, bound by his own civility, Jack sat with the young Rory Ennis for another quarter of an hour, making small talk and taking unnecessary advice about how to ask for and get just the right students for the secret job – whatever it might be – and to ensure that he didn't pay too much.

'What were you talking to Rory for?' asked one of his friends when Jack joined him for a scheduled game of billiards.

'I wanted to know something about the university,' said Jack. 'He works there. In Hamilton.'

'He does the bloody lawns, Jack,' said his friend.

✿

Betty was mortified.

'Jack,' she said in protest. 'I can't afford to pay people.'

'It won't cost much,' said Jack.

'And students! My God.'

'What's wrong with students?'

'I was a bloody student once, wasn't I. I know what they're like. And, anyway, as I said, I've got no money. Remember?'

'I'll pay,' said Jack.

'No!'

'Look, Betty,' said Jack. 'You asked for my help to restore the house. You want it nice for the women's refuge.'

'Oh, they need it, Jack, they really do,' interrupted Betty. 'The space. I was there yesterday and–'

'Fair enough,' said Jack. 'I understand. But first we have to scrape off all the jelly babies and the polyurethane and get rid of it all. It's too much work for you and me – way beyond me to tell you the truth – and yet you don't want anyone local, anyone who knows you, in the house. You want to keep it all hush hush. Secret.'

'Oh, Jack,' said Betty miserably. 'You make it sound so sordid.'

'Bet, I have to be frank.'

'I know, Jack, I know. I appreciate it. I really do.'

It was Tuesday morning at the end of October. Jack was sitting with Betty in her kitchen; he had come to take her to the mission where she was due for her Tuesday shift. She was dressed in a rather grubby-looking primrose-coloured flared pants suit with a matching jacket, with wide and floppy brown-suede lapels, over an acid-orange blouse. Her hair was up, held in place by her tortoiseshell combs, and she was wearing a pale lipstick; Jack thought she looked beautiful. He so wanted to tell her but he didn't. Instead he said: 'There'll only be three or four of them and I'll make sure they don't come from around here. They'll be from Waikato university. They'll probably be country kids who live in the Waikato somewhere. They'll get it done quickly and they won't care what they do. What it's all about. They're poor students. They won't care. They'll just want the money.'

'Oh, Jack,' said Betty in frustration. 'I told you. I haven't *got* any money.'

'And I told you that I have,' said Jack. 'You might be broke but I'm a rich man, Betty. I can't even believe that I'm saying that out loud but I am. Ridiculously rich. It's obscene.'

Betty listened, heard, and shook her head slowly in mild despair. 'Really?'

'Tell me about it,' Jack continued. 'Thanks to Alan I've got more money than I could shake a stick at.'

'Really?' asked Betty again. Pleadingly. She wanted to believe he could afford to help her but was still instinctively reluctant to accept his financial help.

'I said I'd help and I will and that's how I'll do it. I can't do it myself but I can *pay* to have it done. It's as simple as that.'

Betty rested her elbows on the table and her head in her hands. 'Oh, my God,' she said. 'What the bloody hell have I done?'

'I know exactly what you've done,' said Jack to the top of Betty's head. 'It's all quite amazing and I'll tell you about it one day. Soon I hope.'

But the worried Betty wasn't listening. Then, suddenly, remembering something, she looked up. Stood up.

'I've got to feed the chooks before we go,' she said.

And so Jack followed her out to the old garage where he learned that – along with some old, dusty and broken furniture, a rusty bicycle and a dozen or so pumpkins –

she stored the big plastic sacks of wheat and poultry feed. He watched as she scooped out a plastic ice-cream tub-full from each sack and then followed her down the garden paths, a plastic ice-cream tub in each of her hands, around the vegetable plots to the fowl run in the far corner, calling repeatedly "chuck, chuck, chuck", in a falsetto voice, as she went, so that by the time she entered the run – as Jack waited outside – her large hens were clustered together around her clucking with excitement and anticipation.

'Is that what you do every day?' asked Jack when Betty had finished and they were walking back to the house.

'Oh, no,' said Betty. 'Just every now and then. Chooks like all sorts of stuff. Anything. Everything. Wait here,' she said. 'I'll just put these back.'

And so Jack waited in the garden while she returned the ice-cream tubs to the garage.

When she joined him she resumed her talk where she had left it: 'Vege scraps, they absolutely *love* lettuce, cabbage, bread, wandering Jew's a favourite, but most of all they like scratching away in the dirt for insects, grubs and bugs and worms and snails. Anything in the dirt. That's what the tractor's for.'

'What's the tractor?'

By then they were standing at the bottom of the back steps. Betty pointed to what was in effect a lightweight cage on wheels standing behind the garage.

'I got it made in town special,' she said. 'It's exactly the same size as each of the plots so when one of them's fallow–'

'I see,' said Jack, surprised again by his old friend's energy and enterprise.

24

IT TOOK JACK a full week to get everything organized. A three-metre pink bin – dented, dirty and rusty, and the smallest size available – now stood empty (but for a shallow pond of oil-slicked water in the rusty bottom) on the broken concrete of Betty's drive, near her front door, having been delivered the day before, while Betty was out, by a truck of matching pink. Meanwhile three students from Waikato university were due to arrive at the house where Jack was waiting with a box of various-sized and -shaped hand-scraping tools, drawn from his own workshop, a coarse yard broom and a wide-mouthed shovel, and two of his own sturdy and short aluminium step-ladders as well as Betty's own full-size ancient, wooden and somewhat rickety model.

'I have to say again, Jack, I really hate the idea of three strangers working in my house,' said Betty who was about to set off on foot for another day at the mission leaving Jack to his work. 'No one's ever been inside the house in all the time I've been here. More than thirty years.'

'Except me.'

'Except you,' agreed Betty. 'And, yes, I had to get a plumber in once to fix the toilet. That was in nineteen ninety-three. August I think.'

'But you said you didn't start with the jelly babies until–'

'It wasn't just that, Jack. I've *always* liked my privacy.'

'I see,' said Jack who didn't. 'But–'

'I know, I know,' Betty said quickly when she saw that Jack was about to protest. 'It has to be done, I know, and I'll cope, but that doesn't mean I have to like it does it? Because I don't.'

'Don't worry, Bet,' said Jack. 'I'll be here all the time. Supervising. Every minute, I promise.'

'Yes, well, I don't want to be here when they arrive, I don't want to meet them, so I'll go now.'

'But it's only half past eight.'

'There's plenty for me to do,' said Betty referring to her work at the mission. 'I'll work there all day and come back about, what? When do you think?'

'Depends,' said Jack. 'I reckon it'll take them two full days.'

'But when will they be finished *today?*'

'They've got to drive back to Morrinsville or something,' said Jack. 'They'll probably want to finish about four, half past, five maybe, something like that.'

'I'll come back at half past five just to be on the safe side.'

'You don't have to avoid them you know,' said Jack. 'Three intelligent young students. They won't bite.'

'I'm sure they'll be very nice young people but I don't want to meet them. I just don't like the idea of them in my house. Like foreign invaders.'

Jack shrugged. He knew that any discussion – argument, debate – was futile. 'I'll need a key in case I have to lock up before you're back.'

'I'll give you the spare key to the back door. You said you should have one, in case of emergency you said, so I'll give it to you now.'

And as she scratched about in one of the kitchen drawers for the key her eighty-five year-old friend, sitting at her kitchen table, watched her from behind and thought – he couldn't help it – that she looked pretty good in her blue-and-red tartan miniskirt and navy-blue sweater (although he thought her white sneakers with their neon-green laces didn't work) and that she still had pretty good legs for an eighty-eight year-old woman. Tanned. No varicose veins. That'll be all the walking, he thought.

'Here it is,' she said at last as she turned and presented her admirer with a long dull-grey old-fashioned key attached by string to an ancient cardboard luggage tag upon which was printed, in faint but indelible purple pencil: MUM'S.

And then she was gone and Jack was left sitting in the kitchen with three cats who clearly didn't approve of his presence and showed it by sitting on the floor at his feet and staring up at him accusingly.

They all scattered though – one under Betty's cot in the sun-porch and the other two, one immediately after the other, out the cat door – when they, before Jack, heard a car in the drive. He heard it too, in due course, followed by three car doors being shut loudly and the sound of three people laughing and talking. Jack guessed correctly that his young labourers had arrived and so he went outside, down the unnaturally-steep steps, to meet them.

An old dark-blue Ford Laser stood in the drive behind his much older Zephyr – which despite its age looked in better condition than its somewhat battered young relative – and the three young people whom it had carried from Morrinsville sauntered down the drive. Although they were evidently dressed for dirty work, in jeans and old t-shirts, they didn't look like workers. Jack thought they looked like what they were: unmuscled soft-handed students.

They stood in the drive together, the old man and the three students, introducing themselves, stretching forward awkwardly to shake hands, and using only first names: Tim, Liam and Olivia. And Jack.

'Nice car,' said Tim although he seemed the only one of the three to be impressed. 'Yours?'

'Yes,' said Jack. 'Zephyr Six.'

'It's beautiful,' said Tim who was the only one of the three as tall as Jack. 'English, eh.'

'Yes.'

'How old is she?'

The conversation was between Jack and Tim. The other two, Liam and Olivia, stood aside, their arms folded, kicking idly at nothing, waiting.

'Nineteen fifty-five,' said Jack.

'Wow, man,' said Tim, impressed. 'That's more than ten years older than my old man, my father.'

Even Liam and Olivia seemed impressed by that: the Zephyr's unbelievable oldness. They turned together evidently to look for the qualities which Tim had seen at once but they had apparently missed.

'I *love* her,' said Tim which made Jack like him. Indeed, he, likeable Tim, seemed to be the leader of the threesome. 'I really do. I love her.'

'Really popular at the time,' said Jack. 'Built in Lower Hutt, believe it or not, from kits sent from England. Well built too.'

'Can I have a look inside? Only take a minute.'

'Of course,' said Jack. 'Go for it. It's open.'

And so Jack, Liam and Olivier stood together, watching and waiting as Tim got into the Zephyr, sliding onto the bench seat behind the steering wheel where he sat and looked and touched and poked and turned around and looked into the back of the cabin, and then at the ceiling, lightly caressing its soft felt with the tips of his finger, before gently banging the steering wheel with the flat of his hands and getting out fully satisfied.

'She's really beautiful,' he called as he made his way back to the waiting trio.

'Tell me about it,' said Jack. 'I had another vintage car I'm sure you would have liked.'

'What's that?'

'Oh, it's not here. My son has it now.'

'Well, I do love old cars. Not that old wreck,' said Tim referring to the somewhat uncared-for little Ford Laser. 'But one day, Mr Landseer. One day.'

'Good on you, son,' said Jack who had a positive feeling about young Tim whatever his name was the student. 'Anyway, come on in and I'll show you all what's to be done.'

And so, at half-past nine on that Tuesday morning in early November, the work began; using the metal scrapers supplied by Jack, and standing on the short step-ladders when necessary to extend their reach, the three soft-handed students began to strip off the one hundred and seventy-six thousand four hundred and seventy-nine jelly babies which Betty Krilich had so carefully glued to her walls and doors and woodwork in the ten years to twenty-ten. They worked hard, the three of them, not stopping for lunch and pausing only briefly, occasionally, to drink from the water bottles they had brought with them. And so Jack was happily surprised that it took them just that one day; so surprised that he gladly paid them for two.

✿

'So what did they say?' asked Betty when she got home.

She was still worried about what the students might have thought of her house and the job they were required to do; what they might think of *her*. But she needn't have worried; the tired trio – Tim, Liam and Olivia – were almost back in Morrinsville by then, each a round and generous two-hundred dollars richer. So pleased were they with their fee they hadn't questioned or given another thought to the strange nature of their day's work. And anyway they politely suppressed their curiosity. Without discussing it they had each assumed that the house belonged to the man who employed them: the old, kind, evidently eccentric and perhaps foolishly over-generous Mr Landseer.

Jack and Betty were standing together in the kitchen looking down the hall. The jelly babies were all gone but their removal had left as bad a mess as Jack had feared. The printed surface layer of the old wall paper had been torn away in strips by the stiff film of well-cured polyurethane leaving behind a brown and furry substrate. The dark and varnished woodwork was also badly but not deeply damaged, and the old threadbare carpet, coming away from itself in places, was thickly covered in a fine dust. And that was after Jack had swept up everything he could, using his coarse yard broom and a wide-mouthed shovel, and removed it all to the pink bin.

'What about?' asked Jack, answering her question with a question.

'About what they were doing. The jelly babies of course. Didn't they think it was, what? Strange? Weird?'

'They didn't say anything.'

'Nothing?'

'Well, they talked to each other of course. And to me a bit. One of them loved the Zephyr. But nothing about the jelly babies.'

'Why not? They must have wondered.'

'They may very well have wondered, Bet,' said Jack, 'but they probably thought I was the owner, see. So they didn't say anything at all. Not about the jelly babies anyway. Too polite I suppose. Just got on with the job. Worked hard too. Didn't even stop for lunch.'

'I see,' said a relieved Betty. 'And they're not coming back you say.'

'All done,' said Jack.

'Amazing.'

'Now I swept up everything as best I could,' said Jack, happy to change the subject. 'Put it all in the bin with my shovel. The bin's nearly full of it.'

'I saw that,' said Betty. 'Good.'

'But you haven't got a vacuum cleaner so—'

'I haven't got electricity, Jack. Remember?'

'I knew that,' said Jack. 'It's just that the carpet's a mess.'

'It was a mess anyway,' said Betty.

'Yes. But it's worse now,' said Jack. 'But it'll have to come up when we paint anyway. Then we can lay some nice new stuff. New carpet. Vinyl too.'

'Jack!'

'What?'

'Money, Jack. Remember? I haven't got any bloody money for carpet or vinyl. Or paint.'

'And I said that I have and that I'll pay. So shut up.'

Jack made the apparent command gently, with a kind smile, and Betty graciously accepted both the command and the generosity. It was a remarkable double acceptance for a stubborn and independent old woman who always resented being told what to do and had always given but never received charity. So she held up her hands, palms forward, in a gesture of acceptance.

'Alright, Jack,' she said. 'If you insist.'

'I insist.'

'I don't know why you're doing this but, okey-dokey. Because it's not for me, remember, it's for the women's refuge.'

'That's it,' said Jack, happy that Betty had found a suitable justification. 'For the women's refuge.'

# 25

IT'S RIDICULOUS, THOUGHT Betty. I can't get up now. It's the middle of the night. I wonder whose dog that is. Barking away. Sounds eerie. I can feel Norman. He doesn't care. He's snoring. Cats fall asleep so easily. Why can't I sleep so easily? I hate it when I can't sleep. Nights like this. Sleepless.

Actually, come to think of it, I don't feel very well. That must be it. Not good at all. Can't get comfortable. It's so hot. My legs ache. Don't know where to put them. And my arm. Been lying on it I suppose. Such an ache. And the pillow's so hard. Can't relax. Can't stop thinking. Remembering. And why do I keep remembering *that*? Of all things. I don't want to remember it at all. But I do. Like it was yesterday. So ridiculous. Bloody ridiculous. To call her Mrs X. That's what they called her. Mrs X. Go and see Mrs X, they said. She's an expert, they said. No one will know. Take five pounds. Go in the morning and you'll be out in the evening. No complications. I can even remember the address. Twenty-one Toradh Street, Surry Hills. I remember the date too. Monday the twenty-second of February, nineteen sixty. It was so hot. So boiling hot. Gus was busy somewhere. I can't remember where. A meeting. He was always at a meeting. Busy all day, he said. Won't be back till late. So I went in the morning. Got a taxi from the flat. And they were right. She *was* an expert. Five pounds. Looked after me. Made sure I was alright. Came out in the evening. Got another taxi back to Double Bay. Went to bed. So tired. Like now. So tired. Think I've got the flu or something, I said. Maybe that's it now: I've got the flu. And Gus came back and gave me a kiss and tucked me in and never knew. Never guessed.

So hot? What day is it? That's right: Wednesday. Nearly light.

Gynaecological abnormality he said. The specialist. Told me. Then Gus. But he knew, the specialist; the doctors all knew. Straightaway. They *must* have. But they didn't say anything. For my sake I suppose. Ethics maybe. So Gus never knew. But he said he didn't mind. He said he was too old anyway. I was just thirty then. It'd be, what? Fifty-eight by now. Imagine that. Fifty-eight. Bit younger than Jack's Miriam. Could've been just like her. A lovely woman just like Miriam. They might have been friends. Or a boy. I could've been a *real* grandmother by now. What a waste. And poor Gus. He was forty-five. At the very peak of his career as they say. But he said don't worry, darl, I'm too old. But he wasn't too old. Not really. What a fool I was. A horrible selfish young fool. And I was lucky. What if something had gone wrong? The scandal. Gus's knighthood.

Morning. So light all of a sudden. Must have gone to sleep at last. But I'm so tired. So bloody tired. And hot. And my arm. But I better get up. I better get up now.

Right now. I can do it. I can. Feed the cats. And the girls. And then. So much to do. The garden. Needs watering. And the service at eleven. Can't let Mr Widdop down. Then back to the garden all afternoon. It'll be hot there. I'll be so tired. Not enough sleep. But I'll just *have* to get up now. Feed the cats if nothing else. And the girls.

But, shit, I feel so bloody crook.

✸

'Jack? Is that you, Jack? Jack Landseer?'

'Yes. Who's that?'

It was just after lunch; Jack had finished eating and was now enjoying a cup of tea at his kitchen table as he finished reading the paper. He'd spent the morning planning Betty's renovations. He'd rung the bin company – they promised the bin would be removed that morning – and had Betty's permission to go down to the house to roughly measure up each room with a view to getting quotes for the painting and decorating. Indeed, he intended to make a plan of the whole house – room by room – knowing it would come in handy for all the work he planned. He knew she would be home after the Wednesday church service and that she meant to spend the rest of the afternoon in the garden. The day was fine, the weather was hot, he wanted to water the roses and then mow the lawns when he got back from Betty's.

Thus had he planned for a busy afternoon.

The phone was on the wall beside the kitchen table. He didn't get many calls and was surprised that anyone should be ringing at lunchtime on a Wednesday; it occurred to him then that something was wrong with someone somewhere. Why he should have thought that he didn't know; but he wasn't wrong.

He had put down his tea cup on the saucer, which was itself sitting on the open newspaper, and reached up to answer the phone.

'It's Vance Widdop.'

'Vance. Good morning. I mean afternoon.'

Jack couldn't imagine why the young vicar of Saint Peter's should be calling him. They knew each other, but not well, and only through Betty.

'Jack, I'm awfully sorry to trouble you. I'm so glad I remembered your last name. Thank goodness I found your number in the phone book.'

The normally cheerful young clergyman sounded anxious and stressed. His mood was immediately transferred along the copper wire from the vicarage in Church Street to Jack's kitchen in Northumberland Road.

'What is it, Vance?'

'It's Betty,' said the young vicar. 'She wasn't at our service this morning – she plays the organ you know – and I can't help being worried.'

'Oh dear,' said an immediately-worried Jack. He was thinking fast but his thinking was all over the place. Out of control. Confused. He didn't know what to think.

'It's odd you know, Jack, but after all these years I don't actually know where she lives,' said Widdop.

'Yes,' said Jack. 'She's a very private person.'

'You know though, don't you?'

'Yes,' said Jack. 'Of course. It's just down the road from me.'

'Oh, good. She doesn't have a phone see so I can't ring her. And I can't do anything about it at the moment as I have two appointments now. Wedding interviews. I won't be finished until after three.'

'Vance,' said Jack, sounding calmer than he felt. 'I was with her last night. She was fine. She's probably out in the garden. She does an awful lot of gardening you know. Maybe she forgot.'

'I don't think so. She's never missed a Wednesday service before. Not ever.'

'Look, Vance, don't worry. I'll go down to her place right now and see how she is. I'll let you know.'

'Oh, Jack, that would be splendid. I can't help being worried.'

'I'll be in touch,' said Jack, anxious now to get quickly down the road to Betty's house.

'I told you I won't be available until after three or so but can you ring the house and tell Linda, my wife, tell her if you could.'

'You better give me the number,' said Jack.

A few minutes later he had parked the Zephyr in Betty's empty drive. Thank God the bin's gone, he thought. He walked quickly down the drive, unhooked the wire-netting fence, dashed up the three short steep steps to the back door and, using the key she had given him, which he was planning to use this afternoon anyway, he entered the cramped little sun-porch which he knew was Betty's bedroom-cum-living room. There were two cats standing, meowing, beside a single large plastic feeding bowl which was empty but for a few scraps of hard, dry and inedible lumps of something and another large bowl of watery and sour-looking milk. He looked quickly around the small room. Betty's narrow little bed had obviously been slept in. There was a chromed rack of clothes – the sort of wheeled affair he had seen in ladies' dress shops – a wooden chest of drawers with a round mirror propped up on its top. What else? Where is she? And then: another plaintiff meow. It came from the kitchen and there, just inside the door, he found Betty lying on the floor, on her right side, her head resting on her right arm which was stretched out on the floor, her glasses crooked on her nose, her thick hair lying on the floor behind her head in an untamed tangle. A large tabby cat – it was Norman but Jack didn't care for Betty's cats and never remembered their names – was standing at her head, looking down at his mistress with a puzzled posture, intermittently meowing sadly and eerily.

'Jesus Christ,' said Jack loudly. He kneeled on the floor, at Betty's head, shook her left shoulder – it felt thin and bony through her black silk pyjamas – and then suddenly thought he shouldn't be touching her; moving her. But he touched her face anyway; it felt warm. He touched her hands; they felt cold. He noticed her closed eyes fluttering – the only word he could think of – and he knew that at least she was alive; and he guessed – hoped – that whatever had happened might have only just happened.

Ambulance. Phone. No phone. The stupid old woman doesn't have a phone. I should have that bloody little cell phone thing with me. Alan'll kill me when he finds out. But, hell, I don't even know how to turn it on. Neighbours. She never talked about the neighbours. Does she like them? Do they like her? Which side?

He stepped awkwardly, gingerly, down the back steps – no proper builder would make steps that steep and narrow, he thought, with no hand rail – leaving the door ajar, and strode as smartly as he could up the drive deciding as he went to go to the house on his left as it was closer – must be one-seven-four, he thought as reached the footpath and immediately turned down the narrow path of the neighbouring house and went directly to the front door.

Bing-bong.

It was one of those door bells that makes a *bing* when pulled out and a *bong* when released. Through the full-length obscure glass of the front door – sand-blasted with the image of an elegant and stylized flamingo – he could see a blurred figure approaching; a woman. She opened the door; she was a buxom, jolly, woman. Late middle-age. Could be older. She was wearing a floral apron which, as she stood at the open door, she gathered up and used to wipe her hands.

'Scones,' she said breezily. Smiling. 'Sorry. You see my daughter and son-in-law and their little ones are coming this afternoon–'

But she stopped when she saw the dread painted on the face of the old man who was standing on her wooden porch, resting against the door frame and breathing heavily.

'What is it?' she asked fearfully, urgently, as she turned and called loudly over her shoulder. 'Paul. Quick!'

Thank God for them, thought Jack as he walked slowly – he had to walk slowly as he was almost exhausted from the physical and emotional strain of the emergency – back to Betty's house. Mary, the efficient, competent and confident scone-baking neighbour – she who had said: 'Poor old Betty, I knew something like this would happen one day and she won't have a phone you know, she just won't' – had run ahead while Paul, her husband, who had come when called wearing a pair of grey track pants, bare feet, and a singlet, and was obviously retired, and older than his wife, went immediately to the phone.

There were two green-and-yellow-garbed para-medics there already: a bulky man with huge feet in oversized boots and a strong-looking younger woman. Together with all their mysterious machines and equipment they filled Betty's tiny kitchen squeezing Mary and Jack back into Betty's sun-porch bedroom. Eventually they carried out Betty on a stretcher, down the steep back stairs and around to the ambulance, standing yellow, ominous and open behind Jack's Zephyr on the cracked concrete of Betty's drive. And as the big man para-medic did whatever had to be done to make the unconscious Betty ready for the journey ahead – her face covered with a clear plastic mask – the woman para-medic turned to Jack and Mary and Paul, who were by then standing together at the back of the ambulance, watching anxiously, and waiting.

'She's had a stroke,' she said. 'It looks like that anyway.'

'Oh my God,' said Jack. 'How bad is it? She hated the idea of–'

'How old did you say she is?'

'Eighty-eight,' said Jack. 'Is she alright? I mean–'

'She's alright. At the moment anyway.'

'But will she be alright? You know what I mean.'

'Depends,' said the para-medic.

'On what?'

'Well, when it actually happened. How long she was lying there. Her underlying health.'

'How long do you think she's been lying there?'

'All morning I should think,' said the paramedic. 'Looks like she got up this morning and was about to feed the cat.'

'Cats actually,' said Jack. 'But how do you know that?'

'There was a box of cat biscuits on the floor beside her.'

'Was there? I never noticed.'

'Well, that's what it looked like. She got up and was about to feed the cats. They must have eaten what was spilled.'

'Jesus, all morning?' said Jack. 'That's not good.'

'She seems like a tough old thing though. And once we get her to hospital—'

'Shouldn't someone go with her?' asked Jack.

'Are you her husband?'

'No,' said Jack somewhat sadly. 'Jack Landseer. Her friend.'

And when the lady para-medic looked questioningly at Mary and Paul Mary shook her head slowly. 'Neighbours,' she said.

'You can follow in your car if you like,' said the young woman para-medic.

'Where are you going?'

'Auckland City Hospital. Emergency. But we'll be booting it all the way. Siren and lights.'

Jack knew he wasn't up to the long drive on the motorway to Auckland hospital; not the way he felt; and not speeding in the old Zephyr.

Mary knew too. She could see that his face had paled; he seemed to be trembling slightly. Shock. And he was looking about as if he wasn't sure where he was.

'Come on, Jack,' she said kindly, taking his arm. 'Come back with me and Paul. We'll have something to eat and ring up later and see how she is. Then we can decide what to do. Okay?'

They waited for a few minutes and watched as the ambulance reversed out onto Northumberland Road, turned and then set off at speed for the State Highway.

And then, for the first time in his old age, Jack Landseer allowed himself to be a beaten old man, overwhelmed by circumstances beyond his control, surrendering to the inevitable.

He winced and paused when he heard the ambulance's siren from far away – he knew it must have reached the State Highway intersection – and couldn't help thinking of poor unconscious Betty, lying in the back, being carried away from her home to an unknown future.

Walking again, slowly with the stoop of sadness and submission, he felt old and tired, and looked it, as he allowed Mary and Paul – he didn't know their surname – to lead him at last away from Betty's house.

But then, suddenly, he stopped.

'The cats,' he said. 'They might need more feeding.'

'They've run away,' said Mary. 'But I put out some more biscuits before we left. After they took Betty out.'

'But–'

'The Whiskas,' she said. 'The box.'

'And water. Or milk I think.'

'All done,' said Mary kindly.

'I'll come back and feed them tomorrow,' said Jack. 'Every day. I'll feed them every day till she's better. Till she comes home. And the chooks. They need looking after too. Until she comes home. I know what to do. She showed me. I know.'

'Come on Jack,' said Paul. 'We'll worry about all that later.'

But Jack stopped again and so his escorts had to stop with him. Betty took his arm as a steadying precaution.

'Have you ever been into Betty's house?' he asked them.

'Yes, of course,' said Mary.

'When?'

'Just now,' said Mary. 'With you of course.'

'Oh, yes. But you've never been past the kitchen?'

'No,' said Mary shaking her head slowly. Wondering. 'Why?'

'It's a mess,' said Jack quickly. 'We're renovating see.'

'That's alright, Jack. We saw the bin. They came and took it away this morning.'

'She'd be so ashamed,' said Jack.

'We understand, don't we, Paul?'

'Of course,' said her husband. 'Renovating. It's always messy.'

Jack reached into his trouser pocket and drew out his key ring, with an unsteady hand, and showed them the old grey key.

'Can you wait a minute?' he asked. 'I better go back and lock the door.'

And when he returned he held up the key again and said: 'I've got her house key you see. You'll see me coming and going for a while. Supervising all the renovations.'

26

ALL THOUGHTS OF renovation were put aside that day and for many more days.

Betty's kind neighbours, Mary and Paul Owens, took Jack in while he recovered from his shock; and he *was* shocked, visibly.

Mary sat him in her kitchen and had Paul fetch a blanket which she draped loosely over Jack's shoulders and which he pulled tightly around himself and gripped close with one trembling hand. He felt cold, anxious, unsure of where he was and what was happening. And he looked ashen.

'Here, have this, love,' said Mary softly. She was standing at Jack's side with a large yellow mug of something hot.

Jack looked up at her through his rimless glasses and Mary saw a frail, vulnerable and frightened old man; he looked worried and confused.

'What is it?' he asked meekly.

'Beef tea,' said Mary. 'Home made by yours truly. I was going to make soup. It's the broth. Hot and nourishing.'

Jack let the blanket fall from his grasp and took the proffered mug by wrapping both hands around it.

'Thank you,' he said quietly and took a tentative sip. He looked up at Mary and added with a weak smile: 'Nice.'

'Good,' said Mary.

'Oh my God!' said Jack loudly and suddenly. So loudly and suddenly that he gave Mary a fright.

He put the mug of soup down on the table and tried to stand up. The blanket fell from his shoulders and hung on the back of the chair.

'What is it?'

'Oh, I forgot. I forgot.'

'Sit down, Jack,' said Mary as calmly as she could. She pressed gently on his shoulder and replaced the blanket while she called out to her husband, over her own shoulder, in a stage whisper. 'Paul! Paul!' And then she asked of Jack, who had meekly surrendered to the gentle downward pressure on his shoulder: 'Forgot what, love?'

Paul came into the kitchen and Mary looked down at Jack, grimaced slightly, raised her eyebrows and put her index finger to her pursed lips.

'Forgot what, love?' she asked Jack again.

'Forgot about poor Vance,' said Jack, looking up at Mary. 'He'll be worried sick.'

'Who's Vance?'

'Vance Widdop,' said Jack. 'The vicar.'

'Saint Peter's,' said Mary.

'I promised to phone him and tell him what happened to Betty. She didn't go to the service this morning and he phoned me and I came straight here. I don't know what his number is. I left it at home. On the table. I better go.'

He tried to stand again; and again Mary pushed down gently on his shoulder.

'We know the Reverend Widdop, Jack. We know the number. Paul will ring him right now – won't you, Paul – and tell him everything. About Betty. Explain.'

Jack looked around at Paul who was standing behind him nodding. Jack relaxed visibly.

'That'd be so good. Thank you. He'll be so worried. If he's not there he said to tell his wife. Her name is, oh, dear, I can't remember her name.'

'I'll take care of it, mate. Just don't worry. I'll go and ring them right now.'

'And meanwhile, love, you get on with your soup,' said Mary. 'Don't let it get cold now. I went to a lot of trouble to make that soup. Specially for you,' she added with a wink.

And so she retrieved the big yellow mug of soup from the table and Jack obediently grasped it again, in both hands, and took another warm and comforting sip.

'Now I've got things to do, love,' said Mary. 'I won't bother you, leave you alone, but you sit there and relax and enjoy your soup till you feel better.'

Jack sat there, alone in Mary's kitchen, sipping at his soup, looking down at nothing, thinking about nothing. And then he thought about his angina, grateful that it hadn't come on; his out-of-date pills were at home. Then he thought about nothing again.

Mary was busy elsewhere in the house, mostly conferring quietly with her husband who had finished the phone call to Saint Peter's, but every five minutes or so she surreptitiously checked on her guest's welfare. When she saw that he had finished his soup – he had set the yellow mug down on the table – she popped in casually.

'And how are you feeling now, Jack? Better?'

She thought he looked better; there was colour in his face, he didn't look chilled any more, and the ever-so-slight trembling was gone.

'Much better thanks,' said Jack.

He began to shrug off the blanket so Mary stepped forward to take it from him.

'That's good,' said Mary. 'Time.'

She stood beside him while she folded the blanket.

'I'm sorry but I don't even know your name. You were both so good, you and your husband, and I don't even know your names. I know you told me. Isn't that terrible.'

'Natural more like it,' said Mary. 'Anyway, I know you're Jack.'

'How do you know that anyway?'

'I heard you telling the ambulance man.'

'I see.'

'So I'm Mary,' said Mary. 'Mary Owens. And my husband is Paul.'

'I see,' said Jack again.

'We've all had quite a shock haven't we,' said Mary. 'Quite an afternoon of it.'

'Poor Betty, eh,' said Jack. 'I wonder how she is.'

'Well, tell me how *you* are, Jack. Be honest now. It really knocked the stuffing out of you finding her like that didn't it.'

'It did,' said Jack. 'It really did.'

'And now?'

'What time is it?' asked Jack dully. Somehow he couldn't be bothered looking at his watch.

Mary glanced up at the kitchen clock fixed to the wall above the table.

'It's nearly half past two,' she said.

'It's Wednesday isn't it,' he said.

'Yes. Wednesday.'

Jack nodded and began to stand up.

'What are you doing?' asked Mary.

'I've got to go to the toilet,' he said.

'Down the hall on your right,' said Mary.

Paul came into the kitchen at that moment. He had to stand to one side to let Jack into the hall.

When Jack came back to the kitchen he said to his hosts: 'I better get going.'

'Home?'

'Home,' said Jack. 'Yes.'

'What do you want to do about seeing Betty?' asked Mary. 'You do want to see her I suppose.'

'I want to,' said Jack who looked exhausted; worn out. 'But I don't want to go driving into Auckland now. Not now. I don't think I'm up to it.'

'Paul,' said Mary sharply to her husband by way of a prompt.

'Oh, yes,' said Paul quickly. 'The thing is, Jack, I rang the hospital just now and they said that she's been admitted and that she's sleeping and comfortable. But no visitors. Not at the moment. Only family.'

'But she hasn't got any family,' said Jack. 'Only me.'

'We know that,' said Mary.

'But what happened? Did they say? What's going to happen to her?'

'Well they won't say on the phone,' said Mary. 'Not just to anyone.'

'I don't know what to think,' said Jack gloomily.

'She'll be alright, Jack,' said Paul cheerfully. 'You heard what the Zambuck said, eh. Tough old thing or something like that.'

'I don't know,' said Jack. 'Looked pretty bad to me. When I found her. And she didn't wake up did she. They couldn't wake her up.'

'I'm sure she'll be alright,' said Paul. 'In hospital. The best place.'

'Are you okay to drive home now?' asked Mary.

'I'll be alright,' said Jack flatly. 'Thanks.'

'Well, look, you go home now and take it easy. Have you got something for dinner?'

Jack nodded grimly. 'Betty's eggs. Boiled eggs.'

'Good,' said Mary. 'Then have a good sleep tonight, and tomorrow, well, here's what we're going to do.'

◆

'Are you sure you don't mind?' asked Jack. 'All the way to Auckland hospital?'

He was sitting in the front passenger seat of Paul Owens's car.

'I said I didn't mind and I don't,' said Paul. 'The least we can do, mate. Mary and I agreed.'

Mary and Paul Owens had agreed, and had arranged with Jack before he left them the previous afternoon, that Mary would ring him in the morning to see how he was feeling and, if he were up to it, Paul would pick him up after lunch and drive him in to Auckland to visit Betty. Mary had a note of Betty's ward and had checked whether she would be well enough for visitors and the best time to call.

'Well, I do appreciate it alright,' said Jack. 'The old Zephyr doesn't like the motorway any more. I don't like it myself to tell you the truth. And parking at the hospital is a nightmare.'

'Well you don't have to worry about any of that today,' said Paul.

'But you don't have to wait for me,' said Jack. 'Honestly. I'll be fine.'

'But how will you get home if I don't wait?'

'Look, for one thing, I don't know how long I'll be do I.'

'I don't mind waiting,' said Paul.

'No. It's alright. Honest. I'll get the train home.'

'Where from?' asked Paul. 'You'll have to walk all the way down to Newmarket station?'

'Yes,' said Jack. 'Why not? Betty's done it every week. For years.'

'Has she? Why?'

'She was – is I suppose – a grandmother at Starship,' said Jack. 'A volunteer you know. Should have been there this morning as a matter of fact.'

'I didn't know that,' said Paul.

'Better go and tell them why she didn't turn up this morning,' said Jack. 'They'll be wondering. I'll do that later.'

'So how long has she been doing that? Going to Starship?'

'Every Thursday morning for donkey's years,' said Jack. 'This is a nice car,' he added partly to change the subject but also because he really did think it was a nice car.

'Toyota,' said Paul. 'We need a reasonably big job because Mary likes to visit our daughter and grandies a lot. They live down in Tauranga.'

'It's nice alright,' said Jack. 'I love the Zephyr but old cars aren't half as good as modern cars.'

'You've got an old Roller too haven't you?'

'How did you know that?' asked Jack, surprised.

'Oh, we've seen you around,' said Paul. 'You can't get away with much in Karapuke you know.'

'Tell me about it,' said Jack with a laugh. But he couldn't help wondering: if Betty's neighbour had seen him in the Rolls Betty probably had too. But why hadn't she ever said anything?

'Gave it to my son,' he said. 'He loves her as much as I do. But modern cars. They are better I think. Better to drive. Easier to maintain. And safer too.'

Jack couldn't help thinking how relaxing it was to drive on the motorway in Paul's new Toyota compared with the old Zephyr. For one thing, despite the Toyota's comparatively vast power, it seemed so quiet; there was virtually no sound from either the engine or the road. And steady. And the braking was firm, responsive and even; no pulling. Then there were all the instruments; and the air-conditioning. A computer screen. Even a reversing camera. And the individual and fully adjustable front seats were much more comfortable than the Zephyr's flat bench and straight back.

'It's a nice car alright,' he said.

That, though, was the extent of his conversation with the driver until they reached the hospital where Paul stopped at the main entrance to let Jack out.

'Now you know I can wait for you if you want,' said Paul. 'Mary said I should, and I think I should.'

Jack was out of the car holding the door open and so he leaned down to reply to the anxious Paul.

'Thanks, Paul,' he said. 'I really do appreciate everything. I don't know what I would have done yesterday without you. Without your help and that. But, honest, I'd only feel pressured if I knew you were waiting in the carpark for me. I just want to stay with Betty for as long or as short a time as feels right. For her I mean. Then I'll go and see the volunteer people to tell them. And, really and truly, I don't mind walking down to Newmarket to get the train. I really don't mind.'

It was a long speech and Paul Owens had no choice but to listen to it and take the speaker at his word.

'Okay, mate,' he said. 'If you insist.'

'I do,' said Jack.

'Mary won't like it but there you go.'

'Thanks, Paul,' said Jack.

'Take care, mate,' said Paul. 'Now you've got a note of the ward number and the floor and all that haven't you?'

'In my pocket,' said Jack, patting the inside pocket of his sports coat.

'I hope you find her okay,' said Paul. 'Feeling better I mean.'

'She'll be alright,' said Jack. 'I'll see you later.'

'See you,' said Paul as Jack slammed shut the Toyota's door with unnecessary force.

27

THE HOSPITAL WAS busy but by following the signs Jack made his way to the lifts and then up to the correct floor and then by foot to the correct ward. There were six beds in each room of the ward, and the names of the six resident patients were listed at the entrance to each room, but despite going around the ward three times Jack couldn't find Betty anywhere.

'Are you lost?' asked a busy-looking nurse in the corridor who had observed his apparently aimless wandering.

'I'm looking for Betty,' said Jack. 'Betty Krilich.'

'Are you Mr Krilich?'

'No,' said Jack. 'A friend. An old friend. I found her you see. Yesterday. But I couldn't get here until today. She hasn't got a husband you see. No family. No one. Only me. Is she alright?'

'She's comfortable enough,' said the nurse with a slight hesitation and a frown neither of which registered with the anxious Jack.

'But where is she? I can't find her anywhere.'

'Oh, I see, yes,' said the nurse. 'Well, she was moved last night. She's in her own room now. That room at the end of the corridor.'

'The closed door?'

'That's the one,' said the nurse. 'Private. Much nicer you see.'

'Can I go in? To see her?'

The nurse tilted her head slightly and looked doubtful.

'You *do* know she's had a stroke don't you,' she said rather than asked.

'That's what the ambulance lady said but I wasn't sure. Is she alright?'

'She's alright really, considering,' said the nurse. 'You can see her. But it's affected her side. Her right side. You'll see. Not too bad but she can't move her right arm. Or her leg. She can talk but it's a bit garbled. Hard to understand sometimes but you should be okay if you listen carefully. Unless she's tired. Could be worse though. And you might find she cries a bit. Perhaps.'

'Cries?'

'Yes. It's quite normal.'

'But will she get better?'

'You'll have to talk to a doctor about that,' said the nurse lifting and looking down anxiously at the watch pinned upside-down to her breast. 'I'm sorry, I have to go.'

'But–'

'There'll be therapy,' said the nurse.

'So can I–'

'Of course,' said the nurse as she set off down the corridor. 'But, honestly, I think you'll find she's asleep.'

She wasn't asleep. Indeed, she lifted her head from the pillow and turned towards the sound of the opening door.

She looked – squinted without her spectacles, concentrated – but she didn't recognize her visitor.

Jack thought she looked awful. And confused.

'Bet,' he said quietly.

He saw her smile weakly.

'Glasses, Jack.'

Her voice was soft and weak and the words a little garbled as though her tongue were swollen and unmanageable. But she did manage those two words and he did manage to understand them.

Her old-fashioned spectacles, radiant blue – still remarkably unfaded after so many years – with diamantes set into the upswept outer points, were lying on the stand beside her bed. He handed them to her but she had great difficulty accepting them, manipulating them, and then putting them on with only her left hand as there were needles and tubes and other medical paraphernalia attached to, coming from and wrapped around her left arm. Meanwhile her bare right arm was lying heavy, red, swollen and obviously useless, on top of the pale green hospital cover.

He leaned forward and tried to help her put on her glasses and adjust them but he was clumsy and big-fingered, and he had difficulty finding the tops of her ears, and the thin arms of the old spectacles got caught and tangled in her hair which was spread in an unruly mess all over the hospital pillow.

'Hairbrush,' she said as she awkwardly, one-handedly, adjusted her spectacles on her own as best she could.

Jack stood back from the bed and watched. Her obvious affliction made him wince. He knew she was right-handed. How on earth is she going to manage? he thought. And playing the organ?

'I can bring you a hairbrush from your place if you like,' he said. 'Next time.'

He felt terribly inadequate.

Betty managed a crooked and sardonic smile which he understood. He knew Betty needed a woman's support. He thought of Miriam. He didn't mention her but decided that he would ask her for help. He knew she wouldn't mind.

'What day?'

'What day is it today?'

She nodded.

'It's Thursday. All day.'

'Thursday?'

'Yes, Bet. Thursday.'

'Thursday,' she said as if trying to understand the word. And then: 'I'm in hospital.'

'Yes, I'm afraid you are. Are you alright?'

'Tired to buggery. What happened?'

'Eh?'

'What happened?' she asked again.

Surely they must have told her, thought Jack. But he remembered: he'd known other people – men – who were terribly confused after a stroke.

'A stroke,' he said.

'Stroke?'

'Yes. A stroke. But not too bad, Bet. Could be worse they say.'

'Stroke.'

'Do you need anything?' he asked. 'As well as a hairbrush. I'll get you a hairbrush.'

'Yes,' she said with another weak and crooked smile. 'But not you. Not a man.'

At that Jack felt hopelessly inadequate and embarrassed. He decided he would definitely ask Miriam for help. Or perhaps young Mrs whatever-her-name is Widdop. Perhaps she would help. Betty needs a woman's support, he thought. Knew.

'Old people,' said Betty, turning her head slightly on the pillow to better look at the visitor on her left. 'We need help. Young people.'

'I suppose so, Bet.'

'Should have a daughter.'

Jack noticed then that her eyes were unnaturally wet. Not tears exactly but the wetness that wells up in the eyes in the van of real tears.

'I'll get Miriam to come and see you,' said Jack quickly.

'Miriam? Lovely.'

'She is,' said Jack. 'She really is.'

Betty turned away and looked up at the ceiling.

'How old?' she asked.

'Who? Miriam?'

Betty nodded.

'I'm not sure exactly,' said Jack. 'Same as Alan I suppose. Catherine would have known. About sixty-two.'

Betty nodded. 'Sixty-two.' She sounded disappointed. 'Too old.

'Well I could get Vance's wife to come in. I'm sure she'd help.'

'Linda?'

'That's it. Linda.'

'Bloody useless.'

'I don't know anything about her,' said Jack. 'Never met her.'

'Oh, Jack,' said Betty. She tried to lift herself higher in the bed, on one elbow, but failed and fell back exhausted. Jack wanted to help but didn't. 'A stroke,' she said. 'Hell no.'

Jack didn't know what to say – he felt awkward and confused – and so he said nothing.

'I'm *useless*,' said Betty angrily.

She poked her right forearm with the fingers of her left hand leaving white marks in the red and swollen flesh. And then suddenly she moved her left hand to her forehead – dragging the unwieldly medical paraphernalia attached to that arm up and across her face – and began vigorously massaging it with her fingertips as she began to cry real tears.

'Oh, Jack,' she managed to say. 'I'm so ashamed.'

Jack leaned forward. He so much wanted to help but didn't know how. He wanted to take off her silly sparkly spectacles and gently wipe her eyes and wipe the tears from her cheeks; and kiss her tenderly on the forehead; and stroke her tangled white hair; and do all things that a lover would do – even an eighty-five year old lover – to show his love and comfort his beloved. But he couldn't. He didn't think he had any right; any one of the gestures he longed to make seemed more intimate than was appropriate.

She took off her glasses then, using her left hand, and laid them on the bed; then she did her best wipe her eyes and cheeks with her fingers before laying her hand back on the bed and her tired head back on the pillow and closing her eyes.

And so Jack sat forward in his chair and rested his hand over hers and they didn't speak for an unmeasured time until the door opened and they were joined by the nurse who had steered Jack to Betty's room. She came in and Jack had to stand up and move away and shift his chair while she checked the monitor on the wall behind the patient's bed, checked the lines in and out of her arm, adjusted something that was hanging on a hook and feeding something into her arm, before moving to the end of the bed where she slipped out Betty's file to which, after looking up at the monitor, she added some notes.

Then, without having said a word, without a nod or a smile, she was gone and Jack returned the chair to the bedside where he sat and again covered Betty's hand with his. He then saw that she was crying again although her eyes were closed; and sniffing. And so he took his hand from hers, gently took her open spectacles from the bed, where she had put them, closed them and set them on the stand where he had found them, and, without standing, reached across and drew two or three soft tissues from the box that was there. He wanted – longed – to use them to wipe her eyes but instead he put them in her now free hand so she could wipe her own eyes in her own way and in her own time.

Betty took the tissues silently but before using them she opened her eyes and turned her head slightly, to look at her friend through her wetted and unfocused eyes, and said slowly, carefully, if somewhat thickly, and sadly: 'I tried to forget and forgive. So ashamed.'

'Don't worry, Bet. *Please.*'

'You don't understand,' protested Betty meekly as she softly dabbed the crushed tissues to her eyes.

'Yes, I do,' insisted Jack.

'You don't know—'

'Look,' said Jack, interrupting gently but firmly. 'It's all over. The bin's gone. Taken away. All the jelly babies and polyurethane and torn wallpaper and mess. All gone. That's the end of it. No one will ever know anything about it. Nothing to be ashamed about any more.'

'Not that. I want to tell you. It's—'

'Now,' said Jack, gently demanding her attention.

He wanted her to forget her shame about the jelly babies and the state of her house. He wanted her to listen to him. To not talk. Talking was too hard. Tiring for her. Hard for him to understand. And, anyway, he wanted to say what *he* wanted to say thinking only that he was being helpful and positive. Thus he didn't notice old Betty Krilich's sigh of tired resignation. Because she – wanting to explain so much but lacking the strength to insist that *he* should listen to *her*, her will enfeebled by her weariness – was reluctantly forced to surrender to old Jack Landseer's desperate need to promote his own unnecessary and unwanted explanations.

And so – aching with a lifetime's sadness and longing for the understanding which she now knew would never come – she closed her eyes, not needing her spectacles, and silently surrendered to the inevitable.

'Now,' continued the determined old man, his hand over hers, 'with the bin out of the way I'm going to get on with everything else. I'm getting the old carpet and felt underlay lifted and taken away. The carpet people are doing that in the next couple of days. For nothing. When I told them who it was for and that you were ill in hospital and what's happening to the house when it's finished, about the women's refuge, the safe house, they said they'd donate *everything*. The best underlay, the carpet of your choice, the vinyl for the bathroom and that, and all the labour. All for nothing. Isn't that amazing? For the women's refuge they said. But you know what, Bet? I think they're doing it for you.'

Betty's eyes were closed. She didn't respond.

'Did you hear me, Bet?' Jack asked quickly; anxiously.

She opened her eyes slowly and looked at him, or at least in his direction, without turning her head.

'Yes,' she said quietly.

Jack let out a long breath.

'Are you alright? How do you feel?'

'Tired,' said Betty with a heavy sigh.

'Well, you just rest, Bet,' said Jack, 'and I'll tell you everything I'm going to do while you're in here. And you won't have to worry about a thing.'

28

AND SO IT began.

'First,' said Jack to the exhausted patient. 'I'm getting the power connected again. Have to really. For the carpenters. And the painters. A bloke in the club, Steve O'Davies – that's a builder mate of mine, your florist friend Val's husband – he's going to supply all the labour for nothing. And he'll give us all the materials and appliances and anything else you need at trade. Can't do better than that, eh. Mate's rates as they say. He's got chippies and sparkies and plumbers on tap, no pun intended, and he's going to put a few of his blokes into the house to bring it all up to scratch real quick. They'll check all the wiring and plumbing and tidy up all the woodwork and hardware. What with the painting and new wallpaper and the carpets and everything by the time you get out of here, Bet, the whole place will be just like new.

'But the important thing is that he said they'll do it just the way you want. Well, you and the women's refuge people. Four bedrooms, a huge lounge, a separate dining, one big bathroom and one small one, and two separate toilets, you can do a lot with all that. Be real perfect for them don't you think? When you've gone if you know what I mean.

'Then – don't argue – I'm getting quotes for painting the outside too, and fixing the roof. We'll put up a front fence, for privacy, I know that's important, then we'll have to turn the back garden into a lawn for the kids to play on. I'm going to get some playground things, slides and swings and that. Getting quotes now.

'Are you alright?' he asked.

Betty nodded without opening her eyes. And so the old man – with so much he wanted to say – continued his monologue.

'By the way, Bet,' he said, 'I *have* to tell you now that I know about all your money and that. What you did for Starship for a start. I figured it out. It must have come from selling your house in Wellington. My agent – his father was a friend of your Gus – told me all about it. Mansion he said. Eight bedrooms. Servants' quarters. Ballroom. Tennis courts. Swimming pool. Everything. Said you got a fortune for it even back then. So I figured out that's where the money came from for Starship. But first it was the Rolls wasn't it. I never really worked out what you did with that money. You'd probably be surprised to know that it, the Rolls, is worth less now than it was then. Anyway, I've given it to Alan so you don't have to worry. It's in safe hands.

'But the paintings. My God, Bet, the paintings. You know those lumpy old Braithwaites. Two of them. I don't know what you and Gus paid for them in Sydney but I gave you three thousand six hundred for them both and Zelnick tells me that one's now worth forty-eight thousand and the other fifty-five thousand *at least*.

Probably more. Can you believe that? The Steele's worth eight hundred and fifty thousand, the Lindauer nearly three hundred thousand and the McCahon, well, that's worth over a million. A bloody million dollars for that brown thing with the black scrawl. And as for all the others, all the small ones, added all together it's mind boggling. Can you believe it?

'And now, the thing is, Zelnick's going to sell them all for me. I know you know him. Auction them. Not all at once but slowly, release them one at a time onto the market, he knows what to do, and he reckons they'll eventually get more than two and a half million dollars, maybe three or even more. So they'll make a whole lot more money all over again for, well, the thing is, for whatever you like.

'But, first, I've been talking to Alan – actually Miriam mostly – last night, on the phone, and she reckons that we're best to form a proper trust. We'll sell off all the paintings slowly, one at a time, and invest the money cleverly. Alan knows what to do and you can trust Miriam till the cows come home. And then you can support all your friends and charities from the interest which will keep on rolling in forever. Better than selling the house and the Rolls and the paintings for cash and then spending all the money. This way the money from the paintings – pure profit second time around don't forget – will keep earning interest forever.

'And then, together – don't argue cause I've made up my mind – together we can make the interest money do everything you ever dreamed of. Anonymously of course. I know that's what you prefer. And don't argue. They're my paintings to sell and I can do whatever the hell I like with them and the money and what I want to do is what *you* want to do. So don't argue.

'Then you can look after the Starship. They always need stuff don't they. The mission. I don't know what they need but I'm sure you do. And the women's refuge. There'll be plenty to support them until, you know, until they get the Northumberland Road house shall we say. And Saint Peter's. Vance needs a new car, I know that. The church and the hall are okay, according to him, thanks to you he says, but evidently the vicarage needs work. And the hospice. You bought all those flash beds didn't you. That was the last straw wasn't it. The straw that broke your camel's back.

'I know you had your obsession about — you know — abortions and that. I don't know why. But the thing is I had an obsession too. Just as strange as yours in a way I suppose. See I was obsessed with — can you guess? — I was obsessed with you. Or at least the memory of the young Betty Henderson who was so kind to me when I was a kid. Why did I remember that do you think? Why was it so important? I really don't know.

'It wasn't love. I mean I wasn't in love with you or anything like that. I was too young anyway. I suppose I just admired you and your family. You seemed so rich to me. Living in the biggest flashest house on Northumberland Road. Always a new car. Your mother seemed to know everything about everyone and everything and have such good taste. She was known for it wasn't she. Always on committees and things like that. And then when I found out who you married — I was married myself by then — I was so impressed by Gus's knowledge and reputation as an art collector. And so was Catherine. Actually I suppose it was her really. She was fascinated by your life in Wellington, and all the glamour, you two were always in the paper about something. And she followed it all and told me.

'Funny, isn't it, Bet. About you and me. You married Gus and must have been so happy. And I married Catherine and wasn't. I had kids and you didn't. Can't say I blame you. We had the two boys of course. Catherine loved them. You know that. You must know how much mothers love their children. My God, Bet, I wouldn't wish anyone dead but I am so glad she didn't live to see how Michael ended up. You know about that, eh. That wasn't in our plans. Probably wasn't in his for that matter. Bloody kids.

'Anyway, I didn't really understand art but just after Catherine died I heard from Zelnick that you were selling Gus's paintings – I didn't know why then – and I thought if he, Sir Augustus Krilich, thought something was good and worth it then it must be. And that's when I started. I have to admit I didn't really care for them at first but I trusted Zelnick, and Gus's taste, and, you know, they hung in the house for so long that I came to appreciate them properly in time.

'Listen, Bet, I'm starving. And I need a pee. You know what the time is? Nearly four. We've been here chatting all that time. So I better get on home. Got to catch the train. By home I mean your place first. I fed the cats this morning but I better see how they are. And I better check on the chooks too. I put them in the tractor, like you showed me, but they'd probably be better off home for the night. Don't worry. I'll manage.'

He had been sitting at Betty's bedside for most of the afternoon. He didn't want to leave but the call of nature had to be answered before the long walk to Newmarket station and the train ride home to Karapuke.

Before he stood up, though, he looked at Betty's face; really looked. He'd never before seen her without her blue pointy spectacles and their absence made her look vulnerable and made him feel protective. He thought she looked old – properly old now – and somewhat worn out. Her long and wavy white hair looked strangely straight and oily, or wet; it lay on the pillow all about her head in a wild and mad-looking randomness. Her narrow but remarkable smooth face appeared to be a little crooked somehow, and its skin looked as delicate and transparent as the finest rice paper through which he could see the shape of her skull and a tracery of blue and red lines. But her expression was calm and peaceful with no sign of stress or pain. That's good, he thought. No pain is good.

Thus did he gaze at her face for a full minute – thinking nothing coherent – before leaning across the bed to put his large left hand over hers which was still resting on top of the hospital cover. This time, when he thought about it, her hand felt hard, bony and cold under his coarse but warm touch. He squeezed it gently. Tenderly. Affectionately. Sadly.

He was surprised then when she lifted his hand to her lips, briefly, before letting it fall again to the bed. And she opened her eyes – not wide – but obviously looking, searchingly – and he thought he saw her smile faintly.

'You did hear me, Bet, didn't you?' he said quietly. 'I rambled on a bit I know but I wanted you to know that things are going to work out just fine. Just like you planned only better. Much better. I'll make sure of that.'

Her eyes closed slowly, as if she didn't have the strength to hold them open, but he thought she held her crooked smile and gave an almost imperceptible nod.

The nurse came in then and once again did her routine checks. Only when she had made notes in Betty's file, which was stored in a rack at the end of the bed, did she acknowledge Jack who was standing to the side, waiting.

'Mrs Krilich really needs to rest now,' she said, 'if you don't mind.'

Jack wanted to say "Lady Krilich" but he didn't. Instead he said: 'Yes. I'm off. But will she be alright? She can't seem to wake up.'

'She'll be alright. I know she's not responding now but she's heavily sedated and we're monitoring her closely. A good sleep and–'

Dammit, thought Jack as he washed his hands in the toilet on his way out of the hospital, I forgot to go and tell the Starship volunteer lady about Betty. Too late now. I better do it tomorrow.

# 29

THERE WAS A waist-high concrete wall outside the hospital which Jack rested against to think a little before setting off for Newmarket. His thoughts, which were somewhat confused and not at all profound, were interrupted by someone addressing him by name.

'Mr Landseer?'

He looked up from his sitting-back resting position against the wall to see a tall slender young man in a young man's uniform of blue jeans, grubby-looking sneakers and an olive-green t-shirt bearing a printed legend which he didn't understand. The young man had a fresh complexion, with rosy cheeks and pink lips like a little boy, and brown hair, wavy and unruly. For a moment – just a moment – he reminded Jack of a young Michael which gave him a start.

But it wasn't Michael. So he looked up at the tall young man, squinting through his rimless glasses, trying to recognize the young face.

'Are you alright?' asked the young face with a smile that was both friendly and worried.

'I'm alright,' said Jack half-heartedly, rather wanting to be left alone.

'You don't remember me do you,' said the young man whom Jack saw as no more than a tall boy; a boy who reminded him of poor Michael.

'No,' said Jack. 'I'm afraid I don't. I'm sorry.'

'Tim. Tim Richardson.'

Jack listened, heard, looked, but neither the name nor the face meant anything to him.

'My friends and I – Liam and Olivia – we helped you scrape down all the walls in your house. Remember. On Tuesday.

'It's not my–' Jack was going to explain but decided against it. Instead, remembering, and being glad to remember, he added brightly: 'You liked my car didn't you.'

'The Zephyr,' said Tim. 'That's it.'

'I *do* remember,' said Jack.

'Are you alright, Mr Landseer?'

'Not really, son,' said Jack with rare candour. Without turning around or looking he used his hooked thumb to point to the high and wide hospital building looming over him from behind. 'A friend of mine. Not good.'

'Oh,' said Tim sympathetically.

'What are you doing around here anyway?' asked Jack. 'I thought you lived in Morrinsville. Went to Waikato.'

'Liam and Olivia go there. They're friends of mine.'

'Oh.'

'I'm a medical student. Over there.'

He pointed across the road to the grey blocks of concrete which together constituted the medical school.

'I see,' said Jack glancing across the road at the set of sinister-looking buildings. 'But I thought you were on holiday.'

'In the library,' said Tim. 'Studying all day. Have to.'

'No rest for the wicked, eh,' said Jack.

'Exactly,' said Tim with a smile. 'Are you going home now?' he asked.

'I suppose so.'

'Back to Karapuke?'

Jack nodded. He was feeling better – perhaps it was the company and the conversation – so he straightened up and was prepared to stand.

'In the Zephyr?'

'No, no. I got a lift up. I'm getting the train home.'

'Will you be alright?' asked Tim.

'What do you mean?'

'I mean it's late on a Thursday afternoon. The trains will be busy. Could be quite a hassle you know. Especially if you're not feeling well.'

'Ah!' said Jack with amusement. 'You're a doctor.'

'Um, not quite,' said Tim. 'But I can recognize stress and worry and exhaustion in the elderly if you don't mind my saying so.'

'I don't mind, son,' said Jack. 'I *am* elderly. Old.' He looked at his wrist watch and back at the young medical student. 'I suppose you're right,' he said. 'Actually, you know, I don't feel that good really.'

'Are you on medication?'

'Not really,' said Jack. 'I've got angina pills–' he patted his shirt pocket '–but it's not that. I don't need them. Not now. I'm alright.'

'I'm going back to Morrinsville now,' said Tim. 'To my parents. I could drop you off home if you like.'

'In your little Laser?'

'If you don't mind.'

'Don't mind at all,' said Jack who was getting used to being helped. And, anyway, he had a plan.

✡

It was a routine journey for the young medical student – except for the detour to Karapuke – but it was like a test-drive for the old man; an interesting and revealing trip. Indeed, he was even a little disappointed when, an hour and a half after leaving the hospital, the little Ford Laser – somewhat dirty, dented, uncared for but mechanically sound – stopped in Northumberland Road opposite Betty's house.

'No, not here,' said Jack. 'This isn't my place.'

'But I thought–'

'My friend. I'm renovating it for a friend. I live further up. One-thirty-six.'

'You'll have to show me,' said the driver.

'Just keep going up here. Up Northumberland Road,' said Jack pointing ahead. 'Not far.'

And so they set off again for that short distance. And when they got there – to Jack's house – the old man said to the young man: 'Come in for a minute, Tim. I want to show you something. But park on the street.'

And so they both got out of the little Laser and Tim Richardson the medical student – who had easily recognized the symptoms of anxiety and shock in the aged although he could only guess at the cause – followed the old man across the road to his house, up the path and around the back to the workshop. And as they walked, without speaking, the young man slightly behind the older man, following, and wondering what he was about to be shown – something to do with the old man's Zephyr he guessed – Jack fumbled with his key ring getting ready to open the workshop door.

He unlocked the door and held it open for Tim to go in first.

'Left,' he said. 'Through the workshop, into the garage.'

Suddenly the young Tim, who had wanted only to do a favour for a troubled old man, felt troubled himself; uncertain; apprehensive. He was being directed through a dark workshop – he could see sinister-looking machines, and benches along the walls with all sorts of unfamiliar and dangerous-looking shiny tools for cutting and drilling fixed to the walls above – into the adjacent windowless garage which was completely dark. Meanwhile he could sense the old man behind him fiddling with something.

'Hang on, son,' said Jack. 'Let me past. I'll have to turn on the lights.'

And so Tim stopped to let Jack past. He watched as Jack reached around the garage door to find the light switch. Suddenly the garage was lit – brightly lit – by huge industrial-type lights on the walls and the ceiling.

Jack noticed the young man's surprise.

'I need plenty of light,' he said. 'I do a lot of work in here. At least I used to. I restored *her* in here.'

Then he pressed a button beside the light switch and the garage door began to rise, squealing and shuddering. And in the combined electric light and late afternoon sun the young man saw, in the garage that was wide enough to easily accommodate two cars, the her to which the old man had referred: the blue nineteen fifty-five Ford Zephyr Six which Tim had so admired when he saw it, only two days earlier, at the house he had mistakenly thought was Jack's.

The sight of the Zephyr – so clean and shiny with brilliant chrome work – banished all doubt and apprehension from the young man's mind.

'Beautiful,' he said. 'Truly beautiful.'

'It's yours,' said Jack.

He held out his right hand in the palm of which were the two keys he had been taking off his key ring as they made their way into the garage.

'What?'

'Yours,' said Jack. 'I'm giving it to you, son. Now.'

The young man stepped back a little and tilted his head quizzically; he was unsure of what was happening. He did not take the keys from Jack's still-outstretched hand. He didn't want to. He didn't understand.

'Why?'

'Because you so obviously love it and will take care of it,' said Jack. 'Go on,' he added, thrusting his hand towards the surprised and reluctant young man.

'Really?' Tim relaxed a little. The old man seemed sincere.

'Really,' said Jack. 'But there's one condition.'

Once again the young man had his doubts. One condition, he thought. One condition. What sort of condition?

'What's that?' he asked doubtfully. Suspiciously.

'I'll give you the Zephyr if you give me your Laser.'

'What?'

'It's a lovely little car,' said Jack. 'I could tell on the ride just now. As much a classic in its own right as the Zephyr is.'

'Really?'

'Really,' said Jack. 'Yes. We swap cars and I'll have great fun restoring your little Laser.'

'Really?'

'Really,' insisted Jack again. 'I mean it. Honest. Here. Take these. Give me the keys to the Laser. And go.'

Tim pulled a face to suggest apology. 'I've got so much junk in the car,' he said. 'In the back. In the hatch. I'll have to—'

'No hurry,' said Jack. 'Put it all in the Zephyr. I'll wait.'

'Okay,' said Tim uncertainly but thinking he had nothing to lose. 'Only if you're sure. Really sure.'

'I'm sure. Here. Take the keys,' said Jack. 'Back the Zephyr over the road to make it easy. Then come back and give me the keys to the Laser.'

'But what about—'

'Can you do the change of ownership stuff at the post office?' asked Jack. 'Save me the trouble. Bring them to me here to sign or whatever when you're ready.'

'Are you absolutely sure about this?' asked Tim. 'Really?'

'Really,' said Jack. 'I'll enjoy restoring your little Laser. I really will.'

30

BEFORE HE'D GIVEN another thought to restoring his new old car Jack discovered that he thoroughly enjoyed driving it. It may have been old, dirty and dented, with faded paint and a shabby interior, but compared to the Zephyr – which really *was* old – it was a "modern" car; a model which had benefitted from myriad improvements and advances in motor vehicle design, engineering and technology. It had only a small engine but it was economical, efficient and highly responsive; its four-speed manual gearbox put the old Zephyr's sloppy three-speed column change to shame; it had marvellous power steering – Jack had never experienced anything like it in a small car – and disk brakes.

And so, the next day, Friday, he enjoyed the long and relaxed motorway journey to Auckland in a way that was never possible in the Zephyr. He left home in the middle of the morning knowing – or hoping – that the traffic wouldn't be too heavy then; and it wasn't. He thought the little Laser performed wonderfully well on the motorway and was even more impressed, when he left the motorway, by its responsiveness and manoeuvrability in city traffic especially when he reluctantly drove into the expensive multi-level carpark at the hospital. And as he parked the car so easily, and locked it, and made his way to the lift, he felt mildly elated, not only from the pleasure the little car had given him on the long drive from Karapuke but also in anticipation of the pleasure he would get from restoring it, in every way, to its original showroom condition. He wished then he could share his small and harmless pleasure with Alan although, as he got into the lift alone, and pressed the ground floor button, he realized that while Alan would be pleased to see his father happy with his new old car he may not be pleased with the way it was acquired; he knew that Alan coveted the Zephyr almost as much as he had once coveted the Rolls-Royce; but while Alan now possessed the Rolls he could never now possess the Zephyr.

Such thoughts occupied Jack's mind as the lift dropped slowly, stopping occasionally to admit one or two new passengers. And it wasn't until the doors opened on the ground floor and he faced the hospital's grand entrance – crowded with people coming and going, walking fast or swinging along on crutches, or being pushed or pushing themselves in a wheel chair – with its many confusing signs, a flower shop, a book shop, a cafe, a pharmacy, the counter manned by blue-coated volunteer ambassadors, that he remembered why he was where he was.

Suddenly he felt nothing but anxiety; he felt somewhat breathless and could feel his heart beating hard inside his chest. He knew it wasn't angina but an unfamiliar sensation frequently reported to him by others but experienced by himself only rarely and mildly. He didn't like feeling his heart – being so aware of its every hollow, dull and thumping throb – and was suddenly afraid he might have a heart attack and die. How ironic, he thought. To have a heart attack here, right in the hospital entrance in front of all these people. To die here on the way to seeing poor sick Betty. But perhaps not. I mean, he thought, I'm in a big hospital full of doctors and nurses and machines and drugs. They'd probably save me.

Into the crowded lift to go up. To Betty's ward. Jostled by other passengers. Up. Out of the lift. Into the ward. A long corridor. And by then the feeling was gone. Thankfully. But nevertheless it left him somewhat tired and weak.

'She'll be alright,' the nurse had said as he left the night before.

But now?

He was at the closed door. Betty's door. But he was stopped short – surprised, confused, puzzled – by a large brightly white plastic sign fixed at an angle across the doorway.

"STOP!" it said in capital letters, bold and scarlet. And beneath, in smaller black letters: "RESTRICTED ENTRY. PATIENT'S FAMILY ONLY. ALL OTHERS REPORT TO DUTY STAFF NURSE. NO EXCEPTIONS."

Then, suddenly, there was a nurse at his side. A different nurse.

'I'm sorry,' she said. 'Who are you? Exactly?'

'Jack Landseer. I just want–'

'So you're *not* Mr Krilich.'

'No, but–'

'I'm sorry but–'

'But what?'

'Rules you know.'

'What bloody rules?'

'There's no next of kin,' said the nurse. Patiently. 'Mr?'

'Landseer. Say again?'

He started to feel that feeling again. Breathlessness. His thumping heart. Anxiety. He knew what it was. Was he going to faint? Was he going to collapse in a heap on the floor? Was he having a heart attack? Was he going to die?

'Are you alright, Mr Landseer,' said the nurse suddenly. She had a folder which she tucked under one arm while she folded her hand around the old man's wrist meaning to take his pulse.

But he pushed her away.

'I'm alright,' he insisted gruffly.

But he wasn't. The corridor was turning dark and there were fuzzy black and red spots dashing around inside his eyes. He had to move, shuffle, to the corridor wall and hold the rail that ran along its length at waist height.

The nurse gripped his upper arm to help him.

'You look dreadfully pale,' she said.

'I'm alright,' Jack insisted with a worried abruptness which the nurse interpreted as rudeness.

He concentrated. Looked at her. His sight was returning. The dizziness was going. He straightened up.

'Are you alright now?'

'Better. A bit.'

'It says here,' said the nurse when she was sure he had recovered. 'Actually, I can't show you so you'll have to take my word for it.' She released the grip on his arm and was now clutching the stiff folder to her breast in both arms. 'It says here that Mrs Krilich—'

'*Lady* Krilich,' said Jack who was now feeling almost normal.

'Pardon?'

'She's Lady Krilich,' said Jack.

'Is she?' The nurse sounded and was surprised. She looked down quickly at her folder and then at Jack. '*Lady Krilich?*'

'Yes. Lady Elizabeth Anne Krilich.'

'Well,' said the nurse, recovering her professional poise. 'It says in here that Mrs Krilich – Lady Krilich as you say – had no next of kin. No one to be contacted. Nothing.'

'Had?'

Jack looked again at the sign on the door and suddenly understood.

And the nurse suddenly understood that until that moment he had not understood. Hadn't been told. He had simply arrived for a routine visit.

'Oh. I *am* sorry Mr–'

She was surprised and moved to see tears in the old man's eyes. She waited while he took off his spectacles with one hand and clumsily tried to wipe his eyes and cheeks with the fingers of the other.

'When?'

'Just this morning,' said the nurse. 'An hour or so ago. Perfectly peaceful and painless. In her sleep. I *am* sorry.'

'But what about–' the old man sighed, took a deep breath, and, while reaching into his trouser pocket for a handkerchief, with his free hand, added bravely, because he knew he had no rights and so might not get another chance to ask '–the body? The funeral? You know what I mean. What happens?'

The nurse grasped the official-looking folder tightly and tapped it with the neatly trimmed healthy-pink nails of the fingers of her healthy-pink right hand.

'I understand she belongs to a church in Karapuke. Saint Peter's. It says here that the vicar of Saint Peter's will be–'

'Vance. Vance Widdop,' said Jack as he finished wiping his eyes and returned his handkerchief to his pocket.

'Sorry?'

'That's his name,' said Jack as he replaced his spectacles and settled them in place. 'The vicar. Vance Widdop.'

'I see,' said the nurse. 'Well, he'll be contacted this morning. Officially I mean.'

'Eh?'

'Look, I really am sorry you had to find out this way.' And she really was sorry. 'But there's nothing I can do now. Really. If you don't mind?'

Jack looked up at the clock set above the nurses' station. It was almost noon.

✿

He wept as he went down in the lift and then through the busy corridors leading to the hospital exit.

His spectacles in one hand, a handkerchief in the other, he sobbed heavily, aching with sadness, episodically, for the first half hour of his vigil, leaning against the same concrete wall in the same way as he had done the afternoon before.

During the uncounted hours which followed he sat and stared unseeingly at the footpath, the road, at the noisy cars and trucks and vans and buses and motor scooters and motorcycles and bicycles that went busily by, their riders and drivers and passengers unaware and uncaring of the pain and suffering and sickness and death and misery that was present now and always in the grim-looking buildings behind him.

People also passed on foot. Most ignored him; some stared curiously; some glanced away in embarrassment, or fear.

But one, and only one, stopped. A young woman with a very white face; white arms. She was dressed in a pale orange gown and a matching headscarf of sorts, with a red dot painted in the centre of her forehead, brown sandals on her very white feet, and a few early summer roses in her hand.

'Are you alright?' she asked softly and kindly of the sad old man slumped back against the wall. Jack looked up from his sorrowful reverie. At her: the strangely dressed young woman. He thought she had the greenest eyes he had ever seen. Staring at him they were. And an almost saintly white face that was spoiled only by a worried frown.

'Pardon?' he said.

'Are you alright?'

Jack understood and nodded and the young woman saw the redness in his sad old blue eyes — behind rimless glasses which made him look like a professor — the stinging blotchiness on the thin skin of his cheeks, and the unmistakable lines of grief on his face. She looked up at the hospital building behind him and then deeply into his wetted eyes. She took one of his large rough hands in one of hers — small, pinkly white, soft and warm — and transferred a rose from her possession to his.

'I understand,' she said softly. 'Peace.' And she touched his forehead lightly.

There were thorns on the rose's green stem but they were small and soft and benign. And so he held the rose carefully to his breast, as if it were blessed and sacred, and watched her walk away.

'Thank you,' he said quietly but she had moved on and so didn't hear him.

He watched her stop to talk to a young woman wearing a green hospital robe and a pair of fluffy pink slippers who was sitting on a bench at the bus stop; she was attached to a tube which was attached to a plastic bag which hung from a hook at the top of a steel pole which was on a mobile wheeled stand. She was smoking a cigarette. She looked up unsmilingly and grudgingly accepted the rose from the orange-gowned one who then moved – almost glided – away. Jack watched as the beautiful rose was unceremoniously chucked under the bench seat onto the filthy concrete.

He looked away then; looked back and down at *his* rose. The rose he had been given and had accepted and was now holding to his breast. He didn't put it to his blocked nose; he knew it probably possessed only a faint scent which he wouldn't be able to smell. He was familiar with the variety: a rich, creamy rose with a light pink blush on its tender and delicate petals that were as soft as silk.

'Peace,' he said quietly with recognition. 'It really *is* Peace.'

– THE END –